Her First Desire

"Is it just me that you have a problem with, Mr. Thurlowe? Or are you this way with all women?"

Her tone alone was enough to set his teeth on edge. He whirled around, not realizing that she was so close, he practically stepped on her toes—and again, caught the heat of her body beneath that nightdress.

In a blink his mouth went dry. His hands wanted to reach for her. He tensed, holding himself back. And then, calmly, enunciating clearly, he said, "It is just you. I like every other woman I've ever met."

It was a deliberately hurtful thing to say. If she would back away, perhaps then some semblance of his sanity would return. She didn't.

Instead, her chin rose in defiance, and he had a strong desire to kiss her. It would not take much effort. If he tipped his head down, she was right there.

By Cathy Maxwell

The Logical Man's Guide to Dangerous Women
HER FIRST DESIRE • HIS SECRET MISTRESS

The Spinster Heiresses
THE DUKE THAT I MARRY • A MATCH MADE IN BED
IF EVER I SHOULD LOVE YOU

Marrying the Duke
A DATE AT THE ALTAR • THE FAIREST OF THEM ALL
THE MATCH OF THE CENTURY

The Brides of Wishmore
THE GROOM SAYS YES • THE BRIDE SAYS MAYBE
THE BRIDE SAYS NO

The Chattan Curse
THE DEVIL'S HEART • THE SCOTTISH WITCH
LYON'S BRIDE

THE SEDUCTION OF SCANDAL
HIS CHRISTMAS PLEASURE • THE MARRIAGE RING
THE EARL CLAIMS HIS WIFE
A SEDUCTION AT CHRISTMAS
IN THE HIGHLANDER'S BED • BEDDING THE HEIRESS
IN THE BED OF A DUKE • THE PRICE OF INDISCRETION
TEMPTATION OF A PROPER GOVERNESS
THE SEDUCTION OF AN ENGLISH LADY
ADVENTURES OF A SCOTTISH HEIRESS
THE LADY IS TEMPTED • THE WEDDING WAGER
THE MARRIAGE CONTRACT
A SCANDALOUS MARRIAGE • MARRIED IN HASTE
BECAUSE OF YOU • WHEN DREAMS COME TRUE
FALLING IN LOVE AGAIN • YOU AND NO OTHER
TREASURED VOWS • ALL THINGS BEAUTIFUL

Her First Desire

A Logical Man's
Guide to Dangerous Women Novel

Cathy Maxwell

AVONBOOKS

An Imprint of HarperCollinsPublishers

Excerpt from *His Lessons on Love* copyright © 2022 by Catherine Maxwell, Inc.

HER FIRST DESIRE. Copyright © 2021 by Catherine Maxwell, Inc. All rights reserved. Printed in the United States of America. No part of this book may be used or reproduced in any manner whatsoever without written permission except in the case of brief quotations embodied in critical articles and reviews. For information, address HarperCollins Publishers, 195 Broadway, New York, NY 10007.

First Avon Books mass market printing: May 2021

Print Edition ISBN: 978-0-06-289730-5
Digital Edition ISBN: 978-0-06-289686-5

Cover design by Amy Halperin
Cover art by Patrick Kang
Cover photographs © Konmac/Shutterstock (cottage); © karamysh/Shutterstock (garden); © Konstantin L/Shutterstock (sky)
Author photograph by Armaris Narvaez at Five A's Photography

Avon, Avon & logo, and Avon Books & logo are registered trademarks of HarperCollins Publishers in the United States of America and other countries.

HarperCollins is a registered trademark of HarperCollins Publishers in the United States of America and other countries.

FIRST EDITION

21 22 23 24 25 BVGM 10 9 8 7 6 5 4 3 2 1

For Chelsea, Carlos, Trinity, and Josie
Much love!

Her
First
Desire

The Logical Men's Society

The Logical Men's Society started as a jest, as many things do.

Over a pint or two in The Garland, where men gathered in Maidenshop, it was noted that a sane man wouldn't choose to marry. It went against all logic . . . and so the "Society" was formed.

Oh, men had to marry. It was expected and life is full of expectations. A man gave up his membership in the Logical Men's Society when that happened, and he could only return if he was widowed. But in the years before he tied the parson's knot, the Society offered good fellowship that was highly valued and never forgotten.

And so it went for several generations. The irony of the name of their village, Maidens-hop, was not lost on any of its members. The Logical Men's Society provided a place of masculine goodwill and contentment . . . until the women began to win.

Chapter One

London
March 1815

. . . he has passed from this life on earth to his reward in heaven.

The words leaped off the page at Gemma.

Someone had died?

And then, she read *who* had died.

Her legs buckled beneath her. She collapsed onto the desk chair.

She'd been sent to fetch a scrap of paper so that her late husband's sister-in-law, Lady Latimer, and her friends, who were playing cards in the front sitting room, could keep tally of their scores. They were a gathering of elegant magpies who seemed to enjoy making Gemma hop up to do their bidding. After all, as that most pitiful of all creatures, a penniless relation, she existed to do nothing more than to be of service.

The letter had been shoved into the back of the

desk drawer and Gemma had pulled it out thinking that here was something useless that could be used versus taking a fresh page.

She hadn't expected it to be addressed to her . . . or to have been opened.

Dear Mrs. Estep,

You and I were introduced when you paid a visit to your uncle Andrew MacMhuirich some months ago. It is with a heavy heart I undertake the tragic duty of informing you that he has passed from this life on earth to his reward in heaven. I hasten to tell you that he did not suffer but was taken in his sleep.

He shall be missed by our small community. The Garland has been a mainstay in Maidenshop, the center of all goings-on. We shall not know what to do with ourselves without Old Andy, as he was affectionately called.

If I may be of service to you in your time of grief, please know I am your most humble servant.

Sincerely,
The Reverend Gerald Summerall
St. Martyr's Church
Maidenshop, Cambridgeshire
15 November 1814

Gemma stared at the elegant, mannish script, trying to make sense of it all. Her uncle Andrew had died? He had been over sixty, but had been a robust man, a busy one. They had just started to connect as family and now, he was gone. That he had not suffered was comforting to know. He'd been her only living relative. There was no one else.

She reread the date. *15 November 1814.*

For several heartbeats, she couldn't breathe.

She'd already had too much of death over the past two years: her father, then that wee being whose heart had not lasted past a week, and finally her wastrel of a husband . . .

Each death had thrown her life deeper into chaos.

And now she'd lost Andrew, who had been kindness itself when she had so needed a friend. He'd been gone . . . what?—she did a mental count—for at least three months? What must Reverend Summerall think of her? He'd written and she'd not made any reply.

Worse, she wouldn't have known at all if she'd not come upon this letter by mistake.

The back was addressed to her, care of Lord and Lady Latimer. Someone had broken the seal, read the contents, and stuffed it into the desk drawer without one word. Her uncle's death had been dismissed—and for what reason?

Gemma looked around at the room's new furnishings. The drapes, the carpets, the overly ornate furniture. It had all been paid for with her father's money—money that by all that was fair was hers. However, the law had handed it over to her husband, as had been her father's wishes.

Then, when Paul Estep had died, he had left no

will. Scoundrels rarely did. The law had further tricked Gemma by granting what was left of her fortune to Reginald Estep, Lord Latimer, her husband's brother.

Men had done this to her, she realized. Men had conspired together for reasons of gender alone to rob her of what should have been hers.

"Gemma, where is that paper?" Lady Latimer's petulant voice commanded from the adjoining sitting room. "We wish to be on with our game, not sitting here waiting on you."

"Maybe she is tippling," another female voice said. "You know how the Northerners are." Her silly remark was met with giggly agreement because they had all been growing rosy-cheeked off the butler's special punch.

Gemma tightened her hand into a fist around the letter. *Their* husbands would never disgrace them by dueling over another man's wife. *Their* husbands were alive so *they* had a place in society. *Their* husbands saw to their bills.

Those women believed they were superior to Gemma in every way because she'd made the error of falling for Captain Paul Estep's handsome face and believing his lies, including the vow that he would honor and cherish her.

Barstow, the butler, appeared in the hallway door opposite the sitting room. "Lady Latimer is waiting," he prodded. "You'd need go to her now."

None of the senior servants hesitated in giving Gemma an order. They realized she had no power. She wasn't a servant and yet, as an in-law she wasn't quite considered family, either. She was an unwanted burden.

Pride stirred in her. Her father had been a very wealthy merchant. She had brought a substantial dowry to her marriage. If Lord Latimer would give her even a widow's portion of what he'd inherited, she could leave.

"Where is Lord Latimer?" Gemma asked, surprised by how calm her voice was because inside, she churned with anger. "I wish to speak to him."

"His lordship is busy."

Busy? Reading more of her mail?

"He will see me now." Grief had beaten her down for too long. She needed to act. She walked to the door, ignoring the calls coming from the adjacent sitting room.

The heavyset butler blocked her passage with his body. "What is the matter with you? I said his lordship is busy. Lady Latimer bid you to bring her a scrap of paper and you shall do so now. In fact, this is nonsense. Give me what you have in your hand and I will deliver it."

Gemma wasn't about to let go of the letter. She backed away from him, holding up her free hand to ward him off, and then moved toward the sitting room. Seeing she was going where he wished, Barstow straightened his clothes and retreated, all the better for her.

"There you are, Gemma," Lady Latimer said peevishly, her mouth full of sweet bread. "I thought you would never return—No, wait, where are you going?"

Gemma ignored the question as she quickened her pace, rushing straight past the tables of card players, and moving toward the hallway door. She was out into the hall before Barstow, who had trailed behind her, apparently to ensure she did as he wished, realized he'd been tricked.

"Stop her," he shouted to no one in particular since, at this time of day, the sole footman in the house would be in the kitchen flirting with the new scullery maid. And the ladies were not going to move fast, not with all that punch in them.

Behind Gemma, Lady Latimer and her friends were confused. "Barstow, where is she going?"

"Heavens, she looks as if she is being chased by a bear," a guest boozily observed while another complained of there being no way yet to tally her winning points.

And Gemma felt free.

For the first time since her father's illness had taken over her life, she was acting on her own behalf. Propelled by anger and her own sense of self-preservation, she raced down the hall to the library. Lord Latimer usually retired there every afternoon when he was at home. The door was shut. She turned the handle. It was locked.

He was in there.

Probably with Mrs. Sutton, the housekeeper. It was well-known that they enjoyed trysts. The only one who didn't know this was his lady wife.

Of course, Lord Latimer wasn't choosy. Gemma always kept a chair propped against the door handle of her bedroom to keep him at bay, and there wasn't a maid in the house who didn't know to avoid being caught on the back stairs with him.

She pounded on the door. The hardwood shook with the force of her anger. "My lord, I must speak to you," she said with the authority of one who had finally found her voice.

"*Gemma*, you will leave his lordship alone," Barstow commanded, marching toward her.

Her ladyship was right behind him. "What is she doing? What is she doing?" she tipsily repeated.

Gemma wished she did know what she was doing. Pure instinct and a long-dormant sense of outrage were in control now.

She pounded on the door harder. "Lord Latimer, *open up.*"

To her surprise, the door was flung open and the upstairs maid, a new girl by the name of Beth, came charging out. Her lips looked red and bruised. "Thank you," she whispered under her breath at Gemma as she slid by. The maid hurried down the hall as if the hounds of hell were on her heels.

Gemma stepped in the doorway to face Lord Latimer, whose stare let her know she had interrupted him. The library was a big room with huge windows overlooking the back garden, and comfortable seating for enjoying a book by the fire.

His lordship was on the far side of one of those chairs. His jacket was off and his clothes, including the undone top button of his breeches, were in disarray. He was a short man, in contrast to his brother, Paul, who had been close to six foot. Other than the height difference, the brothers had a remarkable resemblance with dark hair and gray eyes. In any quarter they would have been considered handsome, although experience had taught Gemma that "Handsome is as handsome does" was a very true adage.

For once, Gemma didn't defer to him. "How *dare* you open my mail and then *keep* it *from me.*" She held up the crumpled letter.

At that moment Barstow reached her. His thick hands came down on her shoulders. Her response was to send an elbow back and into his side with enough force that he released his hold and doubled over.

Gemma took a neat step away from him. She had quite a crowd watching now. Beyond Lord and Lady Latimer, the card-playing guests, their eyes wide with astonishment, had followed them down the hall. They probably could not believe their luck in witnessing such a scene. Gemma had no doubt that this story would be swirling around London before nightfall.

She didn't care. She was done with being proper and nice. She'd been raised in Manchester where they prided themselves on plain speaking and she had the blood of Scottish rebels on her mother's side flowing in her veins.

It was time to act like it.

"I want my widow's portion of my husband's estate. You owe it to me and *I want it.*"

She'd asked before, of course. She'd asked politely. Humbly. Meekly. In response, there had been excuses, promises . . . silence.

And she'd accepted it all, knowing how precarious her position was. Finding the letter had been the ultimate betrayal.

"You can't just take it from me," she continued. "That money came from my father."

"Who married you off to my brother, changing his will to name Paul his heir. It is not my fault your father did not see to your best interests." He'd straightened his clothing, reached to put on his jacket, and was bringing out his "lordliness." *Or* that your husband left your welfare to me."

"Paul was a philandering, gambling villain who was not a good husband, or even a good man—"

That statement elicited shocked gasps from the magpies—

Gemma rounded on the lot of them. "As if *you* didn't know. I was the last person in the world to know exactly whom he was." To her brother-in-law, she said, "However, even *you*, Lord Latimer, should be able to understand that out of fairness alone, I deserve to receive something."

His lordship looked past her shoulder to his wife. "My lady, don't you believe our guests would be more comfortable in the sitting room? Please, gentle ladies, I am sorry for the interruption of your afternoon. This is a highly personal matter, as you may have assumed. I beg your discretion."

"Yes, let's return to our cards, shall we?" Lady Latimer said, her smile too bright, too false.

Gemma didn't know if it was because of the scene she was creating or the sight of a maid running from the once-locked library.

The magpies didn't budge. They cast knowing looks at each other as if silently agreeing now was *not* the time to leave.

Gemma understood this was her one chance to strike. She'd *shame* Lord Latimer into giving her a widow's portion. "You took my husband's estate and gave me nothing. You left me destitute."

The pleasant smile on Lord Latimer's face hardened. "We have taken care of you, Gemma."

"By keeping my personal mail from me?" Certain the magpies could appreciate how important private correspondence was, she held up the letter. "My uncle Andrew was my last living relative. I deserved to know of his death. Instead, someone opened this letter, *months ago*, and didn't say a word to me."

Lord Latimer came forward, confident. "Absolutely. I am the head of this household. Everything goes through me—and I was bloody tired of seeing you walk around in black for my brother—which you would have insisted on continuing if you had known. I detest seeing women in black. So maudlin. Here now, ladies, back to your cards and cakes." He waved his hands as if he was scooting chickens out of his path. "We take good care of our Gemma. Have no fear. We believe she has had enough of death."

"Yes, we take good care of her," his silly wife echoed, and Gemma had had enough.

"*I can take care of myself* . . . if you will give me the money I deserve."

"That's the point, Gemma," his lordship said. "You don't deserve any money."

That was an outrageous statement. "You purchased a new coach off the money my marriage brought to this family—" she started, only to be cut off.

"I purchased a coach with *my* money." He spoke with finality, his gaze cold. "By the good grace of the law, I inherited my brother's estate. He inherited your father's, and he did so with your father's blessing. If your father wanted you to have money, he should have made a provision."

"He trusted Paul," she said, the words almost choking her.

"*No one* should have trusted Paul. He was a fool, eager to make a fool's decisions. Everyone knew Sir Michael valued the affections of his wife *and* was a crack shot."

Heat rose to Gemma's cheeks.

No, it was not news to anyone in London that her husband had died dueling over another man's wife. However, it was unkind of him to bring it up now, especially with such an audience.

Gemma wrapped herself in pride. "And does everyone in London know you kept the news of my husband's death from me until I came here looking for him? He'd been dead, what? *Six months?*" Her voice shook with the shame she wanted to heap upon him. "Dead and buried and his widow was not told? Is this how you take care of me?"

Lord Latimer's thin lips quirked to one side. "Perhaps I wished to save you from tragic news."

"Perhaps you didn't wish me to challenge your claim on my fortune?"

"It was *never* your money, Gemma. You were never a consideration for your father *or* your husband. That being said, my wife and I took you in out of the kindness of our Christian hearts and this is how you repay us? You foolish, foolish girl."

The magpies tutted their agreement. Of course they would side with him, and the world of *man*-made laws.

Gemma squeezed her hand around the letter, the weight of frustrated tears behind her eyes, refusing to let them fall. "Give me my portion."

He snapped his fingers in front of her face. "You'll receive nothing from me. Now, return to whatever duties my wife wishes of you and in the future, be more appreciative. Without us, you and your precious herbs and spells would be out on the street. Ah, yes, I know what you have been about. Selling potions to houses around the square. I let you do it because several neighbors have mentioned how thankful they are for your help. You may dabble all you wish, until I tell you to stop. Do you understand?"

He referred to the teas, tonics, and salves she made. She'd learned about healing from summers spent with her gran in Glasgow.

Then, leaning forward and in a voice so low only she could hear, "You should also be *kinder* to me."

"Never," Gemma shouted. "You will never touch me." Nor would she let any other man. She was done with the lot of them.

"Such a pity," was his response. Nor did he act humiliated by her outburst. Instead, he turned to his wife. "Come, my lady, let us take your guests back to the sitting room to sample more of that punch Barstow enjoys preparing." He offered his arm to her.

Lady Latimer took it without hesitation, sending a sniff in Gemma's direction, a gesture immediately imitated by the other ladies. Barstow trailed behind them, one hand on his side where Gemma had viciously elbowed him.

She watched them walk down the hall until they disappeared into the sitting room. They would be talking about her now, listening to Lord and Lady Latimer spread whatever story they wished. They would not be kind to her.

Gemma turned on her heel. She dashed blindly for the back stairs. She climbed as fast as her legs could carry her and did not stop to even draw a breath until she was in the haven of the small room tucked under the eaves. She slammed the door, then opened it and slammed it again harder, knowing no one could hear her here.

The action broke her temper and before she could think, she crumpled to the floor by her miserly cot and gave in to a good cry. She wept bitterly for her father, who had always wanted the best for her as long as she followed his will;

she wept for her husband, who had not been the man she'd thought him; she wept for Andrew, who had deserved more than months of silence at the news of his death.

At last, she wept for the child who had once given her hope that she would make her selfish husband proud. Her daughter's story was deep in her heart and she never shared her with anyone.

She wept until she was spent. Exhausted.

Gemma swiped her eyes with the back of her hand, embarrassed now. She was made of sterner stuff. She came from a long line of strong women and here she'd been wallowing on the floor without pride—

Two knocks were all the warning she received before the door opened and Mrs. Nichols, the housekeeper, entered, followed by the footman. With a nod, she indicated the chair in the room, the chair that kept Lord Latimer locked out. The manservant picked it up and left the room.

Mrs. Nichols stayed, her hands folded in front of her. She was twenty years older than Gemma and a practical Irishwoman.

"I tried to warn you, Mrs. Estep. You can't fight those who are better than you. We all have to learn our place. Or how to make the best of it all."

"I don't believe them better than I am. Or better than you."

"Then you will be doomed to unhappiness. His lordship instructed me to tell you he doesn't want to see you in black. You will not be allowed below this floor if you are wearing it." Having delivered her message, she left the room, closing the door behind her.

Gemma's spirit stirred.

So Lord Latimer thought her cowed?

From the hooks on the wall, she chose her black gown, one of five gowns she owned. After all, she'd once been a wealthy man's daughter. She'd barely worn black for Paul. However, she'd certainly wear it for her uncle and as long as she wished—and Lord Latimer could eat pig snouts for all she gave a care.

After dressing, she retwisted her heavy hair high on her head and pinned it in place as if preparing to go out. She didn't doubt that Lord Latimer was a man of his word. He'd be furious about the black. She just couldn't give in to him. If she had her way, she'd walk right out the front door and never return.

But where could she go? She had no one. Only her uncle Andrew—who'd once kindly written to her after she'd arrived in London that what was his was hers . . .

The memory of that letter came to life. Gemma had been touched by the sentiment. Andrew had owned a village tavern. She'd been on her way to London to confront Paul and had spent an enjoyable evening with her uncle. He'd told her that if matters didn't work out with her husband, she could live with him in Maidenshop.

Why hadn't she returned to him immediately upon learning of Paul's death? Too much pride, she supposed. In the beginning she'd believed Lord Latimer when he claimed he'd see her taken care of, except living under the eaves of his house and jumping to do his bidding was not what she had expected. She had only herself to blame. It seemed all her life she'd believed, as a gentlewoman, men would take care of her. How naïve she'd been. Especially after her gran had always warned her that a wise woman learned to take care of herself.

And now Andrew was gone . . . but *the tavern* remained.

What is mine is yours. It was almost as if Andrew whispered the words in her ear.

Gemma fell to her knees and pulled the box holding her most personal belongings out from beneath the cot. She lifted the lid to reveal her mother's miniature, a ruby ring Paul had given her to pledge their troth, and the stack of recipes and wisdom Gran had given her, recipes that had been handed down from one woman in her mother's family to another. And there were letters. Gemma always saved her letters.

Andrew's letter was on top.

She placed the Reverend Summerall's letter into the box and unfolded the one from her uncle. He'd been a sailor in his younger years and had never returned to his native Scotland, but Gran had always held him dear. That is why Gemma had interrupted her journey to see him and she'd not been sorry. Andrew had written to be certain she had made it safely to London, and then he had ended with the kindest words: *We are the last of the MacMhuirichs and all either has of family. What is mine is yours. Never forget I am here.*

The tavern in Maidenshop had been a rambling building in a charming village. The air was clear there. Not sooty like London.

And she was his only heir. This letter said as much.

Suddenly, Gemma was filled with purpose. It was a gamble, but she would not stay here waiting for Lord Latimer to try her door.

She'd been cheated out of much in her life because she'd relied on others. Now she was going to rely on herself. She was going to Maidenshop to claim her legacy.

Gemma crammed as much as she could carry into her large valise. The rest was of no value to her. She emptied out her box of treasures and letters and the precious recipes into that valise. She tucked an embroidered bag that held her herbs, teas, and salves into it, as well. Stoppered bottles of tonics would have to stay. She could mix them again.

For money, she had the ruby ring and what she'd earned from the Mayfair neighbors for her remedies. There was enough to help her make a new start.

Gemma snuck down the stairs without being seen and slipped out into the garden. She traveled through the alley. Within an hour she'd sold her ring. It had not fetched much. The stone was very small. Just like Paul. And his brother.

However, the money did pay her fare on the cheapest seat to Maidenshop—and her desperate hope for a new life.

And later, when she found herself settled on the top of a very crowded post on its way to Newmarket, she thought of the dear man whose death had given her a small ray of hope.

The wind wiped away her tears.

Chapter Two

"*Kiss me*," Clarissa Taylor demanded as she spun around to face Ned Thurlowe. They traveled on a wooded path, not far from the house and yet out of sight from prying eyes.

The unfortunate problem was that Ned hadn't been paying attention to anything she'd been saying on their walk. Including this demand. His mind was on his patients. As the only doctor in the area, his time was always in demand. He also took pride in his work whether it was setting a broken arm, battling a child's fever, or even healing the abscess on a horse's hoof. A country doctor had to be ready for anything, and Ned reveled in the challenges.

Besides, he and Clarissa had been betrothed for a little over two years. Yes, it was an unusually long waiting period before tying the knot, but the truth was, Ned wasn't that excited to marry. He'd only offered for her because after she'd been orphaned by her adopted parents, the Matrons of Maidenshop had decided her best course of action was marriage. She'd been two and twenty, a ripe age for matrimony. As a babe, she'd been left as a foundling on the church steps. The Reverend Taylor and his wife had taken her in and by all accounts had loved her dearly. Unfortunately, they were now dead and she had no family. She was dependent upon the charity of the villagers and lived with Squire Nelson and his family. Understanding what it was like to be a bastard *and* an unwanted member to the family, Ned had agreed with the matrons that someone honorable should secure her future . . . and that *someone* had turned out to be him.

He definitely wasn't an ardent suitor. It had taken him a year to start using her given name. He kept forgetting. And he only had time to call on her once a week, although he prided himself on being punctual. He presented himself to her every Friday at precisely two o'clock in the afternoon for a fifteen-minute social call.

Dependent on the weather, they always walked this path. Usually, Clarissa prattled on about her week and he pretended to listen. He chose to focus his mind on matters that were important to him— such as scientific musings or his lecture series or even the future of The Garland tavern.

Ned was chairman of the Logical Men's Society.

For several generations the Society had called The Garland home. However, now that the owner, Old Andy, had passed, there was concern amongst the members of what would become of this meeting place that was so important to them. Then again, no one had placed a claim on the building. So far it had been theirs to use. Ned didn't know if he should be concerned about the matter or not.

And he didn't want to let his fellow members down. He enjoyed being in the Society. For once in his life, he felt he truly belonged. In London he was trailed by whispers. In Maidenshop, he was a valued member of the community.

So his mind was *busy* when Miss Taylor made her demand and he walked right by her. He took several steps before he realized she was not with him.

Being a gentleman, he stopped—and then he comprehended what she'd said. *Kiss her?*

She'd even closed her eyes and puckered her lips. She waited, facing the direction where he'd been.

What should he do now?

Before he could make up his mind, Miss Taylor's eyes opened. She gave a shake of her head as if surprised he was not where she'd expected him to be. She unpuckered her lips. Her lovely brows came together in vexation. A becoming shade of rose bloomed on her cheeks.

Clarissa was a singularly beautiful woman. She had honey-gold hair, large green eyes, and a smooth complexion. That she found herself promised to him these past few years was not a fault of her looks, but of her birth.

And it wasn't her fault he was not quite ready to marry.

He just didn't really want to kiss her.

And he wasn't certain why . . . except he didn't trust the entanglements of women. Their pursuits were frivolous to him—and, as humans, they could be remarkably cruel.

That didn't mean he hadn't had liaisons. Women liked his looks, and a man had needs. He just kept his affairs far from Maidenshop and always made sure he had the upper hand. He had no desire to copy his father, who had made a fool of himself between London's most famous courtesan and a furious wife. Ned had been an innocent trapped in that triangle and he'd learned hard lessons well.

He also didn't wish to embarrass Clarissa. Was she wrong to ask for a kiss? Any other man would probably have claimed one long before now.

So he returned to her where she stood, leaned forward, and gave her a peck on the cheek.

She didn't hide her disappointment and he understood. He'd felt a bit like he was kissing one of his half sisters—although he was fonder of Clarissa than he was of them.

Her gaze dropped to the ground. Her thick lashes fanned across her cheeks. "I didn't mean like that." There was a pause as if she struggled within herself. "I wished—" She forced herself to meet his eye. "I wished for a firmer kiss."

"Why?"

Again, her brows drew close. "What do you mean *why*? Is that not a reasonable request? It seemed time."

She was right. He had no explanation that made sense.

At his silence, she said, "When *are* we going to marry? I don't want to pressure you. I know we are *not* a love match and you offered for me because the matrons put your back against a wall."

"It wasn't that dramatic."

"Yes, it was." She started walking along the path leading to the house again. She was wearing a gown of green worsted. The early March wind tugged at the ribbons of her bonnet. "You think I don't know that Mr. Balfour had refused on the grounds he was a determined bachelor? Of course, he's changed his tune now and seems happy in his marriage. As for the other suitable bachelor in the parish, the Earl of Marsden, I cannot tolerate that man. He is so selfish."

"Mars is one of my closest friends—"

She held up a gloved hand. "I mean no insult . . . although I don't understand why you or anyone admires him. He really has no purpose in life."

"He does," Ned offered weakly although, as of late, there was truth in her assessment.

"You could have said no when the matrons went after you," she continued. "I would have gone out into the world as a governess or a companion. I could have done that." She spoke as if she was trying to convince herself, and Ned could curse himself because there were times he had wished she had.

Instead, he reached for her arm and swung her around. "That is a hard life and no one wanted it for you. Most of all myself." *That* was true. "I know what it is like to be thrust out into the world. Of course, I am fortunate. My studies equipped me to be on my own. But you don't want to be a companion to some deaf and crotchety old lady. Or live the governess's life of moving from household to household."

"Perhaps it would have been better if I had been born male. Then I could have had the opportunities you had."

She was right.

Clarissa nodded, knowing he understood. "I regret that you have to marry me. It is a burden—"

"It is not—"

She placed her gloved fingers up to his mouth to stifle his dissent. "Please, Ned, let us be honest—"

That is when he kissed her. Ned did know how to kiss and he made this a good one.

Did he feel any great passion? No.

However, she did. Her lips were unschooled and earnest. She leaned in as if hungry for someone, or something.

Ned didn't take the kiss deeper and she wasn't looking for it. She didn't know enough to ask.

His last lover, Emily, a widow in Cambridge, had accused him of being manipulative. The suggestion had upset him. His mother was manipulative. He was just a man with a need, and he'd thought she'd felt the same. Their liaison had started off as a simple arrangement, and then she'd begun prodding him for more.

But what of emotions? she'd asked. *God gave you a handsome face and yet you have a stone heart.*

Ned hadn't understood what she was talking about. Intercourse was a biological necessity. Why should the heart be involved?

Besides, emotions called for trust and there were only two people in this world Ned had learned he could trust—Marsden and Balfour. He'd also been honest with Emily from the start. He'd wanted nothing from her, save the comfort of her body. There wasn't a female on the planet he trusted enough to let down his guard, not even Clarissa— and he liked her more than any others he knew.

Clarissa broke the kiss. Her lovely eyes were closed as if she'd savored every second. Her body leaned against his, her breasts on his chest. She drew in a deep breath. "You smell of the wind and storm clouds. I could wallow in it."

He laughed. She was being fanciful. Sometimes, she wore a scent with a hint of roses or violet. It was nice enough but he had no desire to *wallow* in it, and he wouldn't tell someone if he did—

Suddenly, he realized what Emily had actually been saying. He *was* cold.

Like his mother?

Never once had he wanted to fold himself into a woman because of the way she smelled. *Not completely true*, his medically trained mind argued. He was stirred by a whiff of female, as any man would be.

"You truly don't mind marrying me?" Clarissa asked. She pulled back slightly. In the depths of her eyes he saw her fears, her doubts—and it was his role to reassure her.

"I'm actually honored," he lied.

The tension left her. She smiled and leaned against him again. Ned willed himself to stand firm.

"When?" she whispered. *"When* will we marry?"

Damn it all, more questions.

Correctly reading his hesitation, she prodded softly, "Ned, I can't keep living off the Nelsons' Christian charity for much longer."

"I know." He took a step away. He needed his own space. "A decision should be made, but I can't make it right now." What a relief to say those words! "Our time today is almost up. I can't hash it out in this moment. I must be on my way. The Widow Smethers twisted her ankle yesterday, or, at least, I hope that is what she did. It could be a break. Her ankle was too swollen for me to diagnose. I suspect that a night's rest will make the matter clearer.

"*Then,*" he continued, before Clarissa could make more demands, "I must stop by the Balfours'." He started toward the house where his horse, Hippocrates, was being walked by one of the squire's stable lads.

Disappointment crossed Clarissa's face. However, she followed him, asking politely, "How is

Mrs. Balfour? How is the baby?" Kate Balfour was pregnant.

"Good, although I don't understand why Balfour insists I do the delivery. Midwifery is not my usual line of work but they are very good friends. Kate says I need to listen—"

He broke off, his words coming to a halt as a realization struck him. Ned was not always perceptive, but there were times when he'd have insight. Kate had warned him early in her pregnancy that he must *listen* to her better, something that *was* a challenge for him. He was a busy man. He preferred to diagnose and move on to other patients. Practicing patience and listening to Kate had helped their friendship—as well as his understanding of where her pregnancy was.

Now, he realized he needed to force himself to listen to Clarissa, too. She was right when she said she could not live with Squire Nelson forever and they needed to settle on a marriage date.

Ned reached a decision. "We shall marry after the Frost lecture," he said.

Her response was a frown. "Why wait so long?"

"Clarissa, when do I have time before then? I could be called out for the Balfours' baby at any moment." That wasn't completely true. There was a good month left before Kate Balfour delivered. "Then, there is the Cotillion." The dance celebrated the beginning of summer. It was the highlight of Maidenshop's social calendar. Ned abhorred it, although now it provided a plausible excuse.

"And even then," he continued, "my mind up till then will be completely occupied by the Frost lecture." Which happened the day after the dance. "So we really can't marry before then." Even as he finished the last word, a weight settled upon him, a sense that this was wrong. His gut urged him to retract the statement.

And yet, he was a gentleman. He'd made the offer to her. Any man of honor stood by his word. Two years was enough waiting.

Clarissa's face lit with understanding acceptance and obvious relief—as if she'd feared he was fobbing her off and now thought better. "Yes, I see. Thank you, sir. Thank you. I shall be the best wife ever. You'll have no regrets."

He already did.

She began chattering about how happy the Nelsons would be. He nodded woodenly, moving steadily for his horse.

Of course, he couldn't just escape. When they reached the drive, Squire Nelson was coming out of the house. Clarissa told her guardian the happy news that a date had been set. He shouted into the house for his wife and daughters to come hear the happy news. There were congratulations all around.

And Ned's smile felt tighter and tighter.

He couldn't wait to take his leave. He was also thankful his patients didn't require much from him. The Widow Smethers's ankle was very bruised, but the swelling had abated somewhat and he decided it was not broken, merely sprained. Kate Balfour's baby was simmering along nicely. All was good.

That didn't mean that, try as he might, he was able to ease his mind about marriage. The idea dogged him.

Finally, at the end of his day, he knew he couldn't go home to a solitary supper prepared by his man, Royce. Instead, he headed to The Garland. He hadn't been there in some time.

Last spring, as a way to drum up support for his first lecture, he'd started recruiting new members. A fair number of the village lads had joined. They gathered at The Garland almost every night. The matrons and others complained about the drinking, but men needed a place to enjoy their own company without the intrusion of women, and tonight Ned certainly needed that. He was growing increasingly horrified over the enormity of what he'd agreed to do.

Worse, the word had begun spreading through the parish. Clarissa had wasted no time in telling everyone the date. When he walked into The Garland, the lads there jeered him in the way men do.

"We will be needing a new chairman," cried one of the Dawson lads. "You are leaving the Society, Doctor. Once married, a man is no longer one of us."

"We are disappointed," claimed his brother. "Makes me want to drink."

The group laughed at that quip.

And then, a voice that Ned recognized and was surprised was with the company said, "I didn't think you would be fool enough to walk into the parson's trap."

The Duke of Winderton, confident with the arrogance of youth, leaned against the bar. He was all of one and twenty, dark haired, square jawed, and with the beginning of a bit of paunch around his belly. That hadn't been there when he'd left Maidenshop for the world a few months ago.

Then again, Ned knew he had always been a man whose mother had spoiled him to the point he didn't listen to good sense. Balfour was Winderton's uncle and had served as his guardian, a task that he'd not enjoyed.

Ned removed his hat, hanging it on a peg on the wall with the others. "Your Grace, you've returned from London."

"I've had enough of it."

That seemed an odd thing to say. When the duke left Maidenshop it had been with some ill will. He'd declared the village could no longer contain him. Apparently, London couldn't, either.

"I just saw your uncle. He didn't mention you had returned."

"He isn't my guardian anymore. I've reached my majority, so I no longer have a keeper."

Privately, Ned thought Winderton should still have one—to teach him humility if nothing else.

"You look as if you need a drink," the duke said.

All reservations about Winderton vanished. "I do."

In short order a tankard of ale was pressed into

Ned's hand and he forgot about the duke. Wind-erton was not his worry. He had troubles enough of his own, and the ale tasted good.

Besides the duke and the Dawson brothers, the others included Shielding the lawyer, Michaels, whom Ned never grasped what it was exactly he did, Squire Leonard, Jonathon Fitzsimmons, Nathanial Crisp, and a host of others that Ned didn't really know. The young, new members had brought them in.

Were they drinking too much as the matrons complained? Probably. But tonight Ned felt it justified. Damn the matrons. Damn their manip-ulating ways that had made him feel he must step forward and see to Miss Taylor's future.

He'd done the gentlemanly thing by offering marriage, and now he had to go through with it. He felt as if he'd put a noose around his neck . . . and it was tightening.

Ned reached for another drink.

Chapter Three

Gemma hadn't realized there was a four-mile walk from the Newmarket Road Posting Inn to Maidenshop, a challenging task after a night of travel.

When she'd traveled in the past, it had been by private chaise. Of course, that had been when she'd expected her husband to pick up her expenses.

Four miles was a long way to tramp after the journey she had just taken.

She had assumed that since her post traveled at night there would not be that many passengers. She had been wrong. The coach had been packed and she'd found herself sitting on a narrow bench on top of the vehicle, her valise in her lap and her bonnet in danger of being blown off her head.

The driver had to have been drinking. Their way down the road could be described as erratic and fast. He only stopped to change horses and drop off the heavy mailbags. At each coaching house, passengers scrambled off the coach for food or a moment of privacy. They were warned that if they weren't back on the stage when the driver was ready, they'd be left behind.

Gemma had readily jumped off with the others until, on the road again, she had witnessed a woman sitting on the bench's end seat almost tumble off the swiftly moving coach. The woman had nodded off and the driver had swerved.

Fortunately, the quick-witted passenger behind her caught her arm and saved her. Otherwise, the poor woman would have been left behind in the night. From that moment on, Gemma was determined to hold her seat in the center of the bench.

While Gemma had found it impossible to sleep, the large man to her right curled over until he was practically slumped into her lap, snoring heavily. He also smelled. The smaller man on her left kept jabbing her with his elbow until Gemma had decided to jab back.

Now, after twelve exhausting hours, she faced the walk to Maidenshop. Lifting her heavy valise over one shoulder like a sailor carrying his sea-bag, Gemma considered herself blessed it wasn't raining. This trip was hard enough.

On the Mail, she'd whiled away the time dreaming about what she might do with The Garland. Now it took all her energy to keep moving forward.

Then, just when she thought she couldn't take a step more, she reached the outskirts of the village. There was the spire of the church and down the road she could see the whitewashed walls of The Garland. Her step quickened. She'd made it.

The tavern was a rabbit warren of rooms under a thatched roof. It was a masculine establishment. There were no embellishments such as a welcoming garden by the door. There was a sign, made of aging, splintered wood with the outline of a garland on it. The appearance of the building was spartan and the message clear: people came here to drink.

Gemma started to turn the handle of the heavy wood front door, but then stopped. She needed to be grateful. She closed her eyes. "Thank you, Andrew. May you give your blessing to me as I build a new life."

On that earnest prayer, she opened the door and stepped out of the late-morning light into the darkness of a closed tavern.

When last she'd been here, Andrew had been busy baking rook pies and preparing for a lecture the Logical Men's Society, a local club of gentlemen, was holding.

Apparently, the village doctor organized it. "He is excited for the lecture. He's one of those men who likes to think. However, most of the lads will be here for the ale and my rook pies," Andrew had bragged to her.

"Well, perhaps they will learn something," she had replied.

"You have to be sober to learn," had been Andrew's response.

She remembered that so clearly, just as she

could recall the smell of the baking pies, the late-afternoon sunlight streaming through the windows, the neat tidiness of the tavern's main room, and a sense of peace. The peace was what she'd been moving toward, she realized. She was searching for a haven.

That was not what she walked into.

It was as if she had inhabited a storm in London only to be blown into this place eerie in its silence—and destruction. A pack of wolves could not have caused so much damage.

The rooms of the tavern ran into each other under the low ceiling. There was the main room with a bar, tables and chairs, a taproom, and the kitchen. When she'd visited last spring, the place had the same spare furnishings and decoration but had reflected Andrew's pride of ownership.

Now the seating was jumbled and out of order as if chairs had been tossed around by a giant hand. The tables appeared sticky with spilled drink, and the hearth smelled as if it had not been cleaned since Andrew had died. The ash was at least six inches deep. An effort had been made to shift down the pile for making a new fire only to spread cold ashes out on the floor. Footsteps had walked through it and could be traced around the room.

Ale tankards were everywhere, lining the bar, stacked on a table, thrown on the floor . . .

And the air had the wretched smell of stale drink, old ash—and urine.

She covered her mouth with the scarf around her neck and pushed open the nearest window. That is when she noticed that someone had put a hole in the glass pane.

Her uncle would weep to see his inn now. She felt the sting of tears in her eyes for him. He had always been so proud of his establishment, and now it was in shambles.

Against a far wall was a chair splintered into pieces as if thrown in anger, and she'd wager it wasn't the only one with broken rungs. Soot covered the walls and here and there were handprints. On another wall, behind the bar, someone had made marks as if keeping score.

Gemma dared to move toward the bar and glanced behind it. She wouldn't be surprised to see a body sleeping there. Instead, pewter tankards had apparently been stacked for a bowling game. She hesitated to imagine what had been used to throw at them. The cups that Andrew had once polished until they shone were tarnished and dented as if they'd been the target of many games.

She moved to the taproom that separated the main room from the kitchen.

When last she'd been here, there had been numerous kegs stacked against one stone wall. The kegs were still here except they had been emptied and left in a haphazard fashion so that she had to pick several up and pile them in a corner in order to pass through the room.

A tapped keg rested in a set of brackets to hold it on its side for serving. She turned the spigot and only a few drips came out. They'd drank their fill of every drop in the place and left the tavern a disaster.

She brushed the tap's stickiness from her gloved hands and peeked around the corner. The kitchen, too, was a mess, although Gemma was no longer reacting with surprise. Still, it was better than what she'd seen in the main room. At least the furniture was not in pieces.

Brown pottery plates, some crusted with food, covered the table and cupboard. The hearth was poorly kept but the ash was not as deep. Gemma walked in and looked over the pots and plates on the table. There were signs that mice and who knows what else had been feasting here.

She glanced over at the oven built into the hearth that had been her uncle's pride. She wondered if anyone had used it since his death and was thankful to see the kettle still hung from a hook over the firepit. Gemma remembered the evening she'd spent with him.

Andrew had been kindness itself. She had arrived without warning or fanfare but he'd welcomed her as if he'd been expecting her all along, and she'd felt herself relax in a way she couldn't remember since before her father took ill.

She could even hear her uncle's voice welcoming her. "A sight you are," he'd said, his brogue starting to thicken as he spoke as if seeing her reminded him of the dialect of his youth. "I'm blessed with your visit. Here, sit. A cup of tea? Of course. You are like your dear mother. So much like her. My heart almost stopped when I saw you standing in the door."

"Gran and I always said we would pay you a visit," she'd answered.

"I always meant to travel to Glasgow for a visit, but life got by me until it was too late. I miss my mum." He had set the steeping teapot and a brown pottery mug before her. "Lemongrass and black," he'd informed her. "The way the Mac-Mhuirichs like it."

The tea had reminded her of summers spent with her gran. Her mother had married a man from Manchester and had loved him enough to leave her country, just as Andrew had. Gemma could barely remember Andrew's visit to Manchester back when her mother was alive. She'd died of a fever, just about the time that Andrew had purchased The Garland. Gemma's father had never recovered from losing his wife, and Gran had been Gemma's saving grace. The summers spent with her had been magic times.

In the kitchen, Gemma's eye caught on the pottery teapot on the highest shelf of the cupboard. It appeared unscathed in the middle of the mess, and her throat tightened. Death was a scheming bastard. It had taken everyone she'd loved from her.

She swallowed back her tears. She was done

crying; she was *not* defeated . . . and yet, look at what had happened to The Garland in the short months since Andrew's death.

Look at what had happened to *her* in the three short years since she'd agreed to marry Paul Estep.

Suddenly, Gemma burst into laughter. A mad, untamed sound.

She had traveled from a terrible situation to one that was worse. She'd thought to claim The Garland because she remembered it as it had been. However, like so much in her life, what she'd believed, what she'd hoped for, was a fantasy.

The place was in ruins. Yes, there were four walls and a roof but those walls were probably full of mice, and the roof would leak and she would catch her death from the damp and cold and—

Just as abruptly, the shrill laughter changed into the tears she had sworn she would no longer shed. A huge, shattering sob robbed her of breath and then she saw that she'd not been wrong about the mice in the walls. A trio of them had apparently been hiding and had now decided they had nothing to fear from her. They made a bold dash across the floor heading straight for Gemma as if to chase her out—and they did.

She ran for the back door, shoving it open and practically falling forward. She caught herself just in time, taking a few stumbling steps before she righted herself, and then let out a gasp of surprise.

Where the inside had been filthy and musty,

the world in the back garden was alive with the magical force of a rushing stream. The air danced with the sound of it.

The last time Gemma had been here, she'd been too worried to notice or appreciate the water. Her head had been full of doubts about her husband, and the good expanse of lawn leading to the bank of the stream had been lined with makeshift tables in preparation for the next day's lecture. She'd not even registered the music of the water racing over rocks.

It hit her with full force now.

And everything growing around the stream promised it was ready to spring to life. Buds were already appearing on some of the trees and there was the scent of rich earth and promise.

Here was a safe place for a weary soul. In fact, two worn wooden chairs had been pulled over to the stream as if friends had shared a confidence here.

Oh, how she wished she had known during her first visit what she did now. Then she would never have left Maidenshop for London but would have taken shelter here with her uncle. She would have gardened, creating beds that would rival the ones her gran had boasted—and Andrew might still be alive . . . because he wouldn't have been alone.

She wouldn't have been alone, either.

Gemma removed her gloves and knelt. She dug a bit under the grass. The earth was dark and fertile. She flattened her hand upon it as if she could feel a heartbeat, something she had watched her gran do many a time.

Her mind's eye began to transform the expanse of lawn into a lovely garden full of herbs and flowers, the ones her gran had taught her to blend into healing potions as was the way of the MacMhuirichs.

What is mine is yours.

That is what Andrew had written, a promise he'd made, and she was going to accept him at his word.

She'd not been wrong to come here. He wanted her to have The Garland. She could feel it in her bones . . . and she began to see a vision of what The Garland could be. Over there would be the bed of coneflowers and chamomile. By the door would be the kitchen herbs, the lettuces, the carrots, and peas. She'd have them climbing up a trellis so that all she had to do was reach out the back door to snap off a few for her supper.

She'd nurture the herbs one found in the wild over by the stream. Their powers to heal would increase with the water's magical mist to encourage them.

And The Garland would not be known for whatever foolishness had been going on. No, it would become a place for women to gather, with their families. A place where they exchanged stories and encouraged each other. A place where she could sell her salves, potions, and teas. A place where not only would she heal, she would also be a healer.

Why, she could turn the lawn into a tea garden like the one she'd visited in London. It had boasted a bowling green outside and a place for children to play. There was plenty of space here for such ventures and still room for plants and for tables for guests to enjoy light refreshments.

Besides her healing potions, she would sell scented soaps. Her gran had a recipe that could rival the finest found in London. She even had a laundry day soap that made one want to do the wash.

On the right side of the building where she could see the morning sun was strongest, she would plant a perfume garden full of colors. There would be violets, pansies, daisies, *roses*— and bees. Hundreds of them. All busily humming while they gathered nectar.

A passion for something other than mere survival *finally* coursed through Gemma. She could do this. She could make The Garland the image of her dreams.

It would call for hard work, but she wasn't afraid of that. She didn't have much money. However, if she took everything one step at a time, she knew she could see her way through any challenges.

What is mine is yours.

She pulled the ties of her bonnet and removed it, a sign she was home.

A chilled breeze whipped through the air. It swirled against her black skirts and wound its way around her. The playful wind caught on the loose strands of her hair, gently tugging at it, and for a moment Gemma believed she was not alone. She felt the power of her gran, of Andrew, of her mother and father around her.

This was her place. The peace for which she'd yearned.

With a new purpose, Gemma entered the building. There was much to be done. She'd find seed, tools . . . she'd beg for them if she must. But she wasn't leaving The Garland.

Off the kitchen was a small bedroom where Andrew had slept. She'd used it when she'd visited and it would now be hers. She would eat, sleep, and work her fingers to the bone to create her vision.

Walking through the kitchen, she pushed open the bedroom door. The one window had been shuttered for privacy and the room had a disturbing scent to it. She walked over and opened the window to let in air. Dust motes scrambled as the early-spring sun filled the room.

She was not surprised to see the bed was completely unmade. The sheets were twisted as if someone had suffered a restless night.

She doubted if anyone had touched the room since Andrew's death. A few of his personal things were here. His good jacket was not hanging on the wall hook the way it had been when she'd spent the night in this room. Presumably, he'd been buried in it. Instead, his apron still covered with the splatters of the last meal he had cooked was in its place. She knew a local woman did his washing for him. He had several aprons that he'd said he turned over to her on a regular basis.

Gemma half closed the door to reveal the shelves built into the wall that held a few of Andrew's possessions. She'd not snooped when she'd last visited. Now she opened the carved wood box shaped like a shell that had tempted her curiosity. Andrew had once been at sea. Her gran said that was why he'd left the family. He'd yearned for adventure.

Inside were a few letters and a miniature of a woman who could have been Gemma's mother, except the portrait showed her much younger than in the one Gemma possessed. Her mother had been a wild, redheaded beauty. In the portrait, she had a child on her lap. The child's eyes were blue like the summer sky and her hair as flaming as her mother's.

Gemma immediately assumed the child was herself until she reconsidered, even about the woman in the painting. This could also be her gran and the child her mother, or even Andrew himself. Age had turned his red hair to the color of a mouse pelt and so most forgot that he, too, claimed the MacMhuirich red hair. Stepping back, she started to sit on the bed to investigate the rest of the box's contents when her nose warned her to be careful.

The sheets were the source of the musky smell. She recognized that scent. Someone had been having a heyday with those sheets. And apparently recently.

Gemma gagged. What beast would do such a craven, *vile* thing in her uncle's bed?

Men were pigs. Of course, Paul had taught her that. She'd tried to be all that a dutiful wife should be, and yes, he had been the worst husband in the world. . . . however, she had expected more excitement in the marriage bed than what it had turned out to be. She had imagined her husband taking her innocence and ushering her into a whole new threshold in life such as she'd read in poetry. She was curious and anticipating the experience.

Instead, after her first night with Paul, Gemma had wondered why people bothered. It was messy and dissatisfying. It was over before it started. She likened it to biting into a shiny red apple and realizing it was mush inside. All promise and no—what? Satisfaction. She remembered being disappointed.

Gemma hadn't been able to wait to push Paul's body weight off her. Meanwhile, he'd acted pleased with himself and was asleep almost the minute he was done. There was no romance to the whole act. Just smelly sheets—

"Bloody hell," an angry male voice rang through the rafters, startling her.

He was in the main room, and he sounded furious. Was he upset at finding her valise on the floor?

Gemma put the miniature back in the box and set it on the shelf. Her every sense warned her to be wary.

Heavy footsteps echoed as the man began walking through the room. Furniture was moved, followed by a crashing sound as if something had been thrown in frustration.

She weighed hiding, hoping he would leave her alone, and then ruled against it. This was *her* place. If she was to be here, she had to claim it.

Cautiously, she opened the door and peered out.

A man's form was silhouetted in the center of the main room. He wore a gentleman's great-coat and a broad-brimmed hat pulled low over his brow. His boots were muddy and, to her eye, worn, albeit good leather. He was tall, broad of shoulder, and intimidating.

Well, she could be a bit daunting herself, as well. She straightened her shoulders and moved toward the taproom where she could be seen. Her heart pounded in her ears. She wasn't ready for a confrontation and yet, she'd not back away from it. She was done with being bullied by men.

He was shaking his head in disgust at the scene around him, his scowl deepening—and then he noticed her. They faced each other.

Time seemed to stop.

The mess, the smells, even the disgusting sheets faded from her mind until there was just him standing in the room. They took each other's mea-sure and for a second, she experienced a charge of recognition that had nothing to do with knowing him. Instead, it was as if something shifted inside of her. A recognition that this meeting was important—but why?

She did not know.

He reacted as if caught off balance. His weight rocked back slightly like he was resisting some unseen force . . . the same one that pulled her toward him.

The man removed his hat and raked his fingers through his hair and she was struck by the pure, masculine beauty of his face. He had a strong, straight nose to go with his hard jaw, and eyes as golden as a lion's. Intelligent eyes. Bold ones.

His hair was black and thick. He wore it overlong as if he couldn't be bothered with the details of grooming. Although neither the worn boots nor his shaggy hair detracted from his singular good looks.

However, a handsome face could mask a rotten soul. She'd learned that lesson from Paul. And her guard immediately went up when, in the blink of a golden eye, his manner changed.

He took a step away from her. The movement broke his hold over her, especially as mistrust crossed his face. *"What* are you doing here?"

At his bluntness, she almost offered an apology, until she realized she had every right to be here. He was the trespasser. Proudly, she stated, "I am the owner of this establishment."

"The devil you are."

"The devil I am," she replied coolly. "And you are?"

"Mr. Ned Thurlowe, and *I'm* the owner of this establishment."

Her response matched his coldness. "You lie, sir."

Chapter Four

He was lying.

Ned prided himself on *never* lying . . . because there had been a time in his life when his very existence had depended upon his ability to lie.

Then later, after his father had taken him in under his roof, Ned had learned hard lessons about how civilized society judged liars. Especially lies told by a bastard son. It was because of his lying he'd been packed away to school before he'd turned six. That had been a brutal experience and somewhere along that journey, Ned had vowed he would *never* lie again . . . until this moment.

He *didn't* own The Garland. But this woman's appearance out of nowhere, her bold claim, well, it threw him off. *She* threw him off.

For the first time in his life, he experienced . . . desire. His reaction to her was immediate and strong. It made him feel out of kilter.

She reminded him of the descriptions of ancient sirens he'd read about in his schoolbooks.

Her skin was clear and creamy. The modest black dress and cape could not hide her womanly curves, and his imagination supplied the rest. Her hair was in shambles with tendrils of curls escaping every which way and yet, the light from the greasy windows made it glow like the most brilliant ruby. Her eyes were the color of the clearest summer sky.

So of course he'd lied. He'd been turned inside out. *She* robbed him of good sense. He also had a headache to make Satan proud, induced by last night's overindulgence, and a need to not let the Logical Men's Society lose the only home they'd ever had. He was the chairman. This was his watch, and she was so very unexpected.

In truth, he remembered very little of what had happened last night. He recalled arriving at The Garland and all the lads royally roasting him about finally marrying Miss Taylor. He remembered Winderton being there . . . and that he'd not tethered his gelding, Hippocrates, outside, so that when he wanted to go home, he'd discovered the beast had seen himself back to the stables, something he was wont to do since Ned did not live far from The Garland.

Ned knew he had checked on the horse before stumbling to his own bed because, this morning, Hippocrates had been unsaddled and the paddock bolted. But the details were beyond Ned's memory. When he'd asked Royce, his man who served as butler, valet, and assistant, if he had seen to Hippocrates, the answer had been no.

So Ned hadn't been completely beyond redemption last night. Just a touch out of commission.

Well, more than a touch. He had woken in his bed still wearing boots and clothes. He couldn't let Royce shave him this morning because the scraping of a razor on skin made his teeth ache.

Nor had it helped that as he'd saddled Hippocrates for this morning's rounds, snippets of memory had begun to return, and one snip was alarming.

There had been women present at The Garland last night, or had there been? His drink-fuddled mind had registered the sight of skirts on people hustling in as he was leaving. As if they had been waiting for him to go.

Or had he just imagined it all?

Ned had stopped by the tavern this morning because he wanted to piece together the truth. He hoped it all had been his imagination. The Logical Men's Society stood for male comradery, not loose ways. Heavy gambling and outlandish wagers were also frowned upon.

But now here was *this* woman.

If she'd been here last night, he would not have forgotten her. Then again, he'd been very drunk, and it embarrassed him. He was also taken aback by her claim. He did not own The Garland. He wanted to. He'd asked questions about legally claiming the building for the Society. The consensus was that eventually the Society would assume ownership since Andy had no family. They already considered it theirs.

Her claim, right or not, would upset every-thing.

"I am not accustomed to being called a liar," he said stiffly.

"Then you shouldn't lie." She didn't even miss a beat.

"Who are you? Were you here last night?"

Delicate brows arched as if affronted by his direct demand.

She moved into the main room. "You are Mr. Thurlowe? The physician?" She stopped some five feet from him. He caught the scent of her. It reminded him of a fragrant, potent tea. One that was a treat for the senses. *His* senses.

It took all his power to stand his ground. "You have the advantage of me. Have we met?"

"My uncle Andrew told me about you. He ad-mired you, sir."

Ned ignored the compliment. "You don't sound Scottish." Old Andy had never lost the hint of his homeland.

She smiled. "I'm half Scot. I grew up in Man-chester, where my father had business interests. I spent my summers in Glasgow." She held out a gloved hand. "I am Gemma Estep. Andrew Mac-Mhuirich left The Garland to me. I am pleased to meet you, sir. I am a healer myself."

Andy had left the tavern to her?

Perhaps if Ned hadn't been so drink-bit, he could have accepted the news with more grace. As it was, he spoke his thoughts aloud. "If this isn't a curse, I don't know what is." She claimed own-

ership of The Garland and the title of a "healer."
A *woman*? He laughed, the sound without mirth,
too late realizing she'd offered her hand and he
hadn't touched it.

Her hand dropped before he could make
amends. "Did you find something I said amusing,
Mr. Thurlowe?"

"Just everything," he answered candidly. "The
first being your claim to the power of *healing*. That
is a bald statement, isn't it?"

"I didn't say I had powers—"

"You don't have to explain yourself to me,
Miss—"

"Mrs.," she corrected firmly.

"Ah, *Mrs.* Estep." She was married. Of course.
That was the jolt he needed. He could school his
battered senses now.

"Well, Mrs. Estep, I've known many *healers*
during my time here. The English hillsides har-
bor a host of them. Meddling women who scour
the forests for herbs and claimed their treatments
for warts to cholera could save lives. Although,
how anyone can believe the nonsense they spout
defies my understanding."

Her lips parted in surprise at his insults but
then she said briskly, "You sound jaded, sir. Perhaps you haven't met the right people."

"Trust me, I have. I'm dumbfounded by what
people accept as cures. I've dealt with more rotting sliced potatoes placed on jaws for tooth-
ache, or feet for warts, or for the healing of open
wounds than any man should over a lifetime. I

do not believe that onions cut in half can soak up cholera or that dung packs can be a cure for the French pox, *or* ensure the gender of a baby, *or* be a cure for infertility. In fact, I wager the opposite would be true of infertility. The smell was horrendous."

Cataloging these outrages felt good and let him start a grievance against her. "I've been called in to heal the results of concoctions and potions that only the very gullible or the very ill would believe in. They drank them, they rubbed them on their skin, *they* had faith in their powers to heal because they had been administered by people they trusted—*healers*. Instead," he said, offering his indictment, "they were poisoned."

"I don't offer poisons."

He ignored her. "And here is the part I don't understand. Most of the healers appear worse off than their patients. They have hunched backs, sidewise limps, and fingers gnarled from years of digging through the woods for their precious roots, leaves, and berries. Although, I would never classify you as one of them, Mrs. Estep. In fact, with the right clothing, you could pass for a duchess in any ballroom in the land . . . and do you know, for the first time I understand my father's ill-fated fascination with my greedy courtesan mother."

He hadn't meant to add that last.

It had flowed out of him along with the reminder of how easily women could manipulate situations for their own purpose. Just as Clarissa

Taylor had caught him off guard yesterday and forced his hand. Or how the matrons had preyed upon his empathy to offer for her in the beginning.

"Did you just suggest that I am a woman of low reputation?" she asked as if stunned.

"You can see I have strong opinions," he said gruffly. It wasn't like him to spout off, but he'd not apologize. He meant every word. She'd be wise to leave Maidenshop now. "You say Old Andy left The Garland to you? In all the time I've known him, and Andy and I were close, the man never mentioned any family or the name Estep. In fact, perhaps it would be better if I spoke to your husband?"

"You would have some difficulty, sir. He's in hell." Her tone was clipped. "However, with your attitude, I have no doubt the two of you would have rubbed along well. Thank you for not holding back on your opinions, Doctor. Your words are strong, but so am I. You say you were close to my uncle? Then you must know he is rolling in his grave at the current state of his beloved tavern."

She was right.

That didn't mean Ned was going to trust her. "Well, he has been rolling in his grave for months without a word from you."

That comment drained the color from her face. "I just recently received the news."

Cynically, Ned doubted that. "From whom?"

Her expressive brows came together in annoyance at his tone. Good. He didn't want her to think of him as a friend, because he wasn't. He needed her gone. Vanquished. Never to appear again. And not just because of her ownership claim. *She* threatened him in ways he didn't understand.

Except, instead of disappearing, she snapped, "Reverend Summerall."

Summerall was the cleric at St. Martyr's Church down the road. That was not the response Ned had wanted. "I will check with him."

"Please do."

"In the meantime, let me see your proof that Andy left The Garland to you."

"So you can destroy it? Oh, no."

"Mrs. Estep—"

"Please, call me Gemma. I did *not* like the man I married and carrying his name is a burden I refuse to lift a moment longer."

Ned was not going to call her by her given name. It was too personal and he needed as much distance from her as possible. "Mrs. *Estep,* I am a man of honor. I wouldn't destroy anything of yours."

"Ah, yes, *you* are the chairman of the Logical Men's Society. See? I know exactly who you are. And who *they* are. Such honorable men—"

"We are."

She made a dismissive noise. "Look around the room, sir. Certainly, you of all people can detect the scent of urine. But if not, the sheets on the cot in my uncle's bedroom have been defiled, and recently. I know nothing honorable has been going on here. If anything, I may be saving the reputation of The Garland."

Her accusation clicked his suspicions about

what had happened after he'd left last night. The newer, younger members of the Society had most certainly been abusing their privileges.

At the same time, he was not going to hand over The Garland to her. "Perhaps it is best if we send for the magistrate." The local magistrate was Marsden. His great-grandfather had been the founding member of the Logical Men's Society. He would see matters Ned's way.

"By all means, send for him. I will happily present my proof to him. My uncle was the only family I had left. My claim is valid."

"If your claim was valid, you would have been here *months* ago." He shook his head. "No, Mrs. Estep—"

"*I requested* you call me Gemma." There was fire in her voice.

Ned smiled. Who had the upper hand now? "I am challenging your right to this building and this freehold. The Society members and I wish to purchase this building with the approval of the members of this village. The Garland has a storied history in Maidenshop."

"That story is about to change, sir. I have decided to turn The Garland into a tea garden. For *ladies.*"

"*What?*" Words almost failed him. "What of the Logical Men's Society?"

"You will have to find somewhere else to meet. May I recommend the church? I'm certain the Reverend Summerall would enjoy seeing all of you in the pews."

That was provocative, because Summerall would.

He took a step toward her, changing his tactic, trying to be somewhat conciliatory without giving her anything. "Do you not understand? The Society has been around for generations. You can't close it. Why, even your uncle was a proud member."

Unmoved, she gave a world-weary sigh. "Times change, Mr. Thurlowe. And I'm *not* closing it. I'm giving your precious Society the boot. The Garland will be a tea garden where I sell potions and soaps that appeal to gentle*women*. Perhaps we will start our own society. The Logical Women's Society. What do you think?"

"I think you are ridiculous."

"Well, then you know how I feel about you. *And* your Society that has *destroyed* this place. Now, you may go, Mr. Thurlowe. As you can see, I have my work cut out for me."

"You are ordering me to leave, *Mrs. Estep*?"

She did not like her married name. Her lips curled as if she'd like to take a bite out of him, but then she recovered. "Yes, I did order you to leave. *Go.*"

"Not a worry, *Mrs. Estep*. I shall go, *Mrs. Estep*. First, I will find the Reverend Summerall. Then I will go for the magistrate. You will not take over The Garland, *Mrs. Estep*, without legal grounds to do so."

On that note, because he didn't want her to have the last word, he shoved his hat on his head, turned on his heel, and walked out.

Had he really thought her attractive? Mrs. Estep with her imperial ways was one of the most annoying women he'd ever met. He could spend the day arguing with her or he could muster reinforcements in the form of Mars and the good reverend himself. Once confronted by authority, her claims would fall apart, he'd wager.

He slammed the door firmly behind him.

Hippocrates had been half-asleep at the post where he'd been tied, else he would have wandered back to his paddock. He started at the sound and then snorted his desire to be off. Ned was convinced Hippocrates liked traveling the countryside more than he did.

"You are not going to believe what I just went through," Ned muttered to the horse as he untied him.

Hippocrates stomped one foot as if saying he was well aware.

"We will not go to see Bran and Kate until we pay a call on the Reverend Summerall and track down Mars," Ned informed his horse as if he was a co-conspirator in the endeavor to root Mrs. Estep out of The Garland. Ned prayed that the minister alone would be enough to expose Mrs. Estep as a fraud . . . because he feared the earl was in London. That could be sticky.

He had one foot in the stirrup and was ready to hoist himself in the saddle when he heard his name being called in a sharp female voice. "*Mr. Thurlowe*. Here there, Mr. Thurlowe. I have a bone to pick with you."

Ned swore under his breath. It was Mrs. Warbler, the nosiest of all the Matrons of Maidenshop. She lived right across the road from The Garland and there was little that escaped her notice.

He schooled his features to a politeness he did not feel. Could this day grow worse? He took his foot out of the stirrup and faced the older widow who knew everything going on in the village. "Mrs. Warbler, how good to see you today," he said as if by rote.

"Don't be sweet to me." She'd come out of her house without hat or gloves, a sign of her haste to reach him. Instead, she had her lace morning cap over her short gray hair. She dressed well. Her late husband had been a military officer and she'd done right by him. "*You* know what happened last night."

This was dangerous ground.

"I saw you, sir, and the rest of the rabble. You refer to yourselves as *gentlemen*. Yeomen, lawyers, and drunkards is what I call the Logical Men's Society and I am sorely upset with *you*. It didn't used to be this bad."

"Matters were a bit much last night." And he wished he could remember the details. Or had stayed later to fend off the nonsense, which he was now convinced had most certainly happened. Had it been Winderton's doing? The young duke did as he pleased, and the image of Winderton full of himself and leaning against the bar rose in Ned's mind. There had been something afoot and Ned had been so gone in self-pity, he'd missed it.

"I will talk to the gentlemen." The first code of the Logical Men's Society is that a member didn't give the matrons any ammunition against them, and Mrs. Warbler was one of the ringleaders.

She was not one to be put off. "You had *women* in there and you caroused for hours into the morning. Why, I could barely sleep—"

She was interrupted by the sound of a pony cart. They both looked up the road and he almost swore under his breath. Clarissa Taylor was driving into the village.

Yes, the day could get worse.

She flashed him a bright smile and a wave of her hand. She looked fetching in her velvet cap and cape against the slight chill in the air.

Brazenly, Ned used her arrival to his advantage. "Mrs. Warbler, perhaps we should change the subject. Miss Taylor is here." His tone implied that he was refusing the discussion because of his respect for the delicate sensibilities of his betrothed.

"I thank the good Lord you are finally doing your duty and marrying that poor girl," Mrs. Warbler said through clenched teeth as she smiled and waved at Clarissa. Her frown returned when she looked at Ned. "About time, that's what *we* all say."

Once again he felt the disturbing twist in his gut. Especially when the matron said, "You are putting it off for two months, though? After all these years of making her wait, I say you should meet before the reverend once the banns are announced."

"Well, it is not your decision to make." He kept his voice low lest Clarissa overhear as she came closer to them.

"You would be surprised how much power we have," Mrs. Warbler answered. "We matrons are tired of being nice. And you need to take your *gentlemen*, and I use that term loosely, in hand." On that cryptic threat, she stepped forward to properly greet his intended.

He followed suit, much to Hippocrates's regret. There was no avoiding addressing Clarissa's arrival. The horse gave a withering sigh as Ned greeted his intended with, "You appear in good spirits."

"I am, sir." She looked to Mrs. Warbler. "Good morning, even though it is almost luncheon." She laughed at her small joke. "I came to collect the needlepoint cushion you wished me to finish."

"And I shall gather it for you. However, at this moment I have more important business at hand. I don't want Mr. Thurlowe to brush aside my complaint."

"Mrs. Warbler—" he started.

"What complaint?" Miss Taylor asked, interrupting him. Ned wished he had pretended he hadn't heard Mrs. Warbler's calling him. Why, he and Hippocrates could have tracked down Summerall by now.

"They have been having nothing short of Sodom and Gomorrah in The Garland." Mrs. Warbler's voice rang in the morning air.

"What?" Clarissa asked in surprise.

"She is being dramatic," Ned answered, his voice as firm with complacency as he could make it. "Some of the lads were rowdy last night." He didn't include himself, and he prayed Mrs. Warbler didn't say anything about his presence.

As if reading his mind, the old lady gave him a grim smile. "The ale and gin were flowing freely—"

"We don't serve gin at The Garland." He stepped between the two women, his back to Clarissa. With a hard look, he said to the matron, "I'm sorry your peace was disturbed. You are right when you say the lads may have been carried away. I will talk to them and I will hire Cora and Sarah Belks to clean the place up."

"Cora and Sarah Belks? You would be a fool if you hired them. They were part of the goings-on last night and they looked as if they'd had a right good time when they left in the very wee hours of the morning counting their money."

"Counting their money . . . ?" Clarissa repeated, sounding confused. She truly was a lamb in this world.

"Oh, yes, those girls did very well for themselves—"

"Mrs. Warbler, there is no call to be crude," Ned warned. "Especially in front of Miss Taylor." God, he sounded like a prude.

"I'm not the crude one, sir. You should look to your members for that trait."

She was right. When he saw the lads, he was

going to take them down a peg. And if his suspicions about Winderton were correct? How did one chastise a duke?

He swallowed his pride and addressed Mrs. Warbler. "I'm sorry for the disturbance. I will talk to everyone."

She pointed a finger in his face. "You see that you do. We are not running a brothel in the center of this village."

Clarissa made a shocked sound, her perfect mouth forming an "oh" of surprise, before she responded, "No, we are not."

If this was London, everyone would be turning a blind eye. Not so in Maidenshop. "_We aren't._" And then he thought of Mrs. Estep's complaints about the sheets. "The lads shouldn't have become so rowdy," he admitted.

Mrs. Warbler's answer was a, "Hmmm," as if she questioned his sincerity.

"I will see that it is all cleaned up." An idea came to him. A wicked idea. He glanced at the still-closed tavern door and swallowed a smile. He needed to put his story out before Mrs. Estep could present hers. One could go a great distance with Mrs. Warbler and her network of gossiping biddies on his side. It was a diabolical plan but the Logical Men's Society could not lose The Garland. Nor did he want to be remembered as the chairman whose inaction allowed the loss. He schooled his features into grave concern. "However, I have _larger_ problems to address. We have a squatter in The Garland right now."

Mrs. Warbler's interest was immediately piqued. "What do you say, sir?"

"We have a squatter. There is a woman who claims to be related to Old Andy. She says The Garland is hers."

The matron frowned. "He had relatives? I never heard him speak of one."

"Neither have I. However, *she* is in there and *she* claims she is here to stay."

"What are you going to do?"

"First, speak to the Reverend Summerall. She says he knows of her existence. We shall see about that." In fact, he couldn't wait for the conversation.

"And if he knows her?" Miss Taylor asked.

Ned frowned. "He won't know her. She is a jade, an opportunist. I know her type—"

The door of The Garland opened. Mrs. Estep stood there and the fire in her eyes let him know she'd heard every word he'd just said.

Good.

And then, before he knew what was what, Mrs. Estep took control. She spoke like a town crier laying down the law. "The Garland is now *closed*."

"Closed? What do you mean *closed*?" Mrs. Warbler said.

"I mean the doors will be shut until I am ready to open them again."

Ned lost his temper. "This is *not* your establishment. Your claim has not been acknowledged."

Her answer was an infuriating smile. "I will *nail* the door shut if necessary."

"You can't. We've scheduled a lecture here. The world's leading authority on the cosmos is giving a talk on his paper outlining—"

She slammed the door on all of them. Then there was the scrape of wood as the bar was thrown into place.

Silence settled upon all of them. Clarissa broke it. "Who was that?"

Ned gave up any pretense of control. Who the devil did that woman believe she was? "The most ill-mannered creature you could ever hope to meet. I forbid you to have anything to do with her. Do you understand?" He pointed his finger at Clarissa in the same manner Mrs. Warbler had used on him. "She is an impertinent piece of womanhood. And I assure you, *Mrs. Estep*"—he raised his voice as he used her name because he knew she was listening—"doesn't know *with whom she is dealing*. I understand women like her." Women like his mother, who took advantage of every man who crossed her path. "She will be *out* of there before nightfall."

Then, because no matter how rude Mrs. Estep was, he always remembered his manners, Ned excused himself, saying over-politely, "Mrs. Warbler, Miss Taylor, I beg your pardon. I must speak to the Reverend Summerall immediately."

Without waiting for a dismissal, he mounted and rode toward the church. Wherever Mrs. Estep had come from, he was ready to send her back there.

CLARISSA WAS accustomed to watching Ned ride off. It was all he ever did.

She struggled to not shout after him that *yes*, he was rude. How dare he order her around?

And why was he so angry at this Mrs. Estep? One of the things she admired about him was his compassion. He never pressed anyone to pay for services. The whole village knew that often, if a patient needed food or a bit of help, he'd see that they received it.

Now he wanted to turn out this woman?

She looked to Mrs. Warbler. "Do you have any idea what is going on?"

"Absolutely none," the older lady said. "However, I shall find out." She stepped forward and knocked on the door.

No answer.

She tried the latch.

"Mrs. Estep threw the bar on the other side," Clarissa reminded her helpfully. "Should I go around back?"

Mrs. Warbler didn't answer. She stared at the door as if she could open it with one of her pie-eyed glares before knocking again.

The Matrons of Maidenshop were a remarkably stubborn group of people. Clarissa had observed that, when it came to wanting their way, they would beat on a brick wall until it fell or their fists were bloody. Clarissa preferred a different action.

Without waiting for permission, she climbed down from the cart, tied up the pony, and went around to the back. The kitchen door was wide open and she cautiously took a step inside, before stopping in shock. The room appeared as if there had been a fight and it smelled of rotting food and something else unsavory.

No wonder Mrs. Estep was out of sorts.

"Mrs. Estep—?" Her words broke off in a screech of terror as a trio of mice came out from a hidey-hole and went charging across the floor, heading right for her. Clarissa did not like mice, rats, snakes, or anything that scurried or slithered across the ground. Her fear was irrational. She had no idea why she reacted that way, but react she did, hopping away from the furry creatures.

With a warrior's cry, Mrs. Estep leaped out of a side-room door with a broom. She lifted it like a weapon and brought it down upon the mice. Unfortunately, they were quicker. They raced away, running a full circle around the kitchen table and sending Clarissa up onto the chair.

Undeterred by their quickness, Mrs. Estep went after them with ferocity. While Clarissa cowered, Mrs. Estep chased the mice around the chair until they confounded their pursuer by dashing back into the crevice in the wall.

Mrs. Estep placed the broom in front of it as if to bar the danger of their escape and turned to Clarissa . . . who suddenly felt very silly. Her face burned with her embarrassment.

She climbed down from the chair perch but before she could offer apologies, Mrs. Estep threw her arms wide to take in the room. "Can you believe this? Men are beasts. They are base and disgusting. You will not believe what they were doing in my uncle's bed—"

Mrs. Warbler interrupted them by rushing into the kitchen through the back door, having obviously surmised where Clarissa had gone. "I heard a scream."

"It was me," Clarissa confessed. "I saw mice . . ."

But Mrs. Warbler was not listening. Instead, she looked around the room in horrified surprise. "What in the name of all that is holy has happened here? This is revolting."

In a tight voice, Mrs. Estep said, "Yes, it is." Then she burst into noisy tears.

And if there was ever a way to bring women to your side, it was that action.

Chapter Five

Gemma never broke down, not in front of strangers. It was the English side of her. Or perhaps the prideful Scot. Either way, she knew how to behave.

Oh, she would shed a tear, but to outright bawl? No, never, and yet, here she was.

She was exhausted, hungry, and on the verge of being completely defeated. Her confrontation with the bullish Mr. Thurlowe played to her every fear. In a village like this, the doctor was practically royalty. Certainly, he had access to the gentry and that meant the magistrate. Who would that authority believe? The doctor? Or herself with a rightful claim?

Or at least she hoped her claim was legitimate. She actually wasn't certain. Instead, she had been operating on sheer nerve . . . because what other choice did she have?

If she couldn't have The Garland, she had nowhere else to go.

Hands guided her to sit in the chair. Over her head, the women whispered about the battle of the mice and Gemma's complaint about something having happened in her uncle's bed that had upset her.

"What is wrong with the bed?" the younger woman queried.

"The sheets," Gemma choked out and then refused to go on because it was so disgusting.

"Indeed?" said the older woman in a tone laden with well-placed suspicions, and Gemma knew she didn't need to say more.

The older woman took charge. "Miss Taylor, cross the road to my house and tell Jane we will need a set of fresh sheets here. Also, when you return, bring the tea caddy and the sherry bottle. Tell Jane I want a full one. She needs to bring glasses, as well. We require fortification. I imagine we will not find a bottle here because everything appears to be drained dry."

"Yes, Mrs. Warbler." Miss Taylor hurried to do her bidding.

Gemma tried to halt her crying. It took several minutes before she could finally right herself. She reached for the pocket of her dress for a kerchief or something to blow her nose. There was nothing. She had to settle for the back of her glove and that was the most humiliating moment of all.

It almost put her back into another fit of tears, except for Mrs. Warbler's crisp, "Here now, we can't make things better if you are going to continue to blubber."

Dear God, that was exactly what her gran would have said. Still, Gemma had to indulge in a fit of self-pity. "You won't believe me. Not after what I heard Mr. Thurlowe say."

"Young woman, I am more clever than to listen to what a man says. Are you going to tell me your side of the story or not?"

Such a challenge could not be ignored.

"I'm not usually like this," Gemma said in her defense, raising her head. "I am actually quite practical."

"Does the rest of The Garland look like these two rooms?"

"Worse."

"Then I don't blame you for having a fit. I'm Elizabeth Warbler, the neighbor across the street. I've seen the goings-on here."

At that moment Miss Taylor, breathing heavily from her haste, returned holding a bottle and several glasses. "Jane will be here momentarily," she reported. "However, I thought to carry this myself."

"Excellent idea," Mrs. Warbler said. She took the bottle, broke the wax, and looked around the kitchen. "Ah, a knife." She dared to take one off a dirty plate. With a curl of her lip, she searched for something. Then, not finding it, she removed her lace cap and cleaned the blade of the knife.

"Your cap," Gemma protested. "You will ruin it."

"Priorities, my dear. We need substance." She uncorked the bottle handily with her knife and then poured generously.

"Oh, that is too much for me," Miss Taylor demurred. She was a lovely woman, perhaps the same age as Gemma. Her hair was the color of the richest honey and her green eyes were trusting, but she didn't strike Gemma as anyone's fool.

"Oh, posh," Mrs. Warbler countered. "I have a feeling you will need more than this once we see the whole of the place."

"You will," Gemma assured her. "It is a disaster."

"Then drink up," Mrs. Warbler ordered, handing glasses to the two of them.

Gemma couldn't determine the older woman's age. She must be firmly over fifty. Her skin was thin but still retained a creamy unlined texture. Her short gray hair suited her face, bringing the kindness of her gaze to the forefront. She was tall, thin but not unfeminine.

She looked to Gemma. "You say you are practical. Well, you haven't taken a sip yet, and you need it. It has been a trying morning. However, nothing compared to my being up half the night."

"Up half the night?" Miss Taylor echoed.

"You can't imagine what was going on here last night," was the answer before Mrs. Warbler downed her glass.

Gemma was not one for spirits in any form, except when the occasion did call for something. She tasted the sherry, found she liked it, and followed Mrs. Warbler's action of swallowing it neatly. Rich liquid flowed down her throat. It settled in her empty belly. She placed her hand against her abdomen, afraid she would disgrace herself . . . until she experienced a spreading of warmth.

Mrs. Warbler had poured herself another glass. She was obviously no stranger to enjoying good sherry. "Miss Taylor?" She offered the bottle.

"I'm fine. I think I shall fetch water for tea, if I can start a fire."

"Excellent idea." Mrs. Warbler handed the bottle to Gemma. "Help yourself."

At that moment a serving woman joined them in the kitchen. She was of middle years and held a tea caddy in one arm. Her other arm was full of sheets. She pulled up short at the sight of the kitchen. "Oh, dear."

"I know," Mrs. Warbler agreed. "I would say that this kitchen wasn't cleaned after Old Andy's wake, except *we* saw to it, didn't we, Jane? The two of us together. It was a late night."

"Yes, ma'am."

"The Logical Men's Society has destroyed this place." Mrs. Warbler clicked her tongue.

"Men are beasts," Gemma said, repeating her new refrain, and a fine one it was.

"Right you are," Mrs. Warbler agreed. "Oh, and for introductions, this is Jane, the steadiest of souls in the village." Miss Taylor returned with a full kettle of water and set it on the hook.

"And this is Miss Clarissa Taylor. She is promised to our good doctor."

Gemma would have offered her condolences, except her manners were returning.

Miss Taylor had the good sense to appear

slightly embarrassed. "His outburst was uncharacteristic of him," she offered. She and Jane began building the fire. Apparently, the maid knew wood was stacked somewhere outside and had fetched it. "He forgets himself sometimes."

Gemma chose not to answer because any comment she would have made about Dr. Thurlowe would have been a rude one. Instead, she took another sip from the sherry.

Her limbs had relaxed. Her tears had dried on her cheeks and she held the sherry bottle by its neck in her lap. She didn't even realize she had it until Mrs. Warbler gently took it from her. "So Old Andy was—?" the woman prodded.

"My uncle. My mother's brother." She looked at the women in the kitchen. "I didn't know he'd died until two days ago."

"I'm sorry you didn't know," Miss Taylor said. "That must have been a shock."

Was it? Gemma feared she was beginning to expect death at every turn.

Jane made a triumphant sound at having the fire going. Suddenly too tired to move, Gemma watched as the maid swung the hook holding the kettle over the flame.

"So what is your story?" Mrs. Warbler said. "Do you have a name? Are you married?"

"My name is Gemma Estep and my husband is dead." And before she stopped to think, or because of the sherry, she blurted out, "I don't mourn him, I can tell you that. He gambled away my father's fine house in Manchester and I knew *nothing* about it until a family arrived to move in. I was put out immediately. My husband didn't even help me move. He was in London. He was always in London. Always away, and I certainly didn't matter to him." She wouldn't mind another spot of sherry, except perhaps she'd had enough . . . ?

"Did you know that he was of such low character when you married him?" Miss Taylor asked, her tone shocked.

"No, he was a captain in the Horse Guard and Lord Latimer is his brother. When I was introduced to Paul, he acted the very model of a gentleman," Gemma said. "Father was quite taken with him. Actually, Father was not well and hadn't been for some time. I believe he was most anxious I marry before he died. He wanted to ensure I had a proper husband. Paul Estep appeared in society and, well, he swept us both off our feet and out of our money."

"Yours is a sad story, Mrs. Estep—" Miss Taylor started, until Gemma cut her off.

"*Gemma.* My name is Gemma. I don't claim Estep. Not after what that family has done to me. Paul died and no one told me. He was killed by an angry husband, in a *duel* over the man's wife. I arrived in London expecting to see him, but he had already been buried."

"Good Lord," Mrs. Warbler whispered.

"Oh, there was no good lord involved. Lord Latimer is a hideous man. He claimed my husband's estate and refused to offer me a widow's portion. That money was *my* inheritance and the courts would not let me have it."

"Because you are female," Mrs. Warbler said. She looked to Miss Taylor. "Do you see now, Clarissa, why the matrons have pushed to see you settled with an honest man? A woman, even married, has little rights in society. I'm fortunate that although my husband rarely came home, he took care of me in the will."

"The matrons?" Gemma asked.

"We ensure things are done right in this village." Mrs. Warbler spoke with confidence. "And we know everything. We do," she repeated as if Gemma needed to be convinced. "We know Mr. Thurlowe has grand designs on hosting a lecture series in Maidenshop. He claims his lectures will be more important than anything put on by the Royal Society in London."

"That is a grand dream," Gemma admitted. "But why would anyone come here for a lecture?"

"We are close to Cambridge," Miss Taylor offered.

"Yes," Mrs. Warbler agreed. "There is also, apparently, a number of disgruntled academics who feel the Royal Society is not interested in new voices. Mr. Thurlowe wants to give them a forum for their views."

Miss Taylor nodded agreement. "He is dedicated to the idea."

Mrs. Warbler looked to Gemma. "And that is his story. We want to hear yours. What are your plans for The Garland?"

For a second Gemma balked at being called out. Trust was difficult for her . . . and then she realized that was not the right way to repay these women's kindness.

Miss Taylor stood next to Mrs. Warbler, interested in her answer. Jane was by the hearth, holding a hand up to the iron kettle to see if the water was heating.

Gemma cleared her voice, and said, "I'm going to turn The Garland into a tea garden, a genteel place where ladies are as welcome as gentlemen. I visited one in London and I was quite taken with the idea. There were whole families there for an afternoon outing. They had space for the children to run and a bowling green. The Garland has room aplenty for all of that and my flower beds and herb gardens. The music of the stream is so happy out there, I believe they will grow beautifully."

"The Three Thieves," Miss Taylor whispered.

"What?" Gemma asked.

"The name of the stream is the Three Thieves."

"I imagine there is a tale there," Gemma said, quite charmed with the name.

"If there is, I've never heard anyone say," Miss Taylor answered.

"Well, then, we will have to make one up," Gemma decided, the adventure in the name helping her vision grow clearer. "You see, I'm a healer and I am from a long line of them. My gran taught me how to brew tisanes and make salves. She gave me recipes that go back hundreds of years. I also create teas. There are many healing properties in a good tea. The ones I will serve will not only refresh, but also soothe and ward against bad airs and dangerous spirits."

Mrs. Warbler cocked her head. "What of pains in the joints?" She touched her swollen knuckles as she spoke.

"Ah, that one is easy. I've been making a liniment for sore joints since I was a child. My father was sorely afflicted with pain and swore it was the only thing that could ease his aches. In fact, I have a small tin of it. I would be honored if you were to try it."

"I would be happy to do so."

Gemma stood. The world whirled for a second, a result of the sherry and her tired state, and yet, her excitement over sharing her plans with these women gave her the energy to fetch her valise from the main room. She carried it into the kitchen and set it on the table. She pulled out her embroidered bag that held her healing concoctions. "My supplies are running low," she apologized as she took the lid off the tin for joint pain.

"If you can relieve the pain in my hands, I will consider you an angel," Mrs. Warbler answered.

The balm was an expensive one. It was a combination of ginger, clove, and black pepper oils that had come from India. Carefully, with the women watching, Gemma used her fingertip to circle Mrs. Warbler's knuckle joints.

The older woman remained skeptical, until the oils performed their magic. "I feel it working. My skin is warm."

Gemma nodded. "Keep rubbing it in with little circles the way I put it on." Mrs. Warbler followed suit.

"Is it making a difference?" Miss Taylor asked.

"A *miracle* of a difference," Mrs. Warbler claimed. "Why, it is as if my hands are reforming themselves."

"If only that were true," Gemma replied modestly. "I cannot claim to cure. However, what is happening is that you have a touch of relief and you know how important that is."

"I do. I live with this pain every day. Wait until you meet the Duchess of Winderton," Mrs. Warbler said. "She is one of the matrons and she is always complaining of gout and pain in her knees. All Mr. Thurlowe will do is advise her to stay away from rich foods. She is a duchess! She needs rich food. Do you have anything to help her?"

"Juniper might help." Although Gemma did agree with Mr. Thurlowe.

"Like what they use to make gin?" Mrs. Warbler frowned.

"I brew it into a tonic that is nothing close to gin. My gran had gout and she swore by this recipe." Or, when Gemma thought about it, her gran *could* have been sipping gin. She had been a feisty woman.

"I am in awe of how you have managed to see your way to London and then Maidenshop," Miss Taylor said. "Why, it is as if you have traveled all of England. I don't know that I would have the courage, Mrs. Estep."

"Please, call me Gemma," she reminded them. "And, we all have the courage, when we are angry enough." Gemma looked around at the shambles of the kitchen. A yawn rose in her chest, one that she could not stifle. "I'm sorry. It has been a long journey and now—this."

Mrs. Warbler sat back, rubbing her hand joints in small circles. "Don't you trouble yourself over The Garland or Mr. Thurlowe. One challenge at a time, my girl. You are going to be an excellent addition to Maidenshop. We want you here. Don't we, Miss Taylor?"

"Of course."

"A tea garden is exactly what Maidenshop needs, and it may be a death blow to that ridiculous Logical Men's Society."

Ridiculous? Yes, Gemma liked that sentiment. "Mr. Thurlowe will not agree with you."

"Mr. Thurlowe does not run Maidenshop. The matrons do." Mrs. Warbler stood as if coming to a decision. "We are going to help you, Mrs. Estep—"

"Gemma, *please*."

"Very well. We are going to help you, *Gemma*. The Garland has become a scourge to our fair village, and therefore, we accept your tea garden. In fact, we *demand* it. Don't we, Miss Taylor?"

"I don't believe the Bucks will agree," was the uncertain answer.

"The Bucks?" Gemma asked.

"Mr. Thurlowe and Lord Marsden," Miss Taylor explained. "They are the decision-makers when it comes to the Logical Men's Society. We used to say, 'The Three Bucks,' but Mr. Balfour has married. One must be unmarried or a widower to be a member of the Society."

"So soon, Mr. Thurlowe will not be eligible for membership once he marries you?"

There was a moment of hesitation. A regret. "Yes," Miss Taylor admitted.

Gemma frowned. "Did I say something wrong?"

The younger woman shook her head. "I believe that it is giving up his role in the Society that makes Mr. Thurlowe reluctant to marry."

"Reluctant?"

"We have been promised for over two years. He's . . . not eager," Miss Taylor said. "He's very devoted to the Society."

"Oh, pish posh," Mrs. Warbler said. "It is past high time that man took a wife. He needs to be settled. Both of you do."

"Except he didn't act happy yesterday when I pushed him as you and the others recommended."

"No man is happy about marrying. *All* of them need to be coerced one way or the other," Mrs. Warbler declared. "Indeed, changing The Garland into a tea garden might wake Sir Lionel up to notice that he needs a woman in his life."

"Sir Lionel?" Gemma said.

"He is a widower who is in the Logical Men's Society," Miss Taylor offered helpfully.

"And he needs a wife," Mrs. Warbler said bluntly. A glint came to her eyes. "Like me."

When she spoke that firmly, Gemma wasn't about to argue . . . although she was convinced no woman in her right mind would marry if they understood all the control to their own lives they were surrendering.

Jane had brewed the tea and now offered cups to Gemma and the others.

Gemma shook her head. She had no taste for it. What she wanted was sleep. She looked around the kitchen. Jane had also been quietly stacking the dishes. There was so much to do. "Look at this place. It will take weeks and weeks to put in order. And I don't even want to think about how long I shall need to create the gardens."

"Don't you worry over that now." Mrs. Warbler took Gemma's arm and drew her to her feet to guide her toward the bedroom. "In fact, you appear exhausted, child. Why don't you take a rest and leave all of this to me. Jane changed the sheets. The bed should be comfortable."

Gemma attempted to turn. "I can't. I can't rest when there is so much to do."

"You can," Mrs. Warbler's soothing voice said. "See, the sheets are clean. Doesn't the bed look inviting? Have a little rest."

She was right. The bed now appeared an oasis. Gemma didn't need help to practically fall into it. The sheets smelled of lavender. Mrs. Warbler was a good housekeeper. It would be lovely to take a rest. Her eyes grew heavy. "There is so much to be done."

"And we'll help you," came the comforting answer. "You have friends now."

Yes, friends. Mrs. Warbler and Miss Taylor had

been all that was kind to her. They had done for her what she would have offered if she had been in their places.

Friends. Such a lovely word.

"And our friends will help with The Garland," Mrs. Warbler cooed as if knowing she had won. "The matrons have been looking for a new project and this is a most excellent one."

Gemma wasn't certain what she meant, but she was truly too tired to care, even as she listened to the excited buzz of female plotting.

Mrs. Warbler was giving instructions. She mentioned names and ordered Jane and Miss Taylor to "spread the word. Have them come now with buckets and mops and rags."

Gemma smiled. She could imagine Mrs. Warbler commanding a force of soldiers, or better yet, fairies to scrub from top to bottom. She was having a dream, she surmised. A vision of her tea garden coming to life . . .

Chapter Six

"Our conscience . . . our *consciences* . . . *our* consciences," the Reverend Summerall repeated, testing the words. He paced the length of a small clearing in a wood not far from St. Martyr's. He read from a handwritten paper while gesturing grandly with his free hand. His booming voice filled the air.

Ned had assumed he would find the good reverend in the sanctuary practicing his Sunday sermon. He had not. After he caught Mrs. Summerall in the parsonage, she had directed him here. "Just follow the sound of his voice," she had advised, and so he had.

Summerall was so deep into weighing the different inflections, he didn't realize Ned was there, even after Ned had politely cleared his voice several times.

Finally, Ned spoke up. "Reverend? Reverend? *Summerall.*"

The cleric started at the sound, and then chuckled good-naturedly as he recognized Ned. "Mr. Thurlowe, how fortuitous you are here. Which tonal quality did you think sounded best?"

"Best for what?"

"To make you uneasy. To prick that of which I speak."

"Our consciences?"

"Yes."

"You want the congregants to feel uneasy?"

"Absolutely. My role in Maidenshop is to make the villagers think long and hard about their choices. Of course, that is what I wish them to do every week. You can see how effective I am."

"More of us have devils whispering in our ear rather than angels. Or your voice," Ned observed.

That sparked a bark of laughter from Summerall, and then his manner changed to one of excitement. "*Why* am I going on this way? You've come to discuss the details of your nuptials with Miss Taylor, haven't you?" He put his papers in his pocket and rubbed his hands with anticipation. "This will be a fine wedding. Everyone is ready for it." He chuckled before adding, "Past ready."

Almost churlishly, Ned said, "How has everyone heard the news already? It really isn't even decided."

The Reverend Summerall's manner grew stern. "Not decided? Sir, you have held this woman's promise to you for two years. It is past *deciding*.

Besides, I understand you set a date. The day following your lecture, correct?"

Ned stood in awkward silence. He didn't even understand himself why he wanted to deny it. He was going to marry Clarissa. He had made a commitment.

Then he remembered discussing his marriage was not his purpose here. Without preamble, he said, "There is a woman at The Garland who says she is a relative of Old Andy. She claims he left the tavern to her."

The minister's reaction was not what Ned had hoped. "Mrs. Estep? She is here?"

"You know of her?"

"Is she a redhead with the brightest blue eyes and an intelligent manner?"

"I don't know about the intelligence but the rest of your description is correct."

"Then she is Old Andy's niece. She visited him last spring, the same night as our last Cotillion. She was on her way to see her husband in London. Good family. She's related in marriage to Lord Latimer. You say she is at The Garland? I should go welcome her."

Summerall would have charged away if not for Ned's catching his arm. "But did Old Andy leave The Garland to her? Do you know this?"

The reverend gave him a quizzical look. "Well, I don't know anything for a fact. Andy never confided in me . . . It is possible, I suppose. Is there a will?"

"Not one Lord Marsden and I could find. We searched everywhere. However, she says she has a letter stating that The Garland is hers."

The Reverend Summerall shrugged his shoulders. "Then she might. I considered Andy a friend. However, I was not privy to all the details of his life."

"Damn." Ned pivoted away.

"Is something the matter?"

"Is *something* the *matter*?" Ned couldn't help but repeat. "She wishes to destroy The Garland."

"*Destroy* it?"

"*Yes.*" With an angry wave of his arm, Ned said, "She has no respect for the traditions of the place."

"Such as the Logical Men's Society?" Summerall accurately questioned.

"*Exactly.* She says she is going to change it into a tea garden—and include *women* as patrons—and *then*, she is going to set up shop as a dealer of potions and spells and nonsense."

"Spells—?"

"*Why are women the way they are?*" Ned demanded. The whole lot frustrated him. He could have had Mrs. Estep on her way if not for the interference of Mrs. Warbler and *Clarissa*.

Yes, Clarissa, whom he'd wager was behind everyone in the village knowing of his agreeing to marry her in two months—which was difficult to swallow because he hadn't had a second to process what he'd agreed to. Or, in truth, to determine a way to postpone the marriage ceremony.

He wasn't ready to be a husband.

"In *what way* are women the way they are?" Summerall asked.

"Foolish, wrongheaded, willing to believe in the stars or incantations or the power of grass and leaves."

"Thurlowe, are you feeling all right?"

Ned answered him with a frown. He'd believed The Garland would remain in the control of the Logical Men's Society, that his plans for his lecture series could continue unabated.

She was going to ruin his plans, and in a way he wasn't certain he understood. His reaction to her was too strong. She threatened his sense of peace. He both wanted her gone . . . and *wanted* her.

Lust was an uncomfortable emotion for Ned. Men, such as his father, made fools of themselves over women. He prided himself on his temperate nature. He had no desire to be the rake or the scoundrel. Education and hard work had been his lifeline. Yes, he was accepted, and yet, there was always in the back of people's minds that he was the bastard of an infamous courtesan. Even Summerall had brought the topic up once.

And yet, having met Mrs. Estep, Ned discovered he felt a stronger resistance to marrying Clarissa than he had before.

What the devil was going on with him? Drinking, lusting, acting like every man with a hard dick . . .

"I'm fine, Summerall. It's just that I'm not going to let her walk off with something as important to this community as The Garland."

Summerall responded as if he spoke gibberish. "It is a tavern, Ned. I mean, it is a fine meeting space. However, a tea garden does sound interesting. We can all meet there, including the ladies—"

Ned wanted to roar his frustration. "Are you a *man*?"

"I believe so," Summerall answered, looking as if needing verification. "Why do you ask?"

"Ah, forget it. My apologies. It is not my intention to take this out on you."

"Well, thank you. I think."

"I'm just very concerned about the village. I've worked to bring the very best medicine to Maidenshop."

"And you have succeeded, sir. We count ourselves fortunate to have such a talented doctor in our midst."

"It is just that—*she* is going to change things if we let her stay."

"What do you mean?"

"I know her type."

"Which is?"

How could Ned explain to the earnest cleric what he wasn't certain he understood himself? "She's too—" he started and then stopped. Too what?

Too beautiful? Too bold? Too unsettling?

And those qualities drew him to her in a way he'd not experienced before.

Illogically, he sensed she could prove his undoing because he wasn't one to look at a woman's lips and wonder how they tasted. Or recognize that her hips fit his. Or think of sirens—

"Too . . . ?" Summerall prompted.

Ned ran a frustrated hand over his face. "Everything. Too everything." That was evasive enough to put off questions, especially from a man who was anxious to officiate his wedding. "She says she is a healer. I know the type. She has no formal medical training. She can do great damage."

Alarmed, Summerall said, "Such as?"

"Offering patients false hope, and doing it just for money. London is crawling with charlatans who make dubious claims."

"Yet, without hope, what do we have?" the minister asked.

"Facts. Truth. Reality. It is all that matters."

"I have seen how hope, especially when offered in the deepest, most devout prayer, can be of service."

"As a panacea for fear, yes," Ned agreed. Actually, he'd never given any credit to prayer. Oh, when he was a lad under his father's roof, he'd had a heavy-handed nurse who had urged him to pray. Dutifully. On his knees. Telling him to pray that his "wicked mother's sins" would not be on his little soul.

Now he was a man and he'd realized long ago that prayer had been a way to keep him under control. To keep him humble and not wish for things beyond his station.

Well, he was no longer so browbeaten. "Do you truly believe Old Andy wanted her to do this to The Garland?"

The reverend's brow furrowed in worry. "I fear this is my fault. I'm the one who wrote to her of her uncle's death. I—" His voice broke off in indecision.

Ned was far from undecided. "I know this is *not* what Old Andy would have wanted. Not once did he invite the women of the village to The Garland. It is a man's place. It is not for the gentler sex." Although the lot of them in the Society should have taken more care of the building. The place had looked like a pigsty this morning.

"Except," Summerall suggested wistfully, "it would be lovely to have a tea garden in the village. Deirdre and I would enjoy it."

"You can drink tea at home," Ned answered. It didn't help his attitude that Deirdre Summerall was one of the matrons who had bullied Ned into offering for Clarissa. Right now he was sour on the whole lot of them.

He also realized he was on his own. At least when it came to the married men. Their wives had too much power over them. Even Balfour deferred to his wife. However, Ned liked Kate. She was a sensible woman. And not a matron. At least, not yet.

On the other hand, Mrs. Estep was bringing something to the village that he knew he did not want. She was a danger. "I'm going for the magistrate," he announced, and without waiting for a response walked over to Hippocrates, who had been idly eating his way through clover. Ned mounted and set off toward Belvoir, the Earl of Marsden's estate. The road took him right through the village.

He had not gone far when he realized there was more than the customary activity going on. Women walked the road in twos and threes, their hands carrying brooms and rags. A few had buckets.

What the devil?

Ned nudged his horse up toward a group of them. "Mrs. Ledbetter, what are you all about?"

The jolly woman flashed him a broad smile. "Why, a mission of mercy, Mr. Thurlowe. We've been called to clean The Garland."

Alarmed, Ned kicked Hippocrates forward.

Mrs. Warbler stood in the tavern's front door, welcoming everyone and giving instructions. As he rode up, the old woman stepped forward, her manner one of supreme command. A cadre of females flanked her.

He was outnumbered.

"Mr. Thurlowe, you can see we are busy here," she said cheerfully.

"Aye, that I can. Where is Mrs. Estep?"

"Ah, the poor young woman is sleeping. She's had a hard time of it." She said this to the women around her who took on that look females had of interested commiseration. They were always ready to take up the cause of the indefensible—except he'd wager his horse Mrs. Estep could well take care of herself. See what chaos she had already wrought?

"Unfortunately," Mrs. Warbler continued, "the building has been basely used, as *you* yourself know." Her words sounded sweet but there were glints in her eyes. She held him responsible.

And he hated that she probably knew more about what had been going on than he did. Or that she was right to be outraged.

"We are giving the place a good cleaning," she finished.

"A scrubbing is more like it. I've never seen such a mess in my life," Mrs. Dawson declared. She stood like a master-at-arms beside Mrs. Warbler.

"Or smelled a worse one," a woman said from the door, and Ned could have groaned when he recognized Mrs. Summerall. *Deirdre.*

She wore her silver hair under a sensible mob-cap and had an apron around her ample waist and bosom. "We are going to turn The Garland into a tea garden like they have in London. It is an exciting venture." Heads nodded their agreement. More women joined them.

And then he saw Clarissa.

She came around from the side of the building, a charming kerchief tied around her head. She held a broom and waved her hand in front of her face, coughing at the same time as if she needed some fresh air.

"The smell in the taproom—I can't stand it," she

complained, her step slowing when she noticed Ned. She flashed him her prettiest smile. "Are you impressed with what we are doing? Everyone wishes to help."

Not for the first time, Ned considered how little he knew of his intended. Clarissa Taylor was cleaning?

He hadn't really thought of what she did with her days. He'd never asked, either.

And then, to his surprise, a wagon came down the road with the driver wearing the livery of the Duke of Winderton and none other than Lucy, the dowager herself, sitting on the bench beside him.

She, too, appeared ready to clean.

Ned looked to Mrs. Warbler. She smiled with the satisfaction of a general who had staged a successful coup.

He needed Mars. He needed the magistrate, and he needed him *now*.

Putting heel to horse, Ned galloped for Belvoir, feeling the eyes of every woman in the village upon him.

MARS WAS not in. He was in London.

Ned cursed his bad luck. "I need him here," he told Gibson, the Marsden butler.

"I would be happy to have a message delivered to him," the always polite Gibson offered.

It was all Ned could do. He scratched out a quick post, *Havoc reigns in Maidenshop. The ma-*

trons have taken over The Garland. Please return with all possible haste—T

And now what?

Ned stood on Belvoir's step without admiring the graceful gardens just showing signs of spring awakening that made it one of the most coveted properties in England. Instead, he had a sense of impending doom.

If he was here, Mars would have laughed at Ned's worries and together they would have made it right. Now he was on his own.

There was nothing left to do except see the patients who had requested Ned's attention.

He set out to call on the Widow Smethers. The ankle was doing far better today, which gave him hope. Ankle bones could be tricky. He made certain she had a neighbor checking on her and promised to call on the morrow.

He was on his way to his next patient when the Dawson brothers waved him down. They were in their early twenties and not the most industrious of men. He remembered drinking with them the night before. "We hear the matrons are kicking up dust at The Garland," Mark Dawson said. "Sir Lionel tells us he is outraged. They have no call to enter our domain."

"We want to know what you are going to do about it, sir," his brother, William, said. "You are the chairman, no?"

"I am. And I'm going to talk to the magistrate. Until then, you lads mind your manners."

"Don't seem right, the ladies taking over," William grumbled. "Sir Lionel said they just walked right in."

"It *isn't* right. However, the Logical Men's Society has standards and we will follow them until the matrons vacate or the magistrate helps us to regain the building."

"Why?" William wondered.

"Why what?" Ned asked, annoyed.

"Why do we have standards?"

"Because we are *gentlemen*." How many times had he said that to them, and they still stared at him as if he had sprouted two heads. Did they not understand how important the distinction was? "And don't worry. Lord Marsden should return to the area shortly."

"Won't be soon enough," Mark said. "I liked gathering there. Filled the time. Where are we going to drink tonight?"

It was on the tip of Ned's tongue to suggest Mark attempt reading a book to fill his time, but he knew better. In fact, he'd personally orchestrated the Dawsons' joining the Logical Men's Society. The member numbers had been thin, and wanting to have the best possible numbers in the audience for his lectures, Ned had recruited every single male in the parish he could. One could say that he was also responsible for the wicked, drunken turn the Society had taken, as well. He hadn't overseen things the way he should.

Mars had warned him that he'd been opening the doors too wide. Ned had dismissed the warning as lordly elitism. After all, if someone hadn't given Ned opportunities, he never would have advanced his station in life, and he'd hoped to encourage the villagers in the same manner. Now he realized guilt was an uncomfortable emotion. And he knew exactly what Mrs. Warbler would have to say about the Society's current standards.

"When the earl returns, we will right the matter," Ned repeated. He rode on to his next call for the day—Kate Balfour.

Usually a midwife would take care of parish birthing matters. Unfortunately, the current midwife for the countryside, Mary Thomason, was ancient and had a habit of drinking more than she should. Consequently, Ned had to see to a number of births, and while he didn't mind playing male midwife in emergencies, he'd rather not. He enjoyed every facet of medicine . . . but he was keenly aware that the most respected doctors shied away from this sort of practice. Yet, he also liked seeing babies come into the world. So he struggled with wanting to do his best for all of his patients and being that lad who was always judged and found wanting because he didn't meet the strictures of society. Even for matters that were out of his control, like the circumstances of his birth.

Of course, this baby was different. He would do anything Balfour asked. He just prayed nothing went wrong.

And things could go wrong. Childbirth was dangerous for a woman, especially since Kate was over five and thirty, well past the age of having her first baby.

Ned had suggested Balfour take his wife to London for the birth, but they weren't interested in leaving Maidenshop. They were in the process of renovating a house that Balfour had purchased and thought it important to stay.

"We want our baby raised here," Kate had said. "The child should be born here, as well." So, of course, Ned had agreed to support them in any way possible.

Balfour met Ned in the yard before he could dismount. "Thank God you are here." He was a tall, dark-haired, handsome man. "Kate has been very tense. The baby is kicking."

"That is a good sign."

"I keep telling myself it is. Did you hear of the mother in Thorpton who died of childbed fever last week?"

Ned had heard, and he was sorry they had learned of it. Thorpton was a neighboring village some ten miles away. The mother had been in the hands of the local women—not a midwife, and not a doctor, either. Even though the husband had reached out to Ned at the last minute, it was, by then, too late.

As a physician, he lived closely with death. Still, nothing was more heartbreaking than the loss of a young mother so soon after her child was born. Oftentimes, no one understood what caused those tragic deaths, except childbirth was not easy. Balfour wanted assurances Ned didn't feel comfortable making. Some physicians, he knew, could offer platitudes, but he could not. This was one of his shortcomings, which he liked to believe was also a strength.

"Let's take a look at her," he said instead, and Balfour ushered him in.

Kate waited for them in the privacy of the library. It had recently been painted and was sparsely furnished. The Balfours had planned a trip to London to purchase furniture once the baby was born and Kate could travel again. She sat on the room's only upholstered chair with her feet resting on a footstool.

Some women glowed when they were pregnant. Kate appeared tired and she had several weeks to go.

Ned put on his cheeriest demeanor and enjoyed a cup of tea with her. She was an actress of some renown and she almost convinced him she was doing well.

He took a moment to listen to the baby, his ear against Kate's belly. There was movement, but Kate did not look uncomfortable to him, no matter what her husband feared. This baby was going to be a big one and that, too, could be very hard on the mother.

"Do you think she'll come soon?" Kate asked.

"She?" Ned gently teased.

"I feel she's a girl." Kate rubbed her belly.

Ned sat back. "Well, you are starting to sound

desperate and as if you've had enough of this. That is usually a good sign something will happen."

"Mary Conroy said her midwife told her to walk backward for at least an hour a day. That it would make the birth go easier."

Here was a prime example of the sort of nonsense Ned fought. Instead of barking out his protest, he kept his voice calm. "Does that even make sense, Kate?"

"But wouldn't women know?"

Did he have an answer for that?

"I have never heard of a cure that included walking backward."

"Yes, you are right. It doesn't make sense. I wrote a letter to my sisters asking about it. I posted it today. They all have multiple children. Please tell me they won't think I'm foolish."

"Since they have experienced what it means to be in confinement, I'm certain they will understand."

She nodded and lowered her voice, even though they were alone. "I don't want to lose this baby, Ned. I fear I'm too old. This is our one chance. I'm afraid."

"Don't be, Kate." At least once a week they had this conversation.

"You'll see me through this?"

"I will be right beside you."

"Thank you." The response didn't come from Kate but Balfour, who had come to the doorway. The man loved his wife, and Ned was a bit in awe of his devotion to her.

Would he someday have strong feelings for Clarissa? Perhaps if she carried his child?

Actually, he couldn't picture himself as a father. He'd not been around families very much. He'd been shipped away to school the moment he was in the way and spent most of his holidays there—alone.

That was one of the reasons he felt such loyalty to his friends and the Logical Men's Society. They were his family. It was as if his life hadn't really begun until he'd met Mars and Balfour.

"Forget about walking backward," Ned advised. "Walk forward, take the air. When you are done, soak your feet, and have your maid massage your legs several times a day with a heavy cream. And be ready. It won't be much longer. Maybe a month. Perhaps weeks."

"How about days?"

Ned laughed. "Hours?"

"Oh, no, that might be too soon. I'm not *that* ready yet."

"The babe will come on its own time, Kate. Patience has never been one of my virtues, either, so I can empathize."

Kate reached for his hand. "Thank you."

"You are welcome, and please, both of you, don't listen to stories. Women have birthing tales that would frighten a hussar. I believe many are embellished."

"I just wish I was younger. Then it would be easier."

"Everything is easier when we are younger,"

he responded, and all three of them laughed at the truth of the statement.

There was more small talk. He admired the improvements to the house from the last time he had visited.

However, he was thankful when he could leave. Although the headache from his excesses the night before had left him, it had been a trying day. He didn't think he'd handled Kate's fears as well as he could have. He'd make it up to her when he called on the morrow. As for Mrs. Estep, well, he'd leave that to the next day, as well. Ideally, Mars would return with all due haste and make the woman and her unsubstantiated claim disappear. Then Ned would see what could be done to secure The Garland for the Logical Men's Society for all perpetuity. But first, what *he* needed was a good night's sleep.

Hippocrates knew the way home. The big horse picked up speed the closer they came to Maidenshop. Ned's house, which he let from Mars, was located not far from The Garland. It was set apart from the cottages, and while not grand, it suited his needs. Royce would have a supper waiting as he always did, no matter the hour Ned returned.

His path took him, once again, past The Garland. Ned was determined to not pay any attention to the building. His expectation was to go trotting by—except the street was blocked by what appeared to be every female in the village.

Mrs. Warbler was shaking a mop at the Dawson brothers, warning them off. Off to the side, Sir Lionel and Mr. Fullerton sat in their sedan chairs. Their carriers stood beside them, one of them holding a keg on his shoulder.

Every afternoon since Ned had moved to Maidenshop, the two old widowers were carried to The Garland. It appeared as if today they had been denied entry and the Dawson boys, contrary to Ned's good advice, were taking up their cause.

"This is *our* place," Mark complained.

"Not any longer," Mrs. Warbler answered. "You almost destroyed the place and you don't deserve it."

Clarissa, the dowager, and Mrs. Summerall were not there but the lads' mother was. She came forward to stand right beside Mrs. Warbler. "She's right. Go on with you. Go home. I'm horrified at what I learned was going on in there."

To no one's surprise, her sons did not listen. "You can't keep us out," Mark pressed. "Look over there at Sir Lionel and Mr. Fullerton. Those are old men. They have habits."

Sir Lionel enthusiastically nodded. "We are here every day."

"Well, not today," Mrs. Warbler answered triumphantly. "In fact, it is time for the two of you"—she pointed her mop at the old gents—"to develop some *new* habits."

"If this is your way of making me pay attention to you," Sir Lionel warned, "it is not a good one."

"Come on, Mrs. Warbler," William Dawson

wheedled as if trying to charm her. "You know we are thirsty."

"There isn't a drop to drink in there. You all downed it last night."

"Mr. Fullerton brought a new keg," William answered.

"*No*," she responded and set her mop down like a sentry standing guard.

Seeing Ned, Sir Lionel barked, "*Thurlowe*, do something."

Before Ned could respond, there was another disturbance—Mrs. Estep herself appeared in the doorway.

Her face was flush as if she'd just woken. Her golden-red hair was in one long braid over her shoulder. The last rays of the sun seemed to catch on the color, and there wasn't a man around who wasn't struck dumb.

Ned included.

There were other women present who were as beautiful, even more so . . . except there was an ethereal air about her. She was dressed in her black, but something set her apart from all others.

"Ah, there you are, sweet girl," Mrs. Warbler said in greeting. "Did you have a good sleep? Are you surprised at what we've done?"

"I'm overwhelmed," Mrs. Estep said. There was a huskiness to her voice that seemed to ring through Ned. "This is so generous of all of you and I don't know who you are or why you are being so kind to me but thank you. *Thank you*."

The woman closest to her, Jenny Mandrake,

answered, "Because *you* are one of *us*." Heads nodded. "Welcome to Maidenshop."

And that is when Mrs. Estep noticed Ned sitting on his horse.

Their gazes met. He could not pull his away. Instead, he stared as if hungry for her, and he was.

This was the way of foolishness. This is what had led his noble father almost into social ruin, what had taken many a man down a path of betrayal and shame. Ned had believed himself immune because he'd never experienced such a driving awareness of any member of the female sex.

Apparently, he was capable of being as gulled by a woman as the next man.

If she'd crooked her finger toward him right now, he'd run to her. He would have swept her up in his arms, carried her to the nearest bed, and had his way with her—except he was a thinking man. He may have been a love child, but he did not believe in love or giving in to lust. That way lay folly.

Then her brows came together as if in disdain and it broke the spell. She obviously didn't reciprocate one gram of what he was feeling, and he was damn glad. Or so he told himself. Her attitude saved him from becoming a fool.

Right now he needed to plot his best course.

"Come, gentlemen," he said, taking command. "To my house."

"Yes, go drink yourselves silly again," Mrs. Warbler crowed.

The men ignored her . . . until they were out of

earshot. Then Mark Dawson summed the matter up. "Could you believe the color of that woman's hair? She looks like some fae creature come to life."

"More like the devil," Sir Lionel answered, and Ned agreed.

Chapter Seven

The next morning, the Sabbath, was a cloudy day with a mild threat of rain and little wind.

Gemma had surprised herself by sleeping peacefully through the night. She hadn't believed she would. She'd been too excited about the changes that had taken place in The Garland.

Mrs. Warbler, her friends, and soap and water had worked miracles. The broken furniture in the main room had been removed and what was there now gleamed from a good polish. The floors didn't have a speck of dust, the bricks in the kitchen shone, and the empty kegs in the taproom were gone. She'd even had a duchess direct her servants to help with The Garland.

In one day, the Matrons of Maidenshop had accomplished what Gemma had anticipated would take her weeks, and they had done it out of their enthusiasm for her plans and a strong desire to close down the Logical Men's Society. They had made the latter very clear to her.

This morning, as Gemma walked with Mrs. Warbler to the morning service at St. Martyr's, she brought up the subject again. "I sense there is a touch of animosity toward the Logical Men's Society."

"A touch?" Mrs. Warbler laughed her opinion. She was dressed in a lavender day dress with gloves to match and a deep-purple-trimmed bonnet. Gemma had on her black. She'd pinned her hair up under her black, wide-brimmed hat.

"Why is that? My uncle was proud of the group and the role he played. When I visited, he was making rook pies for a lecture they were having. It was on geology, I believe."

"The lectures are new. They are the idea of Mr. Thurlowe. Trust me, the majority of the members are not interested in any topic but the most expedient way to bring a tankard to their lips. A change that is actually Mr. Thurlowe's fault."

"It is?"

"He is an egalitarian. No respect for principle, for authority. Once he started letting in a less— shall we say—genteel class of gentleman, their meetings became rowdier. Why, there was so much going on the other night, I could not sleep. I am not sorry that they must find another place for their meetings. I also don't care where they go as long as it is not across the road from me."

"Mr. Thurlowe does not strike me as rowdy." Gemma kept her tone neutral. He was not her friend. He'd made himself very clear on that matter. All the same, she resisted seeing him painted with a broad brush.

Mrs. Warbler nodded to a family riding to church in a farmer's cart. "He's not, even though he was born on the wrong side of the blanket."

"He was?"

"Yes, he is the bastard son of the late Earl of Penwell. His mother was a woman of low repute and great renown, Sarah Middleton."

Gemma had heard of the courtesan. Her lips formed an "oh." Mrs. Middleton was rumored to be very beautiful. No wonder Mr. Thurlowe was an uncommonly handsome man.

Mrs. Warbler continued, "He also believes the end justifies the means and I do not agree."

"What do you mean?"

"First, it is silly to encourage men to be happy they are single. That is nonsense. Everyone *should* be married."

Not to Gemma's thinking. She prayed never to marry again, an opinion she realized she must keep to herself. She had no desire to upset her recent benefactress.

"The Society was down to the Three Bucks and Sir Lionel and Mr. Fullerton, who are widowed. When Mr. Thurlowe was voted chairman, he changed things. Can you believe it? He wants to educate the likes of the Dawson lads, which is the most foolish endeavor I have ever heard. Meta Dawson is pleased her sons are rubbing elbows with the upper gentry but she has always been blind to her lads' faults. She also doesn't see what a simpleton her husband is."

Actually, Gemma believed in the value of good education for everyone. Another opinion she kept to herself. "And what was the geology lecture?"

Mrs. Warbler gave a distracted nod of her head. "Something about rocks and the earth. Dirt, maybe. Mr. Thurlowe is keen on the matter. He wastes too much of his time in books."

Reading was a waste of time? Again, Gemma bit her tongue. "Does he allow women to attend these lectures?"

"Why would he?" Mrs. Warbler seemed genuinely perplexed.

"Some women are interested in such topics." She paused a moment and then confessed, "I would be."

"Oh, well, talk to Miss Taylor about that. Supposedly, she was most upset when she learned the lecture was for gentlemen only. She will appreciate a supportive voice when the next lecture rolls around, which it will shortly. They held it the day after the Cotillion last year and will do so again. Come, there is the dowager. Let us pay our addresses." She guided Gemma right into the circle of women surrounding the duchess.

And it felt good to be included by these women. They were far different from Lady Latimer and her shallow friends. Yes, Mrs. Warbler sniffed at egalitarian viewpoints and yet, there was not a woman in front of the church that she did not pull into their circle.

The chatter was about Gemma's plans for The

Garland. Several women were as keen on gardening as Gemma and offered her seeds or plants
from their own gardens. Even their husbands
acted interested. And the Reverend Summerall
seemed almost joyous over the idea of him and
his wife sitting in The Garland's gardens . . .

There was a knot of young men over by the
horses casting sour looks toward Gemma's group.
Some of them were the ones who had tried to stir
up trouble the night before. They appeared to be
doing most of the talking. She noticed that Mr.
Thurlowe was not amongst them.

Nor was he gathered with any of the other gentlemen.

She wondered where he was and yet, didn't
want to be open about her interest—which wasn't
really interest, she told herself. One should always know where their enemies are lurking.

As they made their way into the church, she
asked nonchalantly, "Is Sir Lionel here?" This
was a roundabout method of learning what she
did want to know.

"He never comes. Mr. Fullerton, his companion,
is here." She nodded to the older gentleman in a
back pew, who Gemma noticed had been watching them. Or watching Mrs. Warbler. She tucked
that observation away for safekeeping.

Directing Gemma to follow her into a pew,
Mrs. Warbler said, "Sir Lionel is probably muzzy
from drink and still abed. When I take over his
life that nonsense will come to an end, as well as
that silly red fez he enjoys wearing."

"Ah, the fez." Gemma remembered the fez wearer from the night before. He'd been quite drunk, even before he'd arrived to start drinking.

Miss Taylor and her family were seated in the row behind them and she gave Gemma a welcoming smile.

Mrs. Warbler leaned close to Gemma's ear. "Those aren't her people, you know. Lovely family—Squire Nelson, his wife, and three daughters. I'll introduce you later. They took her in after the Reverend Taylor died. He wasn't her father, either. Found her as a babe left on the doorstep of the church. Sad story."

"Who left her?"

"It is a mystery." Mrs. Warbler then smiled at Miss Taylor as if she hadn't just been gossiping about her. That observation, too, Gemma tucked away.

The service started. Gemma had been raised to attend church, although she had a tendency to use this time to think instead of worship. She always said her prayers and she did believe in a Supreme Being . . . but her idea of what form that took was often at odds with what the churchmen claimed—

There was a disturbance behind her. Someone had entered late and taken a seat in Miss Taylor's pew.

Gemma didn't think anything about it until the small hairs at the base of her neck started to twitch. It was an alarming sensation. She didn't need to turn around to know that Mr. Thurlowe had arrived.

She let out her breath and willed herself to calm, but that didn't stop the uptick in her pulse.

It was almost as if she could feel his eyes upon her. They bored into her. She knew it.

Mrs. Warbler smiled at her over something the Reverend Summerall said about "consciences." Gemma smiled back and used the moment to catch a glance over her shoulder.

Her senses had not lied. The physician sat almost directly behind her.

However, he was *not* paying attention to her. He looked toward the pulpit with rapt interest.

The liar.

She knew her instincts were right. He was plotting against her.

When at last the final "amen" had been said, Gemma was ready to leave. Of course, she was in the middle of the pew. She had to wait for the women in front of her to have their chat. There would probably also be chatting in the churchyard.

A hand touched her arm from the pew behind to claim her attention. Gemma turned to see Miss Taylor smiling at her, and beside her, of course, was Mr. Thurlowe. Right now his attention appeared everywhere but on Gemma.

"You look well rested. I hope you are feeling better," Miss Taylor said with her lovely smile.

"I am, thank you. And thank you for the

work you did. The Garland had been frightfully abused." Gemma took pleasure in saying this in front of Mr. Thurlowe.

"I actually enjoyed the cleaning. I'm proud that we could all come together. It was rather fun. I think even the dowager had a good time, although her servants did the work."

"She and I supervised," Mrs. Warbler said proudly.

Mr. Thurlowe broke in. "Excuse me, ladies, I must leave. Miss Taylor, forgive me. Patients, you know." Before anyone could respond, he was gone. There was no peck on the cheek or loving regret in his manner. He just left.

Gemma realized he must truly abhor her if he was going to dash off and not spend time with the woman he was supposed to marry very soon.

However, he did not travel far before the dowager cornered him.

Miss Taylor began introducing Gemma to her companions. "These are my guardians, and better angels one could not find. This is Squire Nelson and his wife—"

She continued with introductions. However, the duchess had a carrying voice and Gemma doubted if there was anyone in the sanctuary who didn't hear her say, "—Mrs. Warbler shared this salve she received from Gemma. I rubbed it on my knee and it feels immeasurably better. In fact, Gemma"—she turned, drawing Gemma into the exchange—"please come here."

"Excuse me," Gemma murmured to the Nelsons to give the exchange between doctor and dowager her full attention. "Yes, Your Grace?"

"I need more of that salve."

"Unfortunately, I gave Mrs. Warbler all I have."

"Then make more."

"I will, once I have the ingredients," Gemma assured her. "They are expensive."

"I will buy them for you. I need that salve. I can move my knee easily without pain for the first time in ages."

"Well, thank you, Your Grace. *Thank you.*" By now, everyone in the small church was listening to the exchange.

"And you should look into the salve, Mr. Thurlowe," the dowager advised. "It has beneficial properties."

His smile appeared forced. "I'm certain it does . . . However, please excuse me, Your Grace."

"Of course, carry on," the dowager answered and he left with a bow.

From that moment on, Gemma was bombarded with questions about her salve. Apparently, there were more aches and pains in Maidenshop than one could have imagined.

Of course, Gemma didn't believe her salve was for everyone and she said as much. Once her doors opened, she promised she would listen to people's ailments and see if she had a recipe that could help them. She told them about her gran and the healing history of her family and there was much interest. Mrs. Warbler beamed as if Gemma was her favorite child.

In this manner, she joined the flow out of the church. It felt good to be included. She also had the opportunity, now that she had her bearings, to thank many of the women who had given so generously of their time the day before.

At one point the dowager pulled her aside to let her know that she was serious about offering to pay for the salve's ingredients. They stood amongst the gravestones surrounding the church. "I want that salve concocted with all haste. Why, I did more yesterday than I have for an age and I'm thankful to Elizabeth for sharing what you gave her. I could sleep without pain."

"I will do my best, Your Grace."

"See that you do. We are so happy to have you with us, Mrs. Estep—"

"Gemma," Gemma said without thinking and then realized no one corrected a duchess. "Your Grace, I mean, please call me Gemma. I prefer that to my married name."

The dowager's brows lifted with interest. "There is a story."

"And I will happily share it someday."

"Very good, *Gemma*." The duchess swept away.

Gemma drew a deep breath and released it. Over by the church door, people were milling around. She needed this quiet moment to herself and moved toward the back of the church building.

She was doing it. She was rebuilding her life, and it was better than she could imagine—

Her gaze caught on a headstone that was newer than the others. She walked toward it and before she saw the name, she knew it was her uncle's. *Andrew MacMhuirich.*

The only date on it was of his death. That made sense. Gemma wasn't even certain when he was born, either. Beneath the date was carved: *Well-hailed member of the Logical Men's Society.*

That gave her a tickle of guilt . . . because Andrew had been proud of the role he played with the village men. He'd been happy to bake the pies they wanted because he was one of them.

"I'm sorry," she whispered. "I must claim The Garland. I have nowhere else. But thank you. Thank you—"

"We respected him," Mr. Thurlowe's voice came from behind her.

Gemma whirled to face him. She hadn't even heard him approach.

He held his hat in his arms that were clasped behind his back. He appeared serious. Somber. Beyond them, in the distance, was the sound of wagons, carts, and carriages and the other parishioners. They were busy catching up and possibly talking about the changes she planned for The Garland. No one *seemed* to be paying attention to them.

"I thought you were off to your patients."

"I should be. Of course, I was waylaid on my way out of the church."

She held up a hand. "You can't blame the delay on me. I had nothing to do with it."

He shot her a look as if to say, *Can't I?* Instead, he said, "I feel it is important that we talk. Would you?" He indicated with his hand holding his hat that he wanted her to walk farther around the church where they would be shielded from prying eyes.

Curiosity made her agree. She moved forward with him trailing discreetly behind.

Once she'd determined they had gone far enough, she stopped. "We have a modicum of privacy. What do you wish to say?"

The lines of his mouth flattened. It was a handsome mouth. In fact, this close to him, she was struck anew at how physically attractive he was.

But her husband had been handsome, too.

Except, Paul had never looked as grim as Mr. Thurlowe did at this moment. "Do you really believe handing out this rub is in the best interests of these women?"

"It eases pain."

"Two good shots of brandy eases their pain, as well."

She reacted to his sarcasm. "I'll have you know that my gran and her gran and her gran before her worked to create that recipe because of its healing properties. I never said my salve was a cure. The pepper oil mixed with the other herbs offers *relief*, which I would think you would be glad of for your patients."

He made a disgruntled noise. "Pain is part of life. She is growing older. *That* is her problem. Selling her remedies will not prevent her joints from worsening."

"It will help her feel better."

He hummed his doubt, and she had to admit, "As I've said, the salve is not a cure—"

"She thinks it is."

"No, she doesn't. Or else she wouldn't ask me to make more. She just wants to move without pain. What is wrong with that goal? And it won't harm her. Yes, the joints will grow worse because that is the nature of our bodies. However, the salve will be easier on her than soldiering on."

That gave him a moment of pause, but then he came back. "I don't want her thinking she has an antidote."

"She is a sensible woman. She knows what she wants." And Gemma had a sudden insight. "Or would you be speaking to me this way if the dowager was a man?"

"I have no idea what you mean."

"It is my observation that physicians have a tendency to discount the complaints of females."

"What?" He took a step back.

Gemma took a step forward. "If the dowager was a driver or a yeoman or a carpenter or even a stable hand who used his hands all day, would you be more concerned about her joints?"

"Those men are working. They need their hands. They have no choice but to use them."

She hummed her thoughts and asked, "What if the Reverend Summerall had pain? He doesn't labor any more than the duchess does."

He saw her trap. He gave a sound of frustration. "I don't differentiate between my male and female patients. I want to see them all better. However, instead of medicating ailments, I want to see them cured."

"Except you already said yourself, there are some aches that have nothing to do with disease. They are part of aging and if you can cure that, Mr. Thurlowe, then you *are* masterful. My recipe eases pain and works on men as well as women."

"Why do I believe I've just received an advertisement?"

"Why do I believe you will criticize me no matter what I do?"

And she had him.

He frowned and looked away.

"We are not at cross purposes, sir. I might know more than you think I do. Or is your true argument with me based upon my sex? Let me assure you, women have very fine minds."

"I'm not questioning your intelligence." He sounded like a stubborn child.

"Yes, you are," Gemma answered, because she was done with men acting as if she didn't know her own mind. "And you keep women out of everything interesting, such as your lectures."

He sliced the air with his hand. "The Logical Men's Society is not an antifemale society—"

"Then why won't you admit them?" The question just popped out of her mouth.

A more prudent or certainly diplomatic woman would have held her tongue. Gemma felt she'd spent a lifetime holding her tongue—first with her father, then her uncaring husband.

It wasn't that she was just done swallowing her thoughts and opinions. It was that she strongly desired speaking her mind *to* Mr. Thurlowe. He annoyed her, not in an angry way, and not in a completely platonic one, either.

Oh, yes, she was attracted to him.

And here lay madness. He was promised to another woman. He was not for Gemma. She knew that, and still needed to—what? Tweak his nose? Challenge him? Let him know that she was nobody's fool? Least of all *his*?

"I'm not giving up The Garland," she said, her voice steady. "I'm pinning everything I have on it. So let us reach a truce."

His brows came together. "Why should I surrender to you when you have no real claim on the building?"

Any conciliatory thought she'd had toward him vanished. She didn't even like the way he looked right now. "Andrew was *my* uncle and I have my proof."

"Show it to me or be gone."

"You would see me turned out? That is not very handsome of you, Mr. Thurlowe."

"I'm *not* a *gentleman* all the time, Mrs. Estep."

He had snapped the words out and suddenly the air around them had filled with tension. His words had interjected a different emotion. A surprisingly more raw one.

The faintest tinge of color appeared on his high cheekbones. "I didn't mean that the way it sounded."

"How did it sound?" she dared to ask, almost afraid of the answer.

"Threatening."

Gemma was taken aback because she hadn't been thinking in that direction. She turned away from him, shifting her focus to the barn in the field in front of her, and considered her reaction. She hadn't realized the menace in his words. Instead, she found herself wondering in what ways he was ungentlemanly and the thoughts sparked feelings in her she did not trust.

And would not.

She found her footing. Truth. Truth was always the right answer. Bravely, she said, "You don't want me to make the salve because you *fear* for your patients. You just don't want me *here*. It has nothing to do with healing. Correct?" She faced him, ready for his defiance, and realized he was already walking away. She had been speaking to the air.

Gemma was uncertain of whether to be offended that he had just charged off, or relieved she was free of his disturbing presence.

Then she heard a woman's voice calling her name from the other side of the church. "I'm here."

A beat later Clarissa Taylor came around the corner.

Gemma braced herself, certain that Miss Taylor

knew she'd been alone with Mr. Thurlowe. There was no telling how she would react. Gemma knew what response she would have if she suspected another woman, especially one newly arrived to the area, was having a private conversation with a man like Mr. Thurlowe—except Miss Taylor had a smile on her face.

"I told the others I was certain you had come over here to pay your respects to your uncle," she said as she approached and then stopped beside Gemma and looked back at Andrew's grave. "It is always sad to lose someone in the village, but his death touched every one of us. He was a very kind man."

"Thank you. I appreciate your acknowledging him. Maidenshop had become his home. I wish I could have been here for him."

"I'm certain you do. Still, we took good care of him. Mr. Thurlowe paid for his funeral. It was a fine one."

"Mr. Thurlowe did? Because he wanted The Garland?" The tart words were out of Gemma's mouth before she considered them.

"Oh, no." Miss Taylor appeared shocked at the suggestion. "Mr. Thurlowe, he does that for people. If he knows there is a need, he will do what he can to help. I sense he doesn't like having anyone in the parish forgotten. I think it is one of the reasons he works so hard. As you know, he is already off making rounds and it is the Lord's day. He's generous. Kind. That is one of the reasons I admire him."

She was either very secure in Mr. Thurlowe's affections for her, or she might not know that he'd sought Gemma out.

"But let me not forget why I'm here," Miss Taylor said. "Mrs. Nelson wishes me to ask you to join us for Sunday dinner. You can ride with us now, if you wish, and then I will drive you home in the pony cart."

Since she didn't have food at The Garland, this was a generous offer. "I'd be honored. I walked with Mrs. Warbler. Let me tell her where I'm going."

"She has been invited, as well, and I am glad you will join us. I believe we will be great friends."

The pronouncement was like a weight on Gemma's shoulders, and there was no cause for it. She was done with men. She was carving out a life of her own. She didn't need someone stern and heavy-handed in her life, especially toward her healing gifts.

"Yes," she echoed. "Great friends."

She meant those words and, with that, tucked all interest in Mr. Thurlowe safely away.

Chapter Eight

He was a bloody fool.

Ned shouldn't have sought out Mrs. Estep for a private discussion, especially right after the service and in the churchyard where anyone could have seen them. There had been too much risk to it. Wagging tongues told their own stories, and they were rarely the truth . . . and yet he could not have stopped himself from speaking to her.

Nor should he have been surprised the conversation had not gone well.

The woman was impossible.

His long legs ate up the ground between the church and his house as he berated himself for taking the risk. To be certain, Mrs. Estep had not appreciated his criticism or been sympathetic to his reasons for cautioning her—a sign, in his opinion, that she truly didn't know what she was doing.

No one in the village had ever questioned his professional opinion, not like the dowager did today. It pricked his pride that anyone would believe for one second in time that he wasn't doing everything he could for them, and yet, there was the dowager making an issue that she believed more should be done for knees.

In fact, the only true solution would be for him to cut off the dowager's kneecap and replace it with a new one. Unfortunately, there was no way to do such a thing without crippling her for life. However, if she did not start paying attention to her knee's limitations, well, that is exactly where she might end up—crippled.

As for Mrs. Warbler's joints, it was not true that he wasn't doing all he could for her. He'd advised her to wrap her hands in warm compresses. She told him she was. This morning was the first time he'd heard her complain in ages.

Relief was important, and, yes, he knew there were certain oils that had healing properties. He could have recommended them.

He hadn't, though . . . He hadn't really even thought about them—and that pricked his conscience.

He was also honest enough with himself to admit that his argument with Mrs. Estep's methods had nothing to do with why he was practically racing away from her.

Once her clear eyes turned their full attention on him, he found it hard to think, even when she was challenging him. And the words that came out of his mouth were not what he intended to say.

I'm not a gentleman?

He was always a gentleman. He'd worked to become a gentleman.

However, the moment the words had left his lips, his mind had leaped to an altogether sensual meaning to his statement. Other men might think with their cocks; *he didn't*. He was *always* rational. He valued the mind over self-indulgent desire. Life had to have purpose. Man was here for a higher calling, not just hedonistic pleasure.

Ned came to a halt. He sounded like a right proper frump. If Mars or Balfour could hear him, they'd ask when he was going to join the matrons.

They'd also know he was lying to himself.

Gemma Estep wasn't like any other woman he'd met before, and he didn't understand why. Something about her made him both angered and aroused. He, who prided himself on control, had his sights set on her.

It was a shocking realization.

He was like other men.

And he didn't know how he felt about that.

Or was he just having too many late nights? Not to mention how Mrs. Estep's takeover of The Garland was in danger of upsetting his plans, his lectures, and his hope to make a mark on the sciences by providing a forum for free thought.

Yes, that was it. He wasn't attracted to her; he was *annoyed* with her. She was shaking loose some matters inside him that needed to be attended to. She made him aware of how long he'd been alone. Perhaps Clarissa was right and the time *had* come to marry.

And yet, he had little interest in it. Although he seemed to have a *great* interest in Gemma Estep. Even to the point of taking foolish risks with every gossip in the village close at hand.

Ned began walking again, not liking the direction of his thoughts. He needed to take a hold of himself. He had iron discipline. He could not have accomplished what he had in life without it.

He also was promised to a lovely, graceful woman. He should direct his lustful thoughts toward her, although he'd never thought of her that way in the least. Clarissa and *lust* didn't seem to fit together in his mind.

What he needed, Ned decided, was a good night's sleep.

He'd been late to the morning service because he'd had trouble rising from his bed, and that, too, he could lay at Mrs. Estep's door.

After the confrontation with the matrons, he'd herded the Society members to his house. Quarreling with the women would not give them what they wanted, especially since some of those women were their mothers. Ned didn't have a mother figure. Or at least, the one he had didn't give two thoughts for him and he felt even less toward her.

However, he'd spent the evening listening to men who were too full of themselves as they drained the small keg and drank every drop of liquor he owned. They wanted to know how he was going to reclaim The Garland. They relived the confrontation where they were bolder, more forceful. And they ignored every attempt Ned had made to send them home.

Sir Lionel had been the worst. He'd been so drunk, he could barely hold his head up. Yet, every time Ned signaled to his runners they pack him up, the old scoundrel had rallied. Even Fullerton, well into his cups himself, had acted fed up.

Royce had been wise enough to appear in the room with bread, cheeses, and meats. It was a trick Old Andy had employed. Ned had always thought Andy was being a good host. Now he realized the old man just wanted to go to bed, except it didn't work that well with this crew.

Two nights of keeping up with their drinking and antics would make anyone ill-tempered. Perhaps that was why Ned had been unwise enough to take after Mrs. Estep, risking the wrong sort of gossip.

His lack of sleep might also explain why he'd fixated on the clarity of her skin, the fullness of her mouth, and the tempting curves of her breasts—

There he went again. It was as if he couldn't take his mind off her. *Clarissa is a beautiful woman. Think of her breasts* . . . Except there was something fascinating about Mrs. Estep's—

He bypassed his front door and went straight for the stables. He needed to call on the Widow Smethers and see how her ankle fared. Then he would visit Kate Balfour and, if there was nothing else, he'd come home and make an early night of it. He charged into the stables and discovered he had company.

The Duke of Winderton leaned a shoulder against Hippocrates's paddock. The saucy horse was bold enough to rest his head on the duke's shoulder as if fawning around the young nobleman the way Mark Dawson, Douglas Michaels, Robert Shielding, and Jonathon Fitzsimmons were as they stood around him.

"We've been waiting for you, Thurlowe," the duke said.

God help him.

"I was in services, Your Grace," Ned replied, trying not to sound testy, and failing.

"I didn't make it this morning." Winderton stretched languidly. "I blame one of the Belks girls, although I can't remember which one it was. Perhaps both." The duke laughed at his own little escapade, and Ned did not like him.

He'd known Winderton ever since he moved to Maidenshop five years ago. He'd watched him grow from a spoiled, but likeable lad, to this current incarnation of surly, self-indulgent nobleman.

"You are too young to be jaded, Your Grace," Ned said flatly, reaching for a comb to give his horse a quick curry before putting on the saddle. He even shooed the duke aside to enter Hippocrates's stall, something Winderton took with a chuckle. After all, Ned was good friends with the duke's uncle, Balfour.

"We came to talk to you," the duke said. "When are we going to reclaim our tavern?"

"As soon as Lord Marsden returns," Ned said. "I've sent word. He will come when he is able."

"And what do we do in the meantime?" Shielding asked. He was a short man and a bit pugnacious. He was not the best lawyer. He had made mistakes that had cost many in the parish plenty. He was tolerated because he was a village son. "I'll take on her claim for us and put her in her place."

Lord, Ned didn't need that. "The magistrate will deal with it." He knocked the dirt from the comb and reached for the saddle on the rack. "However, if we need more help, I shall turn to you or Michaels."

That seemed to mollify Shielding.

The others were not so easily pleased.

"I think we should run her out," Dawson said. "Just go over there and toss her on her arse. The duke agrees with me."

"Do you agree, Your Grace? We should *toss her on her arse*?" Ned challenged.

"It is a figure of speech," Winderton replied.

"And how will that go over with your mother, who has apparently decided to be one of Mrs. Estep's patronesses?"

Winderton swore under his breath.

"Yes, I agree," Ned said.

"We must stop her," the duke pressed.

"That is my intent." Ned set Hippocrates's saddle on his back and faced the men. They were so

ignorant in their arrogance, they made him feel
ancient. "I don't want her there, either. I was going to purchase the building, remember?" Or at
least he was going to attempt to do so. He was
comfortable but not wealthy.

"Is it for sale?" Winderton asked.

Shielding spoke up. "The property was a freehold. Old Andy won it in a game of cards decades
ago from Marsden's father, who had owned the
property. However, Andy died without a will, as
far as we could find. We were going to wait until
The Garland reverted to the Crown and came up
for sale. Mr. Thurlowe plans on making an offer."

If he could afford it, Ned wanted to add. However, he had been saving.

"That could take ages," the duke said.

"It won't be quick," Shielding agreed. He
looked to Ned. "So she has the will?"

"I don't know. She says she has proof that Old
Andy left The Garland to her. She refuses to show
it to me. She will have to show it to the magistrate. Still, we must do this right or we'll have
the village set against us. Have you forgotten
what happened last night?" He looked directly
at Dawson, whose mother had not been pleased
with him. "The women in the village are excited
about Mrs. Estep's plans. We must be careful."

No one's head nodded agreement.

"Mars might take weeks to return," Michaels
protested.

The duke warned, "By then, the women will be
entrenched. We will never remove them."

Sheepishly, Fitz said, "My mother is already celebrating the arrival of a tea garden. She will be taking several plantings from our beds to Mrs. Estep today."

"See?" Dawson said. "This is what the lot of them were talking about after church. Oh, they are just chirping and planning. Even the husbands were over there. The Reverend Summerall can't do enough for Mrs. Estep. He is practically at her feet."

Ned tried to urge calm again as he cinched the saddle. "Mrs. Estep *claims* Old Andy wanted her to take over The Garland. She says she has proof, but we are going to challenge her claim. You know the earl will see the matter in our favor. I have no doubt on that. Until that time, as chairman of the Society, I want you gents to cool your heels."

"And where do we drink until then?" Dawson asked sulkily.

It was on the tip of Ned's tongue to say that they could try staying sober a night. That would be wasted breath. "Meet at a different location again."

"So we come here?" Fitz said.

"*No.*" Ned had just finished bridling his horse and he turned so fast with his answer, Hippocrates gave a start. He steadied the animal with a hand on his neck. He was not giving up his plans for a decent night's sleep. "After all, you've gone through my larder."

"That is true," Shielding agreed before asking, "Where else can we go?"

"Not my house," Michaels said. "I live with my mother."

"As do I," Fitzsimmons agreed.

"Same here," Dawson echoed.

"You will come to me," Winderton said with great decision. "I'm in the Dower House. I have plenty of food and drink." His statement was met with the sort of acclaim usually saved for conquering heroes.

And Ned had only himself to blame. Mars had warned him. *Most of them don't have the wits to light a candle*, he'd said.

Now, Ned reflected on how sometimes, as an egalitarian, those he wished to help annoyed the devil out of him.

Especially when the duke wondered aloud, "You know, if Mrs. Estep does have proof like she claims, we may lose The Garland . . . unless the proof disappears."

"Exactly," Shielding agreed.

"We could help it disappear," Winderton suggested. Heads nodded as if this was the best idea they'd ever heard.

Ned had been about to put his foot in the stirrup but now he faced them. "Here now, none of that. We do this the right way."

Their expressions said louder than words they didn't think the right way would work.

Ned was done arguing with them. Taking the reins, he swung up in the saddle. "It will all turn in our favor," he promised, and set his horse in motion.

NED'S FIRST stop was Belvoir and, while he wasn't a praying man in church, he was saying prayers up the drive that Mars had returned. He needed an ally. One with common sense. He couldn't bother Balfour with all of this.

Not only was the man no longer a Logical Men's Society member, but now his concerns were for his wife and the coming babe. Then there was the sticky problem that Winderton was his nephew. There was some bad blood between them. Ned had no desire to step in the middle of it.

He knew the moment he saw Mars's butler's face what the answer was. "He hasn't returned."

Gibson's gaze shifted. "No, sir."

"Did he send word *when* he would return?"

"No, sir."

Ned studied the man a moment, a suspicion forming. "Did the messenger actually speak to him?"

Gibson frowned, a servant tight-lipped with his master's secrets.

But Ned was also Mars's physician. He knew the secrets. "He's not at it again, is he?"

The butler shifted. "I don't know that I should say, sir. I don't know that I can."

"Gibson, the last time Marsden disappeared, we both know where he went." Mars had a taste for opium.

Ned did not approve of his friend's occasional proclivities. Then again, Mars hadn't asked for Ned's opinion or permission. He claimed it was his small vice, although Ned wondered why any man, especially one as blessed with good fortune and the favorable opinion of his fellows as the earl was, would be even tempted by the damnable habit.

If he was visiting one of the city's many dens, who knew when he'd return? Men lost days in their opium dreams.

And the Logical Men's Society did not have days to wait.

"Please tell him I called," Ned said to the butler.

"I will, sir."

Ned turned and started down the steps of the stately manor, but then Gibson said, "We all worry. He hasn't done this for some time. Don't think that your influence is wasted on him."

"Thank you, Gibson. We'll both keep trying, eh?" The servant bowed agreement and Ned continued down the steps to his horse.

Now what was he to do? He was thankful the members of the Logical Men's Society hadn't accompanied him to know that there would be delay. And he was not going to be in a hurry to share the news.

He rode his horse back to the road. He was tempted to hunt Mars down, and not just because of The Garland but because he was concerned. That was becoming the bane of Ned's existence. He worried about people. When he was all alone, back in his London days, he'd never given a thought to anyone but himself.

Then again, who knew how long it would take to find Mars? Furthermore, if Ned left and, heaven help him, Kate Balfour went into labor, well, he could not leave her to the local midwife. He couldn't do that. He'd promised her he'd see her baby safe.

Just as Ned reached the road and turned Hippocrates toward a visit to the Widow Smethers, Royce came riding up in a tear. "Sir! I'm glad I found you. Simon Crisp had an accident. His son says his father has cut off his finger."

Crisp was a yeoman on the Belvoir estate and fortunately didn't live far from here—and then Ned had an idea.

He looked to Royce, who was some twenty years older than himself. His assistant had once been in the military. He might be able to do what Ned couldn't. "Royce, I have a particular task that needs to be done and I know it is asking a great deal."

"What is it, sir?"

"I want you to ride to London and find the earl."

"Is he not home?"

"His home right now is an opium den."

Royce was momentarily taken aback.

"I know it is much to ask," Ned continued. "I can tell you where I found him the last time I hunted for him. I know I am asking a big favor. However, we need him here and I can't go this time."

"Of course I will go, sir. Do I just bully him into returning?"

"If he was like he was the time before he'll be docile enough to return with you."

"I shall ride right away."

"Good, thank you. Ride along with me and I'll give you a list of places that I have searched for him before." They both set off for Crisp's cottage while Ned gave Royce the particulars.

They parted company on Simon Crisp's step. "I'll find him, sir," Royce vowed.

"I pray you do."

Ned meant those words. In fact, he meant them even more the next day when he called on the Widow Smethers, who met him at the door practically dancing on her injured ankle.

He'd been able to save Crisp's finger with a few stitches, or so he hoped. One had to be careful of infection. However, he had not been able to call on the widow. He'd sent one of Crisp's sons to her with the message that he would see her on the morrow.

And here she was, looking better than she had for a week. She glowed with good health.

"Mrs. Smethers, I'm impressed," Ned said. "Rest has greatly improved your ankle." And her spirits.

"Yes, Doctor, rest and—" She lowered her voice as if sharing a secret. "A miraculous cure."

Ned's gut gave a sharp twist. "Cure?"

"Yes," she answered, her eyes alive with pleasure. "I met Gemma. She came with Mrs. Nelson when the squire's lady brought a plate of dinner for me. Lovely woman she is. She said she had a soak that would make me better, and so it has. Just look at me." She spun slowly to show the truth of her words. "She wasn't even going to take payment. Just as kind as you are. But then she told me she had a mouse problem at The Garland and I gave her one of my barn cats. That gray mouser will have those mice gone in a blink." And Ned knew that it had begun.

He could tell the widow that *rest* had healed her. That the ankle hadn't been broken, just merely sprained. Her recovery under the circumstances was as expected.

But what did common sense have over *miracles*?

By the end of the day, the parish would be buzzing like a beehive over *miracle cures* and his troubles were just beginning.

Chapter Nine

$\mathcal{N}$ed's most dire predictions came true—and quickly.

Mrs. Estep divided their once-happy community with the majority welcoming her and her "cures" and on the other side were the disgruntled members of the Society.

In truth, the Society had never been popular with the women. It hadn't meant to be. Mars had once explained to Ned and Balfour that his great-grandfather had started it in reaction to the insistence on the local social order to see every male shackled in marriage. It had been tongue-in-cheek but had grown into a club that afforded a strong male bond and good comradery, even though the membership had waned significantly over the past few years. Still, women rarely saw the sense of humor in such things.

Ned's recent regrets over increasing the membership numbers with the local lads turned double-fold as the Duke of Winderton challenged his leadership. The lads hung on to Winderton's every word and even aped his lordly slouch and effortless dismissal of the world at large. It was quite a thing to see yeomen like the Dawsons give ducal "sniffs" in answer to questions. Furthermore, all new gatherings of the Society were held at the duke's lodgings. Ned was apparently the only member to not attend. Well, save Mars, who had still not returned or been found.

Ned didn't have time for nightly drinking, and this sort of male pecking order conjured bad memories from his school days when he'd always felt outside any group. He'd refused to play the games then and he wasn't going to start now at seven and twenty.

He also noticed that the last several times he'd ridden past The Garland, one of the lads, usually Fitz or Michaels, the ones who didn't have any meaningful work to occupy them during the day, stood watch over the tavern, huge scowls on their faces as if they were watching to report to the others. Their appearance was too consistent to not be planned. Ned didn't know what they were up to, but he was certain it was no good.

He wasn't the only one to feel that way. Mrs. Summerall and Mrs. Warbler cornered him one morning in the stables while he was preparing to ride out.

"You need to talk to your members. They should not be loitering," Mrs. Warbler said.

Mrs. Summerall nodded. "Their behavior is disconcerting. If they believe they will discour-

age us from calling on Gemma, they are wrong.
We support her."

"Yes, they are obviously trying to intimidate
all of us, and we won't have it," Mrs. Warbler declared. "The next time I see one of them standing
in front of my window, I'm going for my broom."

"Standing on the road is not a broomable of-
fense," Ned said with a patience he wasn't feeling.
"They are allowed to stand wherever they wish."

"Mr. Thurlowe," Mrs. Warbler said loftily, "I
will use my *broom* however I see fit." On those
words, she and Mrs. Summerall went marching
away.

Ned leaned his shoulder against Hippocrates.
"Do horses have these problems?"

He swore the animal looked at him with com-
miserating pity.

Or perhaps he wanted a carrot.

After mounting, Ned headed out on his rounds.
This time, when he saw Michaels standing watch
over The Garland, he stopped.

"The matrons are concerned that you mean ill
will toward Mrs. Estep."

"I'm just standing here," Michaels said. The
smirk belied his innocence.

"The magistrate will be back and we will take
care of the matter."

"The duke says we might not be able to wait
that long. She's hung curtains in the windows,
sir. *Curtains.* Wait until I report back to the others
about this."

Curtains? Slowly, Ned turned his head and,

yes, there were curtains. In The Garland. "We will take them down," he answered.

"I'd like to take them down now," Michaels answered.

"Not until we have the magistrate's ruling."

"It's been days. When is he returning?"

"Soon," Ned promised, praying he was telling the truth. He hadn't even heard a word from Royce. Ned didn't know if he could keep everyone in line without Mars.

"Until then," he said to Michaels, "don't cause trouble."

"You don't understand—"

"*I do.* And I said stop it. We need the village to look kindly on us."

The mutinous look on the young man's face wasn't reassuring but Ned expected to be obeyed—

At that moment Mrs. Estep came out of The Garland. She had a basket on her arm and wore a wide-brimmed hat. Her hair was down today in a long thick braid over one shoulder. Her black gave her a trim, womanly silhouette. The morning light seemed to shine all around her.

Her head turned as if she felt his gaze. Her step slowed and then she came to a stop.

Ned experienced a driving desire to walk toward her. All he had to do was take the first step—

"Doctor, are you listening to me?" Michaels's plaintive voice said, breaking the spell. "Don't you agree that the duke has enough power in the village to decide where The Garland should go?"

Ned blinked like a man startled out of a trance. It was as if he had forgotten where he was. And he must be imagining things because Mrs. Estep hadn't slowed her step at all.

In fact, Mrs. Burnham, the wainwright's wife, had come running out of her cottage to greet her. They said a few words to each other and then Mrs. Burnham noticed Michaels and Ned and gave them a frown that should have sent them both to hell.

She'd never done that before. She and Ned had always been on good terms.

"Do you agree?" Michaels pressed again. "Because we have to do something. Gemma is turning the village against us."

Mrs. Burnham's frown said Michaels was right.

Grabbing what was left of his wits, Ned tried to make sense of it all, especially Michaels's suggestion about the duke. "No one is above the law," he declared brusquely. "We don't live in a feudal society. Tell His Grace and the others that Marsden will deal with the matter. He is the law. We want the women angry at the law and not at us. Meantime, stop standing out here."

"Winderton said we need to guard the place. Gemma plans on planting flowers. My mother was telling my father last night that Gemma will be off to market day in Fullbourne to purchase seeds and the ingredients the dowager needs for her knee. The dowager is going to send her in her own coach."

Ned swore under his breath, and not because of the flowers.

"Be that as it may," Ned said, "there is a right way to go about this and a wrong one. Standing on the streets trying to intimidate Mrs. Estep will serve no purpose. For one, she apparently isn't intimidated."

"Then we may need to be rougher—"

"*You will not.* Or you will find yourself answering to me."

Michaels mumbled under his breath but Ned chose to ignore him. "I must be off. You go on now." He waited long enough to see the man shuffle away.

Ned looked to Hippocrates. "I may need to have a word with the duke."

Hippocrates shook his head, letting Ned know he was impatient to either ride on or eat grass. The choice was Ned's.

Ned chose to ride.

His first stop was to pay a call on Simon Crisp to check on his hand. He'd saved Simon Crisp's finger, or at least he hoped he had. Crisp had been sharpening his tools when he'd tripped carrying his scythe. The cut had gone to the bone. To ensure Crisp didn't use the hand, Ned had placed a block of wood in the palm and wrapped the hand around it.

Of course, Crisp had complained. He didn't like the restriction. "How am I going to work?" he'd demanded.

"You have sons. Let them be your hands for now," Ned told him. "Besides, that is some of my best handiwork. You should treat it with respect." Crisp had laughed and that had been it—Ned hoped.

He was pleased to see Crisp sitting in his house, taking his leisure. Mrs. Crisp hovered around and the yeoman appeared at peace with letting himself heal.

Ned took the chair that was offered and looked over the hand. No red streaks. That was a good sign.

"Does it hurt?" he asked his patient.

"It throbs."

"That will stop. I hope you are keeping the cider jug close."

Crisp laughed, reached for the floor beside his chair, and held up the jug with his good hand.

"You are a model patient, Simon. I wish they were all like you."

"I'm keeping my eye on him," his wife declared. "We need him well and soon before we start planting." She was a cherry-cheeked woman with a pointy nose and a no-nonsense manner.

Crisp bragged, "My sons have picked up my work and proud of them I am."

"I'm pleased," Ned assured him.

"As I am," his wife said. "I was worried that he wouldn't behave but after he had a stern talk from Gemma, my husband settled down."

Ned's world came to a sudden stop. "Gemma?"

"Yes, Miss Taylor brought her by," Mrs. Crisp

said. "They had heard there had been an accident and so had charitably come to pay a call on us. Gemma is a lovely lady. She approved of your work on Mr. Crisp's hand."

Approved? Ned's genial smile froze.

"She told Mr. Crisp he would be a fool to rewrap his hand without that block of wood. Convinced my stubborn man to listen. Thought you would like to know that, sir," Mrs. Crisp finished. She had been busy darning a sock as she spoke so she didn't notice the impact of her words on Ned.

Gemma approved, of what *he*, a trained *doctor*, did for a patient? He knew he'd better leave now.

Ned stood. Crisp rose to his feet, as well. "I'll see myself out," Ned said.

"I can't have you do that," Crisp countered. "Not after all you did for us, and on the Sabbath, no less." He walked out the door with Ned to where one of the Crisp lads walked Hippocrates. Ned tossed the boy a coin and took the reins.

Crisp nodded for his son to go about his business. Once the lad was out of earshot, he asked, "Is everything all right, Mr. Thurlowe?"

"Yes, fine."

"Your jaw is very tight. It is Gemma, isn't it?"

"Do you mean Mrs. Estep?" Ned flashed and immediately regretted it.

"My Molly does like to go on. She doesn't notice things. I do. I will say, though, that I learned a thing or two listening to the women yesterday."

"And what did you learn?"

"That my Molly has been in pain and worried about it."

Immediately, Ned's attention switched from his irritation with Gemma to concerned physician. "What sort of pain? Here, come back and hold my horse," he said, waving at the boy. He would have started back to the cottage but Crisp stopped him.

"It is the piles, sir. That's all. She had the piles. She won't talk about it with you, sir. She's never said a word to me but suffered in silence. And she'll not be happy that I shared. She was embarrassed speaking yesterday with Gemma." He glanced over his shoulder as if to be certain his wife hadn't creeped up on them, before adding, "I asked why she hadn't told me she wasn't feeling well."

"And her answer?"

"For one, she was afeard she was dying."

Ned frowned. "It is a common ailment."

"Don't I know. I've had them myself." Crisp shrugged. "Who understands the thinking of women."

"I could have helped her. I could have spoken with her about it Sunday."

"That is what I said. She didn't feel comfortable talking to a man, not even her husband, about the matter. You know, it is personal. I suppose women don't like talking about their bums while we men are always going on about our arses. Actually, to be honest, I didn't like talking about it with you when I had them. And I don't want you to take this the wrong way, but I just think she was shy speaking about her privates with one who looks like you."

"One who looks like me? What does my face have to do with this?"

"Mr. Thurlowe, you know the lasses are partial to your looks. They are all sweet on you. I don't mind. I mean, I know my Molly would never stray. I've never believed I had a concern with you and she."

"Oh, well," Ned said, "that is a relief."

"I thought you'd want to know that I trust you around my wife."

"Except she doesn't want to talk to me when she isn't feeling well, and that is a problem."

"Well, she doesn't want to talk about her bum." Crisp laughed. "That is good, no?"

No, it wasn't good. In truth Ned's mind was whirling over the idea that a patient in pain would refuse care because of his looks or her shyness. It didn't make sense to him. Once he started working, all he saw was a body, not the person.

He had to ask, "Did Mrs. Estep help her?"

"She is going to. She has a lotion she makes. Uses cream," he supplied helpfully. "She wants one of the boys to go to The Garland later today to pick up a bottle for their mother."

"I'm right here," Ned had to offer. "I can help your wife." He had an ointment with sulfur in it. He even took another step toward the door. Crisp stopped him.

"Please, sir. She's happy. You aren't a married

man but I'm here to tell you that when the wife is happy, you leave well enough alone. Besides, she'd have my head for telling you."

"I don't know if Gemma's cure will be effective or the best thing for your wife."

"If she is happy, it doesn't matter."

Ned had no choice but to ride away.

"AND WHY does it bother you so much that Mrs. Crisp is confiding in this Gemma?" Kate Balfour asked.

It had been a long day. The conversation with Crisp made Ned question himself. He was now doing something uncharacteristic—unburdening himself. He didn't tell them the nature of Mrs. Crisp's ailment save that it was highly personal.

When he'd called on Kate, she had asked him to join them for dinner. He didn't feel like being good company. However, returning to an empty house wasn't comforting, either. He accepted the invitation, and then, before he knew what he was about, he shared the story of Mrs. Crisp.

"I've taken care of these people," Ned said. "I'm a good doctor."

Balfour handed him a glass of claret. "You are. That is why I'm insisting that you see to my wife and child."

"And I don't think anyone is saying you are a poor doctor," Kate said. She had a shawl around her shoulders and her hair was down. She had picked at her food, even after Ned had gently reminded her that she was "eating for two."

She appeared tired.

Or worried.

Ned watched her closely, even as he sat back in his dining chair and challenged, "Then what are they saying?" He threw the words out and before either of them could answer, snapped, "Because they have all embraced *Gemma*. Crisp and the Widow Smethers were open about it, but others . . . I can sense they hold back around me. They are being duplicitous."

"Duplicitous?" Kate echoed.

"Yes, they seek my advice *and then* they ask hers, as if they are comparing us."

Balfour shrugged. "She is new. People gravitate to the new."

"That's true," Ned agreed. "Except, when I first came here, they put me through my paces. No one trusted me. I worked for their trust—"

He sat up, struck by a new thought. "Is that it? They still don't trust me after five years of my being amongst them?"

"It is nothing like that," Balfour assured him. "You are making too much of this. I've never even heard of the woman. No one has mentioned her to me. Well, save for what you've told me. I don't even understand why she bothers you so much."

"Because ever since I came here, and even when I was in London, there has always been a battle between home cures—which are often based on nothing more than superstition and silliness—and information learned after rigorous study. Do I believe the night air carries bad vapors that cause disease? No. I'm not certain of the causes for many diseases but it isn't the air or we would all suffer from typhus or wasting diseases, and we don't."

"Then what does cause them?" Balfour asked.

"We don't know—yet. Someday I believe we will. It used to be that if you had a growth under your skin or on your breast, it was because you were a sinner and God was marking you. Now we understand that some bodies form tumors that can, judiciously, be cut out of the patient to his betterment. We are learning so much right now about the true nature of illness and disease, it annoys me when someone like Mrs. Estep sets up shop and everyone believes whatever cures she peddles. Cream on piles? Really?"

"There is some truth to what people pass around," Kate countered. "When I traveled with acting troupes, we rarely had the time or money to seek out a physician. There were all sorts of remedies we shared."

"Such as?" Balfour asked.

"Chewing ginger root was a good one. Someone always had it on hand. It seemed to cure a number of ailments such as nausea and sore throat. I even used it once for a headache. And it was good protection against contagion."

Ned shook his head. "I doubt if the ginger protected you from someone else's illness. Or had any effect on your headache, although the strong flavor might have taken your mind off the discomfort. I will agree that it is well-known for helping to settle the stomach."

"And it is true, isn't it, that some plants, when they are steamed, can help breathing."

"Another truth," he could admit. "Eucalyptus is one. The oil in the leaves puts out a strong aroma that seems to help. Some mints can do the same."

"These remedies were known by the locals first, correct?"

Ned had to smile. "I concede your point. Yes, often locals identify those healing qualities first. Still, I must offer two caveats. One is that the steam one is breathing probably does more than the oil from the plant. The second is that eucalyptus has been studied by men of learning. If something is worthwhile, it deserves intelligent review."

"Which can only come from men?" Kate asked.

"Yes, of course," he answered before he realized he was walking into a trap. He threw his napkin on the table and raised his hands. "All right. Correct me."

She didn't hesitate. "My sister is as good if not better an apothecarist than her husband, even though he taught her everything she knows. So perhaps Gemma has studied the cures she offers. Perhaps they have merit. Perhaps not all things come from London."

"She has you there," Balfour said, clapping a delighted hand on the table. "You yourself are frustrated by the stranglehold London has on research and which scholarly papers should be chosen for presentation."

That was true. The purpose of the lecture series he had started was to bring attention to those studies outside the mainstream of academic thought.

"I also think," Kate said, picking up her teacup, "that a tea garden sounds like a lovely idea. It would be an ideal gathering place."

"The Garland is a gathering place—" Ned started.

"But only for you men and just a few of you at that." She set down her cup. "Come, Ned, your thinking is more independent than this. The Logical Men's Society was never meant to be a serious idea."

There was an uncomfortable truth in her statement.

Then she leaned forward and said, "As for the matter you brought up earlier with Mrs. Crisp and her ailment—sometimes a woman wants to talk to another woman. It has nothing to do with your capabilities as a doctor. We can be shy about intimate matters."

"Are you shy around me?" Was that what she was saying?

She blinked at his questions and then laughed and shook her head. "No, I'm fine with you. And you have seen a good deal of me as of late. I'm just saying that country women have perhaps different values. Especially on personal matters."

"I am discreet."

"You are," Kate answered with a small shrug. "But you are still male." Then she added, "A handsome one, too. Yes, I can see some of the local women being very ill at ease."

There it was again: talk about his face. He wanted to say he couldn't help the way he looked or that it made some women . . . Well, he couldn't quite define how it made them feel. However, he noticed Kate suddenly looked exhausted and that was a sign Ned needed to leave.

He stood and Balfour rose with him. "Thank you for dinner. I needed your friendship this evening."

"You are always welcome at our table, Ned," Kate said. Her husband helped her up from her chair. "Will we see you on the morrow?"

"Absolutely." Ned understood why Balfour adored his wife. Kate was the sort of companion who would make any man proud. She was graceful, intelligent, and had courage.

She said her goodbyes at the door while Balfour went out with him to where Hippocrates waited.

Once they were out of earshot of his wife, Balfour said, "The baby . . . It isn't hurting her, is it?"

"No," Ned hastened to say. "It is just a chore to bring a life into the world. No small feat. It also calls for every bit of energy she has. She is tired. What will help is if she eats more." He could also add that she needed to keep her fears at bay.

He was glad he kept quiet when his friend confided, "I had a dream last night. I dreamed she died. It upset me. Thurlowe, if this baby takes her life—"

Ned held up his hand to cut his friend off. "You don't believe in omens, do you?" Was everyone starting to grow irrational?

"Not usually and yet, the dream was very real. Too real."

"Does she know you had this dream?"

"She woke me. She said I was distressed."

Ned took a step toward his friend. "Listen, these last weeks of preparing for a baby can make one anxious. I can imagine how I would feel." He couldn't. Not actually. Ned knew how much was out of the control of mere mortals, and that was the way life was. "Your dream is not prophetic."

"You don't believe so?"

"No, it's probably a sign of indigestion. Perhaps you should chew a piece of ginger root."

Balfour laughed and then sobered, placing a hand on Hippocrates's neck. "There was another baby who died. In Fullbourne. The mother lived."

Ned knew the Fullbourne midwife, a competent woman named Liza Dearman. If she wasn't so far away, he would have recommended Mrs. Dearman for Kate.

"Is this what was wrong with Kate tonight?"

"The news weighs on both of us. Kate is concerned her body is too old. She doesn't want to fail the baby. But here is the truth, Thurlowe. If it comes down to choosing between my wife or this child, save my wife. I can't live without Kate. If there is a choice to be made, I wish you to make the right one. Do you understand me?"

He did. He also knew that if that moment of decision came, so little would be in his hands. "Stop fearing the worst. Have faith, man."

"I don't let Kate see my concerns. Unless I'm dreaming."

Or so he thought.

Ned was now convinced that the secret worries the Balfours were keeping from each other explained Kate's paleness and lack of appetite.

"Childbirth is not easy," Ned cautioned his friend. "However, I will do everything in my power to see *both* mother and babe through. You have my word."

It was a promise Ned had made to Balfour many times before, and one he knew he might not be able to keep.

Fortunately, his friend was mollified. "Thank you. I know you will do everything in your power. Still, I needed you to know how I feel."

"Duly noted," Ned answered, taking the reins and mounting. "I'll see you on the morrow. And thank you for the good hospitality tonight. I needed it." With a wave, he and Hippocrates were off.

As he rode home in the dark, the horse knowing the way, Ned mulled over the weight of what he'd promised his friend. Humans were surprisingly fragile creatures, especially in childbirth. He was sorry that the Balfours had heard of the deaths in Thorpton and Fullbourne. The mothers had been young. He understood why Kate was nervous.

And there was no escaping the fact that Balfour would blame Ned if something happened, even if he did all he could.

Ned tried to imagine himself in such a fevered state over a woman, and failed. He tried to personalize the image and picture himself beside Clarissa Taylor. He couldn't. He never could—

Until . . . A childhood memory, one he hadn't realized was closeted in his mind, flew to the forefront.

There *had been* a woman he had cared for so deeply he'd been inconsolable when she'd died.

He'd been about four. Her death was the reason his father finally came for him.

Ned couldn't remember her name but she'd been important to him. He could also recall her consumptive cough. That rattling, hacking sound had been common in the back rooms of the brothel where he'd been raised up to that date.

The girl had not been his mother. Sarah Middleton was alive and quite well in London, fleecing her lovers.

No, this girl might have been a scullery maid. She'd given him food and at night, he'd shared her pallet. He'd listened to her when she'd scolded him and he had trusted her.

In the dark shadows of the road, he could recall the sounds of adults talking over his head. Their voices echoed in his mind, and then his father, a man he'd never seen before, had appeared. He'd picked Ned up by one arm and dragged him out of the house. He'd taken Ned to his big home and given him a bed to sleep in and the praying nurse to watch over him. She was the first of several until he was sent off to school a year or two later.

However, no one had ever cared for him like the nameless girl.

Certainly, his mother had never given two thoughts toward him.

And it was good Ned had been taken away. His father had seen to his education and had corresponded with him from time to time. What more could a father do for a bastard child? Ned had learned not to mind.

After all, his background was somewhat unusual but hardly unconventional. Besides, he had standing in a community and was to marry a lovely woman, even if he couldn't picture himself beside her or her carrying his child.

They had reached the village. All was dark and at peace.

In a few minutes they would be home. Hippocrates had already picked up his pace. He knew better than to start trotting, except tonight Ned found himself ready to be home, as well. He might let the horse continue to have his head—

The front door of The Garland was thrown open. A dark figure of a man with a hood over his head charged out the door and ran right into the horse's flank.

The man reeled back as if stunned to find

someone blocking his escape—and Ned recognized him. It was hard to disguise the lanky awkwardness. "Fitzsimmons?"

The answer was a shocked gasp at the recognition. Fitz backed away just as a woman's feeble cry went up from inside the tavern. "Help, please, someone help me."

Fitz looked back at the doorway and then went tearing off.

In the next moment the woman herself appeared at the door and leaned against it. She wore her nightdress and little else. Her red hair was in a long dark braid over her shoulder.

A cloud blocking the moon shifted and Ned could see the stain of blood running down her face.

Chapter Ten

$\mathcal{N}$ed immediately jumped to the ground. Dropping Hippocrates's reins over his head, he untied his medical bag from his saddle and hurried to Gemma. The horse would meander where he wished. Ned's first concern was for the woman.

When he reached the door, she fell into his arms. "Someone attacked me." Her voice was breathless, panicked. Her eyes met his and then, recognizing him, she started to struggle as if afraid he would hurt her.

"Please, please," he said. "It is all right. It is me, Ned Thurlowe. You are safe. But I need to stop the bleeding."

She frowned fiercely as if not believing him.

"Gemma, I want to help. Come, please." She didn't relax but she let him walk her back through the door.

All was dark. "Where is a candle?"

"The . . . k-kitchen." Her speech was slowing. She was going to faint.

He swept her up in his arms.

She stiffened. "What are you doing?"

"Making it easier for both of us. Do you know what he hit you with?"

"No," she said softly and then leaned her head against his chest, her braid falling over his arm. Good. She'd given up the fight.

Moving in the dark, he trusted his instinct, and years spent in The Garland, to find the taproom door. From there, he could see the burning embers in the kitchen hearth.

"Can you sit?" he asked.

"Of course." Her voice was still weak, but slightly cranky. He interpreted it as a good sign.

After sitting her in the nearest chair at the table, Ned placed his medical bag on the table and went over to stir the fire. The flames came to life, adding more light to the kitchen. He looked around for the candle and saw it on the table beside her. A beat later he had the candle lit. The room filled with a thin, golden glow.

"My embroidered bag . . . my herbs. In my room."

She was giving him orders. Yes, she would be fine.

"I have salves for cuts." His foot kicked a log that was on the floor.

"That is what he hit me with," she murmured before slumping. He caught her before she tumbled to the floor.

"Come, Gemma. Be strong."

Her lids fluttered and she tried to smile. "He hit . . . me."

"That he did." Bracing her with one arm, Ned held the candle up to take a closer look at her injury. The cut was high on the temple, just at the hairline. "Clean rags?"

She shook her head, sitting back on her own in the chair. Her breathing was still shallow.

Ned removed his neck cloth and dabbed one corner of it on the wound before holding the candle up to see better. The cut was not as deep as he feared. The skin was broken and she'd have a good bruise. To his relief, her eyes were clear. Her confused reaction had more to do with shock than anything else.

"I need you to stay sitting up, Gemma."

She nodded and leaned a supporting arm on the table.

He backed away to be certain she wouldn't fall. She gave him a wan smile. "I'm all right." Her speech was gaining strength and she made eye contact.

Ned went over to the fire. There was water in the kettle. Taking a bowl from the cupboard, he poured water into it, dipped his neck cloth, wrung it out, and started to clean her wound. His voice gentle, he warned, "This may hurt—"

She flinched.

"Still, it must be done. You know that."

She nodded. A tear ran down her cheek. She'd been given quite a fright.

And it made him furious at Fitz. And whomever else was behind him.

She lifted her head, turning it for him to have better access to the light.

"The cut is right on the temple," he explained. Her brows came together. She reached up and took his neck cloth from him, pushing it against her wound herself.

He threw the water he had used out the back door and poured more. It was his habit to tell his patients what he planned. He found it reassured them. "I will make certain the wound is clean. Considering that you were hit with a log, I don't want splinters or dirt. That could lead to infection."

She nodded.

He took a flask out of his bag and unscrewed it. "Here, sip this."

"What is it?"

"The best medicine in the world. A good brandy—"

The sound of bootsteps scuffling on the taproom floor interrupted him. Ned looked to the doorway, braced for anything.

Jonathon Fitzsimmons stepped out of the darkness. He held the hood in one hand at his side. His manner was that of a chastened ten-year-old. "Is she all right?"

"No thanks to you. What was this about?"

Instead of answering Ned, Jonathon entered the kitchen and fell to one knee on the brick floor beside Gemma. She recoiled while Ned put a protective arm out to block the man from touching her. "Fitz—"

"I didn't mean to hurt you." Fitz's tone was stark, repentant.

She didn't answer him.

His face crumpled. "Please. I didn't mean it."

"What were you doing here?" Ned asked.

Fitz acted relieved to take his attention away from Gemma's pale face. "I thought I would find the will that gave The Garland to her. I—"

His voice broke off, and then he finished, "It was an idiot's idea. I just thought it would be a way to do something for the lads." Again, his gaze sought Ned's for understanding and then dropped to the floor. "To fit in."

And Ned remembered the conversation in the stables where he had said clearly not to attempt a stunt like taking her proof from her. "Did the others egg you on?"

"I'd rather not say, sir."

"Did Winderton promote this idea?"

"He did not tell me to do it."

"Did he imply it?" Ned had to ask.

Fitz's expression grew pinched. "I should be able to think on my own, sir."

"Yes, you should," Ned readily agreed, convinced that the lot of them had cooked up this scheme. Fitz was just the messenger.

The man had the good sense to look ashamed. He turned back to Gemma and caught her staring at both of them, her expression wary.

Wary. The word described her manner from

the first moment he'd met her. She didn't trust men. It was clear to him now.

He didn't trust women.

They were a fine pair.

"Mrs. Estep?" She didn't respond. "*Gemma.*" He made his voice deliberately sharp. She blinked, looked to him—and what he saw in her eyes almost broke his heart.

He understood betrayal. He knew it well. Whatever was going through her mind, it was bigger than a knock on the head.

Ned spoke to Fitz. "Since you are here, make yourself useful. Pick up the candle and hold it high. Gemma, keep drinking."

She dutifully took another sip from the flask while Fitz did as bidden. Ned could now see the cut more fully. No sign of imbedded splinters. "It is clean."

He had pulled a second chair up so that he could sit facing her, the two of them knee to knee, and reached inside his bag.

Gemma stirred. Her knee hit his, then rested. "I would put charcoal on it."

"Not from the hearth," Ned countered, pulling out a small bag.

"Certainly from the hearth." Her spirit was returning. "Where else would you find it?"

He poured the contents of his bag in the palm of his hand. There were three small charcoal pieces. "I'm a bit choosy about what I use. I prepare this myself from good oak wood."

For the first time since the incident began,

she looked at him, *truly* looked at him. He took a small mortar and pestle from his bag. It was a third of the size of a normal one. He ground a chunk of the charcoal, adding a spot of water to create a paste.

She watched, a small smile forming. When he was finished, she said, "Why, Mr. Thurlowe, I'm surprised you would use a healer's remedy."

"I use whatever has been *proven* to be good medicine."

"So that means you keep leeches in that bag?"

"Not in my bag."

She raised a skeptical eyebrow. Yes, she was feeling better, and he did have leeches at his house. Every doctor kept them. "I rarely use them. I prefer to see if the body heals itself first. Sometimes the best cure is patience."

"That is a comfort." She turned her head for him to apply the charcoal. Fitz, his prominent Adam's apple bobbing, held the light. He was good about not letting any wax drop on both doctor and patient.

After Ned gingerly applied the paste to her wound, he unrolled a clean bandage from his bag. He wrapped it around her head. She touched it as if judging his skill and then smiled. "It helps."

"Fitz, fetch a mug." Ned took the flask and poured a bit of brandy in it. He handed it to the lanky man. "Here, you look as if you could use a bit of a restorative."

"Thank you, sir. I could. I didn't like seeing what I did."

"She is lucky you didn't do worse."

"Yes, sir." Fitz downed the brandy.

And was that his imagination, or did her mouth twitch as if she held back a smile?

He placed the flask in her hands. "Drink."

"Yes, Doctor," she replied, as if being dutiful. She took a sip, tasted it, and then took another. "It is restorative." The fear had left her eye.

Fitz hovered. "Will you accept my apology, Mrs. Estep—?"

"Gemma," she corrected him perfunctorily. She leaned back in the chair and closed her eyes as if letting the brandy flow through her being.

"Gemma," Fitz repeated.

He really did sound pathetic and Ned could see Gemma softening toward him. For that reason, he said, "I am certain you are sorry, Fitz. However, this will be a matter for the magistrate when he returns. You can't go around bashing heads."

Poor Fitz appeared ready to dissolve. "I regret what I did. I wasn't thinking. My mother will be disappointed."

"Still, you did it."

Gemma had opened her eyes, watching Ned carefully during this exchange. Not Fitz. She watched him.

"I've never been in trouble before," Fitz said. He appeared ready to bolt.

Ned shrugged. He had no words.

Gemma did. "Why did you attack me? I understand you were trying to steal, but you *hit* me?"

"I didn't mean to attack you. When you came

out of your room, you startled me. I thought you were with the other women gathered at Smythson this evening." Smythson was the ancestral home of the Duke of Winderton and where his mother resided.

"Ah, so that is why Mrs. Warbler hasn't come running over," Ned murmured. The color was definitely returning to her cheeks. He was now certain she would be all right. One always had to worry about concussion.

"I was supposed to go with them except I was tired. Thank heavens I was here, although you would not have found the letter from my uncle."

That caught Ned's interest. A letter? That was what she had?

And then he pushed those thoughts aside. There had been enough of this nonsense for the night. Almost wearily, he said, "The Earl of Marsden will deal fairly with you, Fitz. Of course, what you should truly fear is the wrath of your mother and the other matrons once they learn what you have done."

Fitz pulled at his hair. "Oh, God, sir, Mother can't know. She will not be pleased." He looked again to Gemma. "I will do anything to make this right to you. I'm not afraid of paying my dues."

"Just not in front of the magistrate or your mother, eh?" Ned observed.

Fitz ignored him, appealing directly to Gemma. "Please."

"Your friends might believe I deserved a whack on the head," she said quietly.

"No, ma'am, they would not think it honorable. And it wasn't," Fitz answered.

Gemma considered him a moment. She took another sip of brandy and then said, "I could use help here. Show up on the morrow and we shall see if we can work something out. I would not wish to trouble the magistrate over the matter."

Fitz's shoulders sagged in relief. "Thank you. *Thank you*—" Ned thought he sounded pathetic in his gratitude. "I will be here. In the morning?"

"Oh, yes, half past seven. I'm an early riser."

Fitz nodded. "Thank you, Mrs.—Gemma. Thank you."

"The lads will believe you a turncoat," Ned pointed out. He wanted Fitz to realize exactly what he was committing to.

"They can think what they like. I'm sorry I did it." With that, he took off as if escaping before she could change her mind.

They were alone.

He suddenly became very aware of that.

And although she wasn't the first female patient he'd been alone with in her nightdress, she was the first where he'd registered how thin the material of a gown was. Or wondered how naked the body was beneath it.

He should leave.

He'd done all he could.

Instead, he lingered, sitting right where he was. Close to her, her knee still familiarly against his.

Ned knew his face attracted women. He'd had

plenty throw themselves at him, something he found embarrassing and that had blessedly been curbed by his betrothal to Clarissa. Except, right now he wondered if his face appealed to her? And would *she* throw herself at him? Would she become giddy and a bit reckless like some women did? Then he thought of the wariness in her eyes, her lack of trust.

They were cut out of the same cloth, he realized with a start. Neither of them trusted easily. He'd heard her husband had been a complete villain. The women he'd known in his life—his mother, his father's wife, the half sisters who would have nothing to do with him—they'd hardened him. He'd learned that if he let people, especially women, too close, they would betray him. They would ferret out his vulnerabilities and use them against him.

Except, he didn't want to believe that about her. That made her even more dangerous.

With the bandage around her head and her toes peeking out from beneath her hem, she appeared young and defenseless. He'd liked the weight of her body in his arms. He now knew the silkiness of her hair and the scent of her, a blend of the herbs she distilled.

So, so aware of her, even to the beating of her heart against the very sensitive skin where her jaw met her neck. He could almost count the beats, and his fingers longed to touch that delicate place.

There was a slight flush to her cheeks, probably from the brandy. She seemed to study some point on the brick floor.

What if he pressed his palm against the smooth skin of her cheek? What if he turned her attention toward him?

And then she moved. Her head tilted up to him, her eyes clear now. "Did *you* think I was away this evening?" She set her flask on the table. "Did you have a hand in putting him up to stealing my papers?"

Had he almost let down his guard? That was a damn idiotic thing to do. Bloody women were all alike.

"What?" Ned came to his feet, so offended he didn't know where to start. Here he'd been thinking—well, it didn't matter what he was thinking because he'd certainly misread all the signs.

"It is convenient that you were so close," she observed.

"You think I was waiting to see if the deed was done? Is that what you are imagining? Oh, and of course, I rushed in to make it appear as I was not involved." He used his most sarcastic tone, mocking her.

She didn't blush. Instead, her gaze was steady, expectant.

"Good God." He had to take a step away. How could he have been so deceived by her? One second she was weak and malleable and now she appeared ready to spit fire.

Perhaps he was more like his gullible father than he had imagined. "I am not devious. I've told you exactly what I'm going to do from the very beginning."

"Which is to see me thrown out of the village."

"I don't know if I like your manner. You are very direct."

"And you're not?"

"Of course I am. I'm male."

"Ah, I was wondering what the difference was between the two of us. Men say what they think and women waffle on, right?"

Ned narrowed his eyes. "I'm not pleased with you."

"Pity," she responded.

His temper, which he rarely lost, rose like a thundercloud. He had to take another step away from her. "I'm not treacherous. From the beginning, I have told you what will happen. Once Marsden returns, this will be straightened out—in *my* favor."

She came to her bare feet, and he was no longer entranced by her toes. "I'm not giving up The Garland."

"You will not have a choice. There is no will, is there?"

Her chin lifted. She didn't answer.

She didn't need to. She'd already told him what she had and that was a letter. He crossed to the table, avoiding her as if she was a leper, and started to pack up his medical bag. Through clenched teeth he issued his doctor's orders.

"You might have a headache on the morrow. I have a powder for that, which is good mixed with mulled wine. Do you have any wine?"

"What is in the powder?"

She questioned him? Of course.

"Crushed lavender from *my* garden," he said, his jaw tight.

"Lavender for headaches?"

"No, the mulled wine will take the edge off your headache. The lavender is to add scent and make you believe that you are drinking something special."

"Actually, lavender does soothe the senses."

He knew that. "Do you have wine?"

"No."

"I will have a bottle of wine brought over to you."

"It is not necessary."

Suddenly, he remembered he didn't have anything to drink at his house. The lads had sucked it all up and nothing would be replaced until Royce returned. "I'll leave the flask." It was the best he could do.

He moved toward the door, careful to stay as far away from her as possible. She could be standing there stark naked and he would not touch her.

"I'm not attempting to be difficult," she said, following him as he moved through the taproom. "The Society is still free to meet here. Of course, there will be rules."

Ned stopped at the main room entrance, offended that she was offering him a bone. "Sorry, we don't enjoy tea and treacle."

"Well then, let me assure you, the Society's goings-on that *I* have heard happened *here* will not take place under my ownership."

"Mrs. Estep, I *don't* condone recent events." That was true. "That doesn't mean that the Logical Men's Society doesn't have a right to exist and to meet. It is an old and revered tradition in this village."

"How old? Mrs. Warbler said it has only been around for fifty years. A teardrop in English history."

"Fifty years is old enough." He walked into the main room, wanting to be done with this conversation. How could he have ever thought her attractive? She was a shrew through and through. He kept his manner brisk and professional. "I will check on you in the morning to see how you are doing—"

"Is it just me that you have a problem with, Mr. Thurlowe? Or are you this way with all women?"

Her tone alone was enough to set his teeth on edge. He whirled around, not realizing that she was so close, he practically stepped on her toes—and again, caught the heat of her body beneath that nightdress.

In a blink his mouth went dry. His hands wanted to reach for her. He tensed, holding himself back. And then, calmly, enunciating clearly, he said, "It is just *you*. I like every other woman I've ever met."

It was a deliberately hurtful thing to say. If she would back away, perhaps then some semblance of his sanity would return. She didn't.

Instead, her chin rose in defiance, and he had a strong desire to kiss her. It would not take much effort. If he tipped his head down, she was right there.

He was startled at how easily their bodies would mesh together. She was just the right height. And while she accused him of not liking her, parts of his body liked her very much. In fact, he'd never experienced *liking* this hard—

"I believe *you* are a very poor sport."

That was it.

A mountain of snow could not have cooled his ardor faster.

"Good night, Mrs. Estep." He turned and walked out of the tavern.

She followed him. Of course she would. "Good night to you, sir." She sounded almost pleasant.

And then she slammed the door behind him and threw the bar.

For a beat Ned stared at the door as if he could burn it up with his eyes. What was the matter with that woman?

He should fall on his knees now and thank the good Lord that he hadn't surrendered to base impulses and attempted to kiss her, because he'd been close.

Close to opening himself to her. Close to letting down his guard. Close to making a fool of himself. A barred door was the only way to deal with her.

Of course, he was now standing alone out in the road. Hippocrates had ambled home.

Swearing under his breath, Ned began the short march to his doorstep.

GEMMA FELL against the barred door. Her heart pounded and her head throbbed. She couldn't tell which was more disconcerting.

That man.

If she wasn't careful she would once again fall for a handsome face. There had been a moment, when they were alone, when he'd sat so near to her she could detect the scent of horse and fresh air about him, when she could look into his eyes and see every shade of golden brown even in the candlelight, when she was tempted to reach out to him.

And true, earlier when he'd lifted her in his arms, she had never felt more safe. Never with Paul and not even as a child with her father. He was solid, strong, protective. She'd allowed herself to relax, and to momentarily trust.

Except, he was not her friend. She had no worse enemy in the world. He had just said as much. And she would bet all her possessions that he had some sort of role in the attack on her tonight. Oh, perhaps he didn't plan it. He sounded genuinely surprised and quite angry at Fitz's actions.

However, wittingly or unwittingly, he'd had a hand in it, or so she wanted to convince herself . . . because to think differently was dangerous.

Yes, she knew there was more to Ned Thurlowe than his looks. He *was* a man of substance. The villagers spoke of him with respect. Even Mrs. Warbler, who seemed to have a low opinion about everyone.

Furthermore, Gemma had seen his handiwork. He was a good doctor. A caring one. He was the sort of man she could admire, save for one glaring fact—he was also promised to another woman. A delightful woman who was eager to befriend her and had been kindness itself.

What sort of man looked at her the way he had when he was to marry someone as special as Clarissa Taylor?

So there it was, the truth. All men really *were* alike. Paul, his brother, Mr. Thurlowe. Even her beloved father had been capable of not being honest with her. Why else would her father have not told her he'd left everything to Paul in his will? He'd let her believe she would have some control over her own future.

Gemma had learned her lessons the hard way. And she'd best keep as far from Ned Thurlowe as she could. Lashing out at him accomplished that feat.

She pushed away from the door.

Chapter Eleven

*T*he more Ned walked, the angrier he grew.

It didn't help that lust still coursed through his veins. He was half-mad with it. His step was strong and hard, his breathing heavy with extra exertion, his muscles still so tense they felt like tightly coiled springs.

He stormed straight to the stables, thinking he would both unsaddle Hippocrates and put his fists repeatedly into the wood walls. Then maybe he'd cool the anger and satisfy the need for—what? Wishing he'd been able to choke off Gemma's ugly accusations? Or pound sense into Winderton and his gang of barely literate locals—?

Ned didn't know. He was on edge, annoyed, and bitter—

He came to a full-on stop.

Hippocrates had already been unsaddled and was too busy munching grain to even nicker a pleasant good-night. Not so with the other horses there. Royce's animal was standing asleep, his back hoof cocked. However, Bruno, the Earl of Marsden's animal, put his head forward and whinnied.

Mars was here.

Ned's anger evaporated. A resolution to his quarrel with Mrs. Estep was at hand.

He charged to the house. Royce had been waiting for him and opened the door almost before Ned came into the lamplight.

"You brought him home," Ned said in relief.

"It was a challenge," Royce confessed in a low voice.

"Where did you find him?" Ned was afraid of the answer.

"Actually, he found me. I searched every wicked den I could find. I finally circled back to his house to let them know that I had failed. That is when I caught him returning home on the arm of a watchman. He insisted on coming with me but, well, he's worn thin." He nodded to the sitting room. "He is in there. He's too wrapped around the axle to rest and more than a bit touchy to learn there is no port or brandy."

"Wait until he discovers why." Ned handed Royce his hat and coat and then inwardly braced himself before greeting his friend. Mars could be tricky even when he was feeling his best. Ned had nursed him the last time he'd needed to recover from his overindulgence. It had not been a pleasant experience. He entered the sitting room.

Mars was ensconced in Ned's favorite uphol-stered chair before the fire. His stockinged feet rested on a footstool. He was coatless and with-out his neck cloth. What had once been a fine vest was unbuttoned and appeared as if it had been slept in then ridden in for several hours.

He'd rolled the sleeves of his lawn shirt up and his arms rested over the sides of the chair as he complained, "You have kept me waiting." He was a tall, broad-shouldered man with hair the dusty color of winter wheat and eyes that could turn to ice when he was crossed. Right now they were red rimmed and a pale blue. "Who drank all the port?"

"Winderton." Ned came around to sit in the identical chair next to Mars's. "He's back in Maid-enshop. He is staying at the Dower House and he is an idiot."

"He's an idiot wherever he stays," Mars an-swered. "Of course, he is young. Not ancient like you and I."

Mars *did* look ancient and Ned forgot his ar-gument over The Garland. It was suddenly un-important in the face of his friend's disheveled appearance. He angled his chair to face the earl and leaned forward. "Why, Mars? Why do you do this to yourself?"

"Why does a wild March hare run out in the open across a road?" The earl shrugged.

"You have everything any man could ever want. There is no need to lose yourself in opium."

Mars looked away. For a few seconds there was silence and then he said, "What do you know of what I need?"

"Then tell me."

"I do it because I wish to."

"No, there is always a reason. Something deeper."

Mars frowned as if he didn't quite believe him, then said, "A reason. Such as watching my father shot and having no right or ability to make the man responsible pay?" He referred to Lord Dervil, a neighbor who spent most of his time in London. He'd dueled with Mars's father over a property line and killed him dead. If Dervil had his way, he'd own the village. Only Mars stood in his way, and even though the earl had ascended to the title when he was fifteen, he'd stood up to the powerful lord then and he stood up to him now. He just couldn't make him pay for his father's death.

But Ned was not going to let his friend drift off in self-pity. "Many people see their father die and don't turn to the pipe."

The earl sat up and shook his head and shoulders as if stretching before pinning Ned with an aloof gaze, a nobleman's stare. "I don't do it often. At least, not anymore."

Ned refused to have his concern dismissed. "And never on a whim, I imagine."

His friend snorted his answer and settled back into the chair, any good humor gone. Here was the true man. Mars may smile and be genial in public but there was a dark side to him. "You don't understand."

Ned sat back. "Possibly. Then again, you never had to play witness to your mother's entertaining. Or have your father shove you out of his life to please his lady wife. Your sire was an honorable man. Mine was a fool, his wife a disgrace to the word, and my natural mother a whore. You should also thank the Almighty that you are an only child instead of having half brothers and sisters who would adore to see you six feet under."

His statement didn't faze Mars. He knew Ned's story. "Your mum is a whore who is still celebrated to this day. And everyone knows Sarah Middleton can take care of herself. It is said that Nottoway is now keeping her. He is twenty years her junior."

"If ever there was a woman who could teach a man something, it is the ewe that birthed me."

"At least she gave you life."

"Aye, and she never made that mistake again or gave *me* a sideways glance."

There was a beat of silence. Then Mars leaned forward abruptly. "But don't you ever want to take them all on?" he challenged. "Give them a good hard shake? You are a brilliant man, an excellent doctor. Why hide yourself away here in this farcical little society?"

"Because this is my home."

The earl fell back. "We are both doomed." He said the words with such dry, comic effect that Ned had to smile, and Mars answered it with a wan one of his own before admitting, "You are right." He paused. "Do you know I tried to hire Royce away from you? He is too devoted to your service to leave. In fact, you are ten times the man your lordly half brothers are. *You* are the one who would have made a father proud."

"I ceased caring about what any of them thought decades ago. When I was seven, in fact. That was when I finally realized no one was going to return for me. Ever. My sire paid for my studies and that was enough. You and Balfour are my brothers. I have little need of any others. And that is why I must beg you to stop indulging in pipe dreams, even if it is on a rare occasion now. Do you know what Maidenshop would be like if Dervil was allowed to reign unchecked? As it is, he stays away from us because he stays away from you."

"You believe Dervil is afraid of me?" Mars returned with a half laugh. "I doubt it."

"He knows you want to kill him."

"Someday, I will find a way."

"Then you need to keep your wits about you."

"And what do I do until then?"

Ned thought of Clarissa's complaint about Mars, about how he had no purpose in life, and realized she might be right. "You find something that gives your life meaning. That is what you do."

"*You* are saying this to *me*?" Mars shook his head. "What of you, my friend?"

"Me?" Ned didn't understand. "I have my

medicine. I have my patients. My studies of science and mathematics. My plans for my lecture series. *Those* are the passions of my life, and it is a very full life."

"Or merely a busy one to fill empty space. Don't you find everything a trifle boring?"

"How could I?" Even as Ned answered, he experienced a niggling of doubt, one he pushed away. His life was *not* empty. "What we understand of the world is in constant change, especially over the past few decades of this modern age. There is so much to learn. I can barely wait for the Frost lecture. Which brings me to the reason I sought you out—"

Mars cut him off. "I am not ready to discuss why you dragged me back here. We are on a theme of particular importance. I may dance with the opium pipe from time to time, but I don't lie to myself. Not like you are."

"What the devil do you mean by that?"

"That your patients, your medicine, your lectures, well, they are your opium, aren't they?" He spoke as if he was laying out something clever.

Ned sat back. "I think your skull is cracked. What a ridiculous thing to say."

"No, what an honest one to say. Look at us, Thurlowe. Two old roués—"

"We are not old. And I'm not a roué. *You* may be one."

"I *forgot*," Mars said with great exaggeration. "You are the monk."

"I'm not a monk."

The earl raised a skeptical eyebrow. "When was the last time you dipped your sword?"

"Do you mean had sexual relations? I take back what I said. You *are* old. *Dipped my sword?* How quaint."

"Answer the question."

"I see. I'm being interrogated."

"For your own good." Mars pretended to dust off his hands. "Isn't that why you sent Royce to hunt me now? For my own good?"

"I've dipped my sword."

Mars took his feet off the stool and leaned forward. "When?"

"It is none of your affair."

The earl considered that a moment and then repeated, "You aren't a lothario, Thurlowe. I'm not accusing you of that. I'm the rake in the room. But you are a man with a man's needs. So one week? Two weeks—?"

"Stop this."

"Six weeks?" Mars paused, considering. "I'm absolutely certain you haven't been with the saintly Miss Taylor." He gave a shiver.

"I don't know why you don't like her," Ned answered, pleased to have a change of topic.

"She's boring." He spoke as if there was no worse epithet. "She offers nothing."

"I'm marrying her the day after the Frost lecture."

"*God.* And I'm not using the Lord's name in vain. I am praying for mercy on your ever-living soul. I thought you were wrong to offer for her. Now you will spend the rest of your life with the future matron to end all Matrons of Maidenshop? You poor fool."

"I made a promise and I'll honor it." Ned sounded dogged to his own ears.

"She has appalling taste."

"What?"

"Yes, she does. Have you ever looked at what she wears? Prissy, silly, girlish."

Actually, Ned hadn't really paid attention to what Clarissa wore. "You seem to notice her more than I do." Then again, he could recall the stitching in Gemma's nightdress. He gave his head a hard shake, wanting to dislodge the image.

"Are you all right?" Mars asked.

Ned wasn't going to answer, not after the comments of him being a monk.

Mars gave a small yawn. "Enough small talk. What is going on in sweet Maidenshop that has made both you and the matrons come searching for me?"

"They tried to contact you?"

"Letters, missives, threats, entreaties. All of it. There was a stack of letters in my hall when I returned. I didn't read any of them. Royce wanted me to leave right away. What has their skirts twisted now? I'm certain it is the Logical Men's Society. What have we done?"

"What have we *not* done, especially with Winderton at the helm."

"Winderton?"

"He's learned some bad tricks during his time in London. He's drinking too much and that is never a good look. And the reason the matrons were trying to reach you before I could is because a Mrs. Gemma Estep claims that Old Andy left The Garland to her. All the matrons support her claim. Mrs. Estep is planning on turning our tavern into a tea garden and there doesn't seem to be a female breast for a hundred miles around who hasn't discovered a sudden, ardent desire to drink tea—and displace the Logical Men's Society."

"The devil you say."

"I do say. That is why I sent for the magistrate. *You.* Mrs. Estep refuses to show me the proof that Andy left the building to her. I need you to set her straight. The lads and I want The Garland back. We are counting on you, Mars. There is a good amount of foolishness going on because of this." He thought it prudent not to mention Fitz's head bashing. "You know how we can be around here."

A gleam of interest had come to the earl's eye. Ned was glad. He liked his friend vital, engaged, and away from his vices. "We shall solve the issue in the morning."

"That is what I was hoping you would say." Ned raised a hand as if to toast the air. "Here is to our success."

"Well, here is to hoping the law is on your side."

"I beg pardon."

"I must be impartial, no?"

Ned didn't like this response. "Well. Yes. In all fairness. Except, she doesn't have a claim, Mars.

She couldn't. Old Andy would never have left The Garland to a woman."

"No, of course he wouldn't," Mars replied, yawning. He came to his feet. "I assume I can climb into my usual bed?"

"Of course." Ned considered the room at the top of the stairs as the one for his friend.

"Then I shall seek it out." He picked up his boots and started out of the room but then Ned stopped him.

"I want The Garland."

"I understand." There was a beat of silence and then Mars said, "You know Andy was like a surrogate father to me."

"He was a good friend to all of us."

"True, and yet, there were times I would have gone completely over the edge if he hadn't been there for me. Opium is a poor substitute."

"It is no substitute at all."

Mars gave him a bland smile and changed the subject. "Well, good night, Thurlowe. I am glad we had this conversation. As much as I complain, I do enjoy your efforts to keep me on the redemption road. Just remember, heal yourself, physician." He left the room and took the stairs.

Ned wasn't certain what he meant, but was too tired to ask. He found his own bed, expecting to fall immediately asleep. Instead, he stared at the ceiling, thinking about the confrontation with Gemma Estep and wondering why he was so bloody aware of her. He could too easily picture himself standing beside her, as if they were a couple, something he would never do in his right mind . . . and yet, there was the image, worming its way into his brain.

Consequently, the next morning he overslept and didn't wake until he heard shouting.

He rose up from his mattress, groggy. There were more shouts in the hall. Feminine voices. It took him a moment to grasp that he wasn't dreaming.

A beat later Royce pounded on the door. "Wake up, sir, wake up. The matrons have stolen the Earl of Marsden. I tried to stop them but they pushed me aside. Some of those women are very strong. I felt overpowered."

Ned scrambled to dress.

GEMMA HAD not enjoyed a good night.

After Mr. Thurlowe had left, she'd had trouble falling asleep, and she wasn't certain of exactly why.

She should have been disturbed over the idea of being attacked. That was enough to keep anyone wide awake in their bed . . . except that wasn't what was preying on her mind.

No, what had her tossing and turning was reliving the conversation with the good doctor. He was her enemy. She understood he was determined to reclaim The Garland for flimsy reasons, and she would fight him.

And yet, she sensed a connection with him. A pull. Almost as if she'd been destined to meet him. Her gran had talked about destiny that way. She'd married her second cousin, a healer himself, and she'd claimed she could have married no other. Then again, perhaps what had kept Gemma up was regret. It would be a horrific thing if Paul had been her destiny. Her one and only.

She discovered in the wee hours of the morning that although she'd vowed repeatedly that she was done with men, a part of her still yearned for love. For someone she could trust. For someone with strong arms and a giving spirit . . . like Ned Thurlowe.

Actually, there wasn't a woman in the village who didn't find Mr. Thurlowe attractive. Whether he was aware of it or not, they all watched him closely. Several had even made comment to her about the private conversation between her and Mr. Thurlowe after Sunday services. There was no missing the envy in their voices. Of course, if they'd known the level of hostility he held for Gemma—

Well, they might still be jealous.

So she was up and ready to greet Mr. Fitzsimmons at half past seven, even if her brain was a bit muddy from lack of sleep. She set him to work turning over earth for the flower beds. She then brewed a cup of strong black tea. Mrs. Warbler had sent over a loaf of fresh bread and preserves on Monday, and Gemma now made a breakfast with the last of it. Sipping her tea, she determined she wouldn't give another thought to the doctor. He was not hers to think about.

Instead, she focused on her plans for the day.

She wanted to set up the main room. She would have tables for patrons . . . but she'd also decided to put together a special nook for her soaps, creams, and other concoctions that she would sell. Her gran had such a place—

The door opened in the main room with the merry jingle of the small bell Gemma had purchased from the tinker. She'd just tied it on that morning. If she'd had it in place last night, then she would have been warned before sensing someone was in her home in the dark.

Now, at the sound of it, she tensed. Then she heard Clarissa's voice. "Gemma?"

"Back here."

Clarissa rushed into the kitchen, her eyes alive with anticipation. She was wearing a fetching dress of blue worsted. It was high necked and quite modest. Gemma was in her black. "I hope you are ready for this."

"For what?" Gemma asked.

"Heavens, what happened to your head?"

Gemma had taken off the bandage. She believed cuts healed better with air. She was afraid to look at it even in the small glass in the bedroom thinking it was better not to know what she looked like. "I bumped into something."

"It must have hurt."

"It did," Gemma could say honestly. "So what should I be ready for?" she asked, bringing Clarissa's attention back to her business.

"The earl has returned from London. Mrs. Warbler says they will bring him to you at once."

"Bring him to me?"

"Yes. He's the magistrate and you can show him your proof that your uncle left The Garland to you. Once he makes his decision, no one will question your claim ever again."

For a second Gemma froze, struck dumb. The magistrate was coming to her?

This morning?

Now?

She'd pushed her way into The Garland. She'd claimed it, pronouncing to one and all she had proof that Andrew had left it to her.

She believed he had. She *hoped* he had.

But would the magistrate agree?

After all, she only had a letter. *What is mine is yours.* The desperation that had initially driven her deserted her. In its place was fear . . . because if she lost The Garland, she'd lose her dream. Then what would become of her?

"Gemma, aren't you happy? This will all be settled."

Before she could answer, she heard the sounds of voices outside and she knew that her reckoning was on her doorstep.

Gemma looked to Clarissa. "What if he refutes it?"

"Why would he do that? If your uncle gave it to you, The Garland is yours."

"But it will be the men who decide," Gemma answered, feeling slightly faint. "It is always the men who make the decisions. And they choose against us."

Clarissa put her gloved hands on Gemma's arms above the elbow and gave her a little shake. "Not this time," she said as if she understood Gemma's fears. "This time you have *us* with you. The matrons are strong. Look at what they have done for me. Think of your dreams, Gemma, and don't be afraid."

"I've never met a man I can trust." She looked at Clarissa. "Do you trust the earl to be fair?"

"I can't abide him. A more self-centered person you will never meet."

"That is not reassuring. And, isn't the earl a member of the Logical Men's Society?" She hated the hollow feeling in her stomach.

"Yes, it was started by his great-grandfather. But don't expect the worst. We are *all* on your side, Gemma. The matrons found Lord Marsden at Mr. Thurlowe's house and they are bringing him to you. We believe in you. *I* believe in you. You have made me see that a woman doesn't just have to do what people tell her. She can have a dream. She can, if she is fearless enough, take care of herself."

Gemma was barely attending. The fear had left her. In its place was fury. "The earl was at *Mr. Thurlowe's* house?"

"Yes, apparently, he returned from London and spent the night there as a guest," Clarissa confirmed helpfully.

"And the good doctor knew that all along?"

Clarissa looked momentarily confused. "He should have. The earl was under his roof."

And here he had been all that was solicitous

last night. Gemma could have growled her anger. She'd almost trusted him.

The bell on the main room door tinkled as it opened. Gemma went through the taproom to see the matrons come pouring in, chattering happily. They brought with them a tall, unshaven nobleman who definitely appeared the worse for wear.

Chapter Twelve

The dowager and Mrs. Warbler took immediate control, herding everyone into the main room. There had to be at least thirty ladies present, perhaps even more. They fanned out, lining the walls and standing by the tables as if awaiting orders.

There were some gentlemen in the crowd, as well—the Reverend Summerall, Squire Nelson, several husbands, who stood beside their wives.

Gemma was a bit taken aback to realize she knew most of them, at least by name. She'd made their acquaintance in the short period of time she'd been in Maidenshop and now here they were to support her. She blinked back the sting of tears, not wanting to be too sentimental, and yet, deeply humbled. It was as if they were saying they *wanted* her to be a part of them.

They wanted her.

The last place where she'd truly felt wanted was at her gran's. Her father had loved her, of course, and yet he'd judged her with a critical eye.

In Maidenshop, she'd rediscovered that lovely sense of belonging.

The Earl of Marsden stood amongst the organizing, swaying slightly and not offering any help. Instead, he yawned and watched with sleepy interest. Gemma was surprised at how young he was, and how tall. She had pictured him as gray and stodgy. Instead, he was actually handsome albeit a bit rough-looking. He had the loose air of a highwayman, or someone accustomed to doing whatever he pleased.

"This is the man you can't abide?" she said to Clarissa.

"Look at him. He is slovenly. He's not even wearing a hat. How can anyone respect or trust him?"

"I pray we can do both." Gemma's words were heartfelt.

When things were arranged to the dowager's satisfaction, she said, "Lord Marsden, be so kind as to sit here." She indicated the chair behind a table in the middle of the room. A fitting location for a hearing.

"I could not sit in the presence of so many lovely ladies, Your Grace." He sent a waggish smile around the room.

His charm did not deter the dowager. "*Sit.*"

He sat, flopping down in the chair and pushing his long legs out in front of him.

"Very well, everyone. Pay attention." The dowager faced Gemma. "We are here to see this done right. My lord, this is Mrs. Gemma Estep, the niece of Andrew MacMhuirich. Gemma, this is Lord Marsden, usually a pillar member of our small community when he apparently hasn't been obviously hugging a bottle all night—"

"Is it that obvious?" he said, unchastised and unconcerned.

"He also serves as the local magistrate," the dowager finished, undeterred in her mission. "My lord, you are here to settle the matter of ownership of The Garland. Gemma says her uncle left it to her. As you undoubtedly know from conversation with your recent host, the Logical Men's Society intends to challenge her claim. Presumably, they wish The Garland for themselves. We expect you to hear Gemma out and make a fair decision."

"Presumably in her favor, I take it," he drawled, looking around the room at the women. Their expressions were serious. His brows came together as he realized that they were not in the mood for his humor, such as it was. He turned his gaze to Gemma. "Well, it is a pleasure to make your acquaintance, Mrs. Estep."

"Please call me Gemma."

"A bit too familiar, isn't it?"

"I don't like my married name any more than I liked the man I married. I'm sorry it was ever visited upon me."

The earl looked around the room, puzzled. "Am I in the same village?" he asked. "When I last left Maidenshop, there was nothing but biddable women living here. Things seem to have changed."

"You are exactly right, my lord," Mrs. Warbler said without missing a beat. "And *we* are here to be certain that Gemma receives all that she should."

"And we don't want *you* stalling or patronizing any of us," Clarissa declared. Everyone in the room looked at her with startled expressions as if puzzled by her forthrightness. As if answering their silent surprise, she said, "Well, we don't," to the others.

Heads nodded in agreement.

The earl gave her a cynical look. "Coming into your own finally, eh, Miss Taylor?"

Her answer was a tight smile, even as she leaned close to Gemma and whispered, "I can't stand even looking at him."

Lord Marsden took charge. "Let's be on with it. First order of business—is there anything to drink?"

"I think you've had enough," someone muttered from the crowd.

"*Au contraire*, I have not had a drop for almost twenty-four hours. It is one of the reasons I look this way."

He was so cocksure, so completely himself, that Gemma did fear for her claim. "I have tea brewed," she offered.

The earl looked at her as if she spoke gibberish. Clarissa helped him understand. "Tea. It is served in a pot. One may drink gallons of it and stay sensible."

The corner of his lip curled up. "I don't know

how sensible it would be to drink gallons of any-thing. I would prefer—"

"Tea would be excellent," the duchess finished for him, a stern warning on her face.

Gemma could see him wonder if it would be worth doing battle with a duchess, and then he murmured, "Tea would be nice."

And Gemma had the chance to escape and gather her wits. She practically ran to the kitchen, Clarissa on her heels. "It's happening," she said. "It's my opportunity."

"Yes," Clarissa answered, equally excited.

"I need my letter. I need a mug and tea."

"I'll pour the tea. Your hands are shaking too hard."

"Yes, thank you. I need to fetch my letter."

Ducking into her room, Gemma pulled out her bag and the stack of letters. The promise from her uncle was the one on the top, or so she had thought. Now she wasn't so certain. She couldn't find it. What if she'd lost it? Her heart pounded in her ears.

They were going to take The Garland from her.

No, they were not . . . but where was the letter she needed—?

Mrs. Warbler's hand came down on hers. Gemma looked up, surprised, to the woman in the bedroom with her. "Don't be afraid," Mrs. Warbler said.

"What if I lose?"

"Well, that could happen. I don't have the faith in Lord Marsden that the duchess enjoys. Granted, he appears rougher than he usually does and he is one of *them*, the Logical Men's Society. However, he should hear us out. He has always been fair. He also has to live in this village. He knows the dangers of crossing the matrons. We are with you."

Gemma nodded, afraid to voice her fears lest they take on life. She looked down at her letters and realized the one she searched for was right there in her hand. "I have it."

"Then let us go present it to the magistrate."

Just as they entered the main room, the front door flew open, the bell jangling wildly, and Mr. Thurlowe stormed inside. He was not alone. Several of the men who had stood sentry across the street over the past several days filed in through the doorway behind him.

"Thurlowe," the earl called in good-natured greeting. "You are right on time for a cup of morning tea."

Ignoring Lord Marsden, the doctor demanded, "What is going on here? Why was a guest in my home kidnapped?"

The dowager looked down her nose in a way only a duchess could manage. "Your hat, Mr. Thurlowe?"

He frowned as if not understanding what she'd meant, and then realized he was wearing his hat. He practically grabbed it off his head as if he couldn't be bothered. The other men removed their hats.

"As for the charge of kidnapping," the dowager

said, "what nonsense. He was not kidnapped. We asked him politely to come with us."

"*All* of you?" Mr. Thurlowe demanded.

"Of course. We didn't want him to refuse," the duchess answered. Hands came up to hide smiles—and Mr. Thurlowe knew it. His jaw hardened.

He hadn't looked at Gemma. In fact, he seemed to be studiously ignoring her. Good.

She needed to ignore him, as well . . . instead of noticing that although he'd had a late night, he was impeccably dressed and appeared rested. Which was far from what she was feeling.

His men clumped around him, pushing their way into the room and crowding the matrons. One, a gentleman so short that he had to crane his neck to see what was going on, announced, "I'm here. What is going on?"

"We need your services, Shielding," the doctor said. "There is about to be a legal hearing over who owns The Garland."

Mr. Shielding took in everyone and then his officious gaze landed on the earl. "I didn't hear you were back, my lord. I'm to represent the Society."

"Ah, yes, good," the earl replied. He looked over to Mr. Thurlowe and said in a false whisper, "You couldn't find someone else?"

There was no answer but again, smiles were hidden.

The door was finally shut, only to be opened again by none other than the Duke of Winderton.

He didn't mill about but sauntered in as if the proceeding waited for him. He looked around as if surprised at the crowd. "The village has gathered, eh? Is there anyone left on the streets?"

Gemma had come to know him by sight but they had kept their distance from each other. There was something very angry about him, and she did not trust angry men.

The people in the room acted diffident with curtseying and bowing. "Good morning, Your Grace," the Reverend Summerall said.

His mother was unaffected. "How nice of you to rouse yourself, Your Grace."

"Always trying to please you, Mother," he answered and looked around the room, his gaze landing on Mr. Fitzsimmons. The young man had been out toiling on Gemma's behalf and he appeared the part. He stood on the opposite side of the room from his fellows. "Hello, Fitz," the duke said. "We were expecting you to return last night."

His words brought a flush to Mr. Fitzsimmons's face.

"It appears he has changed sides," said one of the Dawson lads—Gemma could not tell which one was which yet.

"Ah." And then the duke's gaze focused on Gemma. Did he notice the nasty bruise on her head? Did it matter to him? Mr. Thurlowe had implied last night that the duke might be behind the stunt. Seeing him this close, she'd place money on that suspicion.

She glared right back. And he'd not receive a curtsey from her.

His answer was the half smile someone would save for a kitten who amused them.

Well, she was no kitten.

Winderton turned his attention from Gemma to the group as a whole. "Did I interrupt?"

"No, you arrived just in time," Mr. Thurlowe said. "Let's be on with it."

The earl frowned. "Why, thank you, Mr. Thurlowe, for making my work here easier. Ah, here is my tea." Clarissa placed the hot mug on the table before the earl and backed away.

At that moment one of the Society members made a pretense of wiping his nose on one of the curtains. Gemma charged forward, ready to grab the man by the ear and give it a twist for having the manners of a schoolboy, except to her astonishment, Lord Marsden was ahead of her.

"Sweeney, leave the building."

"My lord, I need to be here."

"No, you don't. Not until you have some manners about you. Out."

Sweeney appeared ready to keep contesting the issue until Mr. Thurlowe stepped in. "You need to leave."

For a second the man hesitated, casting an angry look around the room. He then grabbed the curtain, giving it a hard enough yank to tear it off its rod, and bolted out the door, the bell heralding his departure.

"Great. We have that done," Lord Marsden

said as if he wasn't troubled at all by the make-shift circumstances. "Very well. I believe we all understand what is at stake. This situation is a bit unorthodox but I see no reason to postpone this hearing for me to shave. Mrs. Estep, please tell me your story."

"Gemma—" she started to correct him and stopped. Let him call her whatever he wished if it meant she could have The Garland. She stepped forward.

Lord Marsden gave her a very male look-over. She ignored him, choosing to focus on a spot over his head as she told her story.

"My uncle Andrew MacMhuirich was the only family I had and the same was true for him." She was proud that her voice didn't betray her inner turmoil. "I visited him last year around the time the village was holding the big dance of the season. I helped him make rook pies and it was a good evening between us. The next day I continued my journey to London. I wrote a letter to my uncle Andrew that I had arrived and shared with him the news that my husband was dead—"

A sympathetic murmur from the women went around the room.

"—and had been for some months prior to my traveling to see him—"

"Estep? Captain Paul Estep?" the earl interrupted.

Gemma blinked in surprise. "Yes?" she hedged, wary.

"I knew him. He was probably the most disreputable scoundrel in the Horse Guard and they have more than their share. You actually married that man? He never acted married."

Dear God, this was a terrible turn, and Gemma decided only the truth was her ally. "No, he didn't. And yes, by all accounts, including mine, he was a scoundrel." She braced herself, waiting for Lord Marsden to reveal to one and all the disgraceful way Paul had died.

He didn't. Instead, he nodded. "Go on with your story."

"My uncle wrote back and this is his letter." She held the letter up. "He expressed his condolences and then informed me that what was *his* is *mine*. That is what he says in this letter."

"A letter?" Mr. Shielding challenged boisterously. "No will? Only a letter? Well, then there is our case. A letter is not a will." He smiled his superiority. Mr. Thurlowe stood with his arms crossed. He didn't pay attention to Mr. Shielding but watched the earl.

"May I see it?" Lord Marsden asked. She handed the letter to him and he took his time reading it. That might have been necessary. Andrew had not had the best penmanship.

At last, he placed the letter on the table and looked to Mr. Shielding. The earl's manner had undergone a change from under-the-weather rakehell to a man in control of his intellect. "Mr. Shielding, you are serving as the spokesperson for the other side? Or will it be Mr. Thurlowe?"

"You are the lawyer," Mr. Thurlowe said to his compatriot.

Mr. Shielding was happy to take charge. "Our case is simple, my lord. The Logical Men's Society has been using The Garland for close to fifty years. It is our home, as it were. We believe Old Andy wished the building to go to us. Furthermore, I say again, a letter is not a legal will."

"No," the earl agreed. "However, a letter of *one's wishes* does speak to the man's intentions. Is that not true, Mr. Shielding?"

The lawyer looked uncertain. "His wishes are best outlined through a will."

"Or a letter of one's wishes," the earl answered. "We are here to determine what Old Andy wanted, will or not."

"Property should not be left to a female."

"That old saw?" The earl shook his head. "Many women in this country own property. Some purchase it themselves and others inherit it. Your views are outdated. Furthermore, The Garland is not some grand estate, although if Mrs. Estep keeps making her improvements, such as curtains, it may begin to look like one."

Mr. Shielding frowned. Apparently, he wasn't expecting the earl to be so reasoned, especially in Gemma's favor.

Neither were the women in the room. Eyebrows were raised in surprise and lips lifted into smiles of hope.

Mr. Thurlowe spoke up. "May I address the

matter, my lord?" The doctor and Lord Marsden were great friends. Gemma held her breath for what Mr. Thurlowe would say against her.

He didn't mince words. "Then the question is, what were Old Andy's wishes? He purchased this tavern from your father, my lord. Did they not have an agreement?"

Lord Marsden sat back in his chair. "Actually, my father lost The Garland in a game of cards to Andy, and they did have an agreement. Andy was to allow my father to drink his fill whenever he wished."

"And to use The Garland as the base for the Logical Men's Society, no?"

"Father supported the Society. He was a member when he was single. However, when he sold the tavern to Andy, he was *married* to my mother. So he was *not* a member. Such is the problem with our rules of membership. You know, having to be a bachelor or widower and all that?"

"But your father didn't *disapprove* of the Society," Mr. Thurlowe pressed.

"No, my mother did." That drew laughter from the ladies.

"She did," the dowager chimed in.

Mr. Thurlowe ignored them. "Andy was a member of the Society. We were his friends. He wanted it to go to us. I'm even willing to pay Mrs. Estep for her claim, either valid or not."

"I understand your position," Lord Marsden said. "However, this letter says differently. Andy's intent according to his own hand—and we can all recognize it, few people had a scrawl like Andy's—is that whatever he owned, which includes The Garland, he wished to go to his niece."

There was a pause of dead silence.

Gemma could scarcely believe her ears.

"It is my judgment that Mrs. Gemma Estep is entitled to the tavern and all its contents." Lord Marsden rapped the table in front of him with his empty tea mug as if he had a gavel, and it was done.

She owned The Garland.

Gemma wasn't the only one stunned, but then a great cheer went up from her supporters. Both Clarissa and Mrs. Warbler put their arms around Gemma and gave her a squeeze.

Several of the Society members had things to say that were not congratulatory, but no one paid attention to them. The duke opened the door. With a nod of his head, he silently ordered them to follow him, and out they stomped. The door's merry bell tinkled its goodbye.

Gemma saw the dowager watch her son leave. The duchess frowned and then sighed heavily as if there was some burden there. As she turned, her eye caught Gemma's. "We won," she mouthed.

Beside her, Clarissa murmured, "I wonder why Lord Marsden was so reasonable. It is certainly out of character."

"Well, today is a good day for him to turn a new leaf." Gemma moved to Lord Marsden, who was listening to Mr. Shielding carrying on about the "unfairness" of such a verdict and how it would destroy good order in the village. The earl seemed to welcome her interruption.

"Thank you, my lord," she said. "Thank you."

"We *will* challenge this," Mr. Shielding declared.

"That you can," the earl agreed. "But why?" He'd risen from his chair in that lazy way of his and offered the letter to Gemma, who gratefully took it. "I'd keep that safe if I were you," he told her, before addressing Mr. Shielding. "There will be a circuit riding judge from London through here sometime soon. You may put your petition to him. Or give it your all and take the matter to Chancery Court. Of course, it will cost money."

"But we could try."

"Yes, you may. Still, the result will be the same. Andy wrote an eloquent Letter of Wishes. He was my friend, and I shall honor it. Now, I find a need to search out my valet. I'm also certain that Gibson, my secretary, and a host of others have tasks they have been waiting for me to perform. If you will all excuse me?" He didn't travel too far to the door before Mrs. Warbler stopped him by practically wrapping her arms around him.

"You have saved our village," she declared.

Lord Marsden acted embarrassed by the hug and from there beat a hasty path out the door.

"I have sherry at my house," Mrs. Warbler announced. "Please, everyone, come and join me for a toast to a new day in Maidenshop." She led the way out the door and many followed.

Gemma moved forward until she saw Mr. Thurlowe. He'd not left with the others.

He held his hat in his hand, his stance awkward. "Congratulations." There was no good humor in his voice.

She mimicked his tone. "Thank you."

"The cut on your temple looks better this morning than it did last night."

"Yes, thank you." She wasn't going to give him one inch and would have gone on after the others except he moved to place himself in her way.

"You know I was planning to hold a lecture seminar here."

Gemma tensed, waiting. "Yes."

"Perhaps we could make arrangements?" He did not wear humility well.

And the truth was, yesterday, before the attack, she would have been open to the idea. Now—? "You spoke against me."

His expression tightened. "I spoke for the Society."

"You *hid* the magistrate from us. If my friends had not gone for him, you wouldn't have said a thing until you had coerced him into your way of thinking, using your friendship as inducement. Certainly it would be easier than bashing someone over the head."

He really didn't like that. "I say again, I had nothing to do with Fitz's action last night."

"Perhaps. But I'd wager that if he'd found my letter, you would have looked the other way. You would have denied me of what was rightfully mine. You and your friends would have happily seen me turned out."

A dull red crept up his neck. Was it shame? Or anger that he hadn't won? "I said before the magistrate that I would have paid you for The Garland."

"Am I to believe that? Or trust you would have paid me what it is worth? Do you have that sort of money, Doctor?"

"I have enough to have seen you happy. I also have a better character than what you believe."

"I doubt if you will ever convince me of that, sir. And I shall never let you or your *Society* have a foothold in The Garland again. I am not one to entertain my enemies. And no, you may not have your lecture here." With those proud words, she dismissed him with a, "Good day, sir," and left to follow the others.

HUDDLED IN the crossroads down by the church, Winderton and the younger members of the Society were working themselves into a lather over Mars's verdict. Even Sir Lionel and Fullerton had joined them. Apparently, the old members had just caught word that there had been a meeting.

Shielding was boasting that he wasn't afraid to take the matter all the way to London, a bit of silliness if ever Ned had heard of it. "A woman shouldn't have the right to inherit property. Or at least property important to the village," Shielding was saying, punctuating the air with his finger for emphasis.

Heads nodded. Ned walked right by them. They could grouse on their own. He had his own concerns. His lecture series was ending before it really started.

However, they weren't going to let him go. "Thurlowe," Winderton called.

One had to stop for a duke.

Ned turned. "Yes?" He took a beat and tacked on, "Your Grace?"

"Where are we going to meet now?"

"Yes," Sir Lionel said. "Where shall we gather now that we've lost The Garland?"

Ned didn't hide his exasperation. "Where have you been gathering?"

"At your place," Sweeney said helpfully.

"That is not going to happen." Ned saw no reason to mince words.

"We met at your place a time or two, Your Grace," Dawson said.

"Aye, and a good time we had." Winderton smiled and then turned serious. "The truth is, we shall have to find a new location. I say we head for the posting house and we do so now." The posting house was some four miles away. It was a busy inn along the Newmarket Road.

"I could use a drink to wash down that nonsense," Sweeney said. "Can you imagine tossing me out over a curtain?" He still held it in his hand. The others glumly nodded agreement.

"*To the posting house,*" one of the Dawson brothers shouted and like a clan of crusaders, two of them in sedan chairs, they went off down the road.

Everyone, that is, save the duke and Ned. "You aren't going, Your Grace?" So far Winderton had been ready for any party.

"Oh, I'll join them. Except I'm going to ride." He looked at Ned. "As chairman, Thurlowe, all of this is your problem. You need to talk to Mars and change his mind. We can't have the women thinking they won."

"They did win, Your Grace."

"Not if Mars reverses his opinion."

"He won't."

"You could change his mind. I expect it of you." On that thought, the duke began walking toward the smithy, where he must have left his horse that morning.

For a second Ned considered the matter. Could he convince Mars that he was wrong? Ned didn't know.

As he had expected, he found Mars was in the stable. Bruno was saddled. Mars was just handing a vail over to the stable lad who came in every morning to see to the chores. Mars waved the lad away and calmly faced him.

"What happened?" Ned demanded.

"The law happened."

"Letter of Wishes?" Ned snorted his doubts.

"There is such a thing in the law. And last night you were encouraging me to have a purpose. Now you know the truth. I do take my position as magistrate seriously. I always have. And don't believe Shielding or anything he claims. He has the wits of a knob of wood. Besides, Andy's letter was very clear he was fond of his niece."

"I'd never heard him speak of her before her arrival in the village and I saw Andy almost every day."

"Well, you didn't see him the evening of the last Cotillion Dance, because she was there."

"Summerall said he met her. Did you?"

"No, I learned about her the day of the rook hunt. After breakfast, I stayed when everyone else left. Andy was preparing to make the pies and he said he was expecting his niece. He was excited. The next day, at the lecture, I asked where she was. He said she had already traveled on. He'd also said their meeting had been good. He was proud, and sad. You know how we men are."

"No, I don't know. I don't pine after my family, such as they are."

"Well, Andy did."

"What the devil is this about?"

"Last night you lectured me. Today I lecture you."

"No, you *betrayed* me."

Mars's easiness vanished. "Be careful, my friend." His warning was soft, and meaningful.

Ned stepped back. "I beg pardon. That was unnecessary. However, what becomes of the Society?" He paused and then added, "Of my hopes for the lecture series. I asked if we could still hold the lecture at The Garland. Mrs. Estep flatly refused."

Mars grunted his thoughts. "When did you ask?"

"After the verdict."

"There are times when you have more hair than wits. Give her a few days or even a week then ask her again. She'll change her mind."

"How do you know that?"

"Because you will work on her. You will show your handsome face and jabber on about the importance of building fine minds or whatever it is you say that convinced all of us to support you, and she'll agree to hold the lecture."

"My face has never convinced anyone to do anything."

"Only because you are afraid of using it. You could have a harem of women with your looks. And then you wouldn't have to settle for Clarissa Taylor. I swear, the biggest mystery is why God gives gifts to people like you who won't use them."

"You don't have trouble with women."

"Because I use the gifts I'm given." Mars walked Bruno out of the stable. "Truly, Ned, I know what the lecture means to you. Wait a bit. Ask again. Everything will work out as it should."

"Another difference between us—I'm not an optimist."

Mars laughed on that one. "Let her cool off," he advised. "If it comes to the worst, we hold the lecture at the Posting Inn."

"We won't be able to."

"Why not?"

"First, it is too busy a place for concentration and serious discussion. Second, Winderton, Dawson, and the lot of them are heading there to drink. They will ruin any goodwill we have with Peavine." Peavine was the proprietor of the Posting Inn.

"Fools."

Ned nodded his agreement. He watched his friend mount before saying, "She's changed us. This woman is changing the village."

"Perhaps it is time to change." Mars picked up the reins. "For all of us. And thank you for fetching me. I lost myself a bit this time in London. I needed someone to make me return." On those words he rode off.

THAT NIGHT Gemma slept better than she had for ages.

The Garland was *hers*.

After sherry at Mrs. Warbler's, she and Mr. Fitzsimmons had returned to work. He was actually a rather nice young man who was easily influenced. He was also sincere in his regrets and was willing to do what she asked as atonement. Most of her garden beds had now been turned and were ready for planting, her favorite task. Her new friends had seen that she had all the seeds and plantings she would wish.

She'd not had Mr. Thurlowe's predicted headache so she hadn't finished the brandy in the flask. She did so before she went to bed because she was certain after all the hard labor of gardening, she would wake with a few muscle aches.

Of course, and perhaps since she was not accustomed to spirits, the drink seemed to have given her strange dreams.

She dreamed of chickens. Thousands of chickens. She could hear them clucking. They were off in the distance and she wasn't quite certain what *she* was doing or what was happening . . . until a rooster crowed, and she realized, she *wasn't* dreaming. But waking at her customary early hour.

Gemma sat up and wiped the sleep from her eyes—and then she *did* hear chickens.

Jumping from the bed, she opened the door and found in the kitchen she had cleaned the night before . . . chickens. Red hens, black ones, brown ones roosted on the table and chairs. There weren't thousands but there were enough to make a mess of the place. They clucked and ruffled feathers and one pooped right there in front of her. The bird just put her chicken tail over the edge of the table and did her business. It landed with a plop on the brick floor.

At the sight of her, their clucking paused and then they took up again.

A very beleaguered Athena, the gray mouser Mrs. Smethers had given her in gratitude for the foot soak, had been hiding under the cupboard.

She now raced to the open bedroom door for shelter even as one of the hens tried to peck at her.

A rooster called from the main room.

Still in a state of disbelief, Gemma gingerly walked to avoid droppings through the taproom and almost collapsed in shock. There had to be a dozen, maybe more, hens on tables or chairs, while the rooster stood proudly on the back of a chair and crowed his "good morning" to her.

Dear Lord, the floor was a mess with feathers and droppings. All her cleaning had been for naught.

And she knew who to blame.

Never before had she experienced such white-hot fury. *How dare they do this to her.* She'd presented her case in front of the magistrate, a requirement *they* had put on her, and now, because they didn't like the verdict, *this* is the way they behaved? Children had better manners.

Gemma marched back to her room and dressed quickly. Her hands were shaking as she laced the back of her dress. Her braid was a mess after a night of sleep. She didn't care. She put on her shoes without bothering with stockings.

Out in the kitchen, she opened the back door, grabbed a broom, and started shooing hens into the garden. There were three eggs in the new bowl Mrs. Warbler had given her. Another two on the table. One on the chair rolled off and broke. She would have to scrub the floor later or else it would smell.

However, right now she had something more important to do.

In the main room, Gemma shooed the chickens, including the arrogant rooster, out the front door—and then she began picking up eggs. She made a basket out of her skirt. There were nine eggs in total.

Holding her skirt so she couldn't lose one of them, she set off for Mr. Thurlowe's house, scattering chickens picking at the earth as she left.

The hour was early. There were few people up and about. Mrs. Burnham was sweeping her step while her husband was walking to the smithy. Jane, Mrs. Warbler's maid, waved as she carried a bucket into the house.

A rider came down the road toward her—Mr. Thurlowe. How fortuitous.

He was obviously beginning to make his rounds. His wide-brimmed hat was set at a cocky angle. His boots were polished and he looked the very image of a country gentleman.

That was about to change.

With a grim smile, Gemma took up a station in the middle of the road and when she felt she had a good shot, she picked up one of the eggs from her skirt and threw it at him with all her might.

Chapter Thirteen

It was a beautiful March morning as Ned rode out on the day's rounds. The air held an actual hint of spring.

Ned didn't know what he was going to do with the Logical Men's Society, but he was tired of worrying about it. Instead, Royce had found a bottle of decent port and, after two small glasses, Ned had gone to bed and had the best sleep he'd had since Gemma Estep had entered his life.

He'd even managed to not think of her once, which was a feat considering what had happened the day before. No, he had more pressing concerns, such as deciding *if* he would hold the Frost lecture. He didn't want to give it up and he didn't want to change what he had envisioned, which had included The Garland.

Last night he decided he would ask Mars if it could be held at Belvoir. In fact, the more he thought about it, the better he liked the idea. Then he could establish the protocols for participation exactly as he wished.

No wonder he'd had such a good night's sleep.

Not even the sight of Gemma Estep in her familiar black leaving The Garland could upset him. He might have to tip his hat out of courtesy, but he was not going to engage with her . . . although she appeared rather disheveled. She wasn't wearing a hat and her wickedly red braid looked as if she'd just rolled out of her bed. She held her skirt as if she was carrying something. Probably herbs for more of her "potions."

He sniffed his dismissal. His intent was to ride past her.

And then she took something from her skirt, pulled back her arm, and threw it at him with all her might.

A white object shaped like a round, smooth stone came flying through the air. Before Ned could move, it hit Hippocrates in the chest.

The horse startled, turned around. Fortunately, Ned had a good seat, and then, he felt something hit him in the back. He couldn't discern what it was because Hippocrates had decided he wanted to return to the barn. Ned's legs pressed his horse around, stopping him from bolting, even as another of her missiles hit his arm and broke into a wet, gooey mess.

Eggs? She was throwing eggs at him?

"What are you doing?" he shouted at her.

"Giving you back what you left behind." This time the egg hit Hippocrates's neck.

The gelding was not meant to be a war horse. He'd never learned how to stand his ground.

Realizing that he was losing the battle with his mount, Ned slid off before he was tossed off. Hippocrates didn't wait but turned tail and went running for home.

Even then Mrs. Estep didn't let up. She tossed two more eggs at him in quick succession. She'd moved closer and they hurt. She had a strong arm.

"*Enough,*" Ned ordered.

She picked up another egg, tossed it in the air, and deftly caught it in one hand. "Not even enough." She threw the egg and it landed on one of his boots. The boots Royce had freshly polished. She'd aimed right for it.

By now they were gaining attention on the street.

Ned's hat had been knocked off when he'd scrambled down from his horse. He ran an exasperated hand through his hair and said, "Mrs. Estep, stop this."

"How *dare* you," was her answer. She picked up another egg.

He held out his hand to ward her off. "Dare what? Why are you doing this?"

"Oh, you know. You know exactly what you did." She started to pull her arm back.

"I don't have a clue what you are talking about."

Her arm came down. "I don't believe you. I don't believe any of you. However, this was *petty*. Childish even. I will never let one of you through The Garland's door. Not while it is in my name." She threw her egg.

Ned managed to duck from this one and then he rushed her. She'd grabbed another egg and let down her skirts, so this had to be her last one.

Before she could let it fly at him, he reached for her arms and captured her by the wrists. She struggled against him, an angry wasp of a woman. His boots protected him from her kicks but he had to jump from side to side from her knee.

"Stop this," he ordered.

Of course, she didn't listen.

"What is this about?"

That caught her attention. She pulled back. "Oh, you *know*."

"I don't know."

"You *have* to know. They wouldn't have done it without your permission. What infuriates me is that it is so spiteful. Especially after I was attacked the other night and you *knew* about it. I can't believe you put them up to this."

"Put them up to what?"

Her answer was to glower mightily at him.

"I don't know what you are talking about," he said. Her eyes narrowed as if she was measuring the truth of his words. *"I don't."*

"Someone, or some*ones*, entered The Garland last night and filled it with chickens."

Ned didn't believe he'd heard her correctly. "Chickens?"

"Yes, chickens. Over a dozen of them. And a rooster."

"Someone gave you chickens?" he repeated, trying to make sense of what she was saying.

"They didn't *give* them to me. They turned them loose inside the building. The place is a mess. All my hard work is for naught. And I think we know who would play such a mean prank."

"Who?" Ned was baffled.

"*You* and your *Society*." She bit the words out. And then, taking advantage of his loosened grip on her wrists, she slammed her last egg into his chest.

Ned released his hold, feeling the crunch and the slimy wetness through his shirt. "Why did you do that?"

"Because it pleased me." She turned on her heel and went walking to The Garland with her head high.

Close at hand, a woman said, "Oh, dear." Ned looked up and was shocked to see how many villagers stood on the street gaping at him. But he wasn't going to let an audience stop him. Mrs. Estep's behavior was outrageous and she needed to answer for it.

He went after her. He scattered a little gathering of chickens and caught her just as she was entering the front door. "What are you talking about?" he demanded.

"See for yourself." She pushed open the door, and his jaw dropped in surprise.

Chicken droppings were all over the place. He frowned, trying to make sense of it.

"I woke this morning to have chickens in my kitchen and in the main room. Someone came in while I was alone and asleep. And it will not happen anymore, do you understand me, sir? I will not stand for it."

"Nor should you," he agreed swiftly.

Winderton had to be behind this. Winderton, who challenged Ned on everything and who was destroying the reputation of the Logical Men's Society. When word of this reached the matrons their gossip would set a bonfire in the village.

Ned's own temper ignited. "Come with me," he said, taking Mrs. Estep by the elbow and directing her out onto the street.

She tried to balk, but now *he* was in charge. "Where are we going?" she demanded.

Ignoring the curious stares following them, he said, "I'm going to settle this matter once and for all. He will not take over my village."

"He who?"

"The Duke of Winderton."

"You are saying he is behind this?"

"I'm certain of it. However, let's find out."

She cast him a speculative look but matched him step for step.

Fortunately, Hippocrates had not made it all the way home. He had stopped to nibble the grass growing in the churchyard. The reins were still around his neck. Ned was lucky they hadn't been broken. He mounted and then offered a hand to Mrs. Estep. "Come along."

"What do you have in mind?"

"I'm going to talk to Winderton and I want you there when I do."

"Why?"

"Will you believe my denial that I had anything to do with this without hearing for yourself?"

Her response was to give him her hand. He lifted her onto the saddle in front of him. Together they rode to the Dower House on the Winderton estate.

Of course, everything was quiet. The hour was too early in the morning for the likes of the duke to be up.

Ned's suspicions were solidified when they approached the house and found Mark Dawson and Shielding fast asleep on the front step, leaning against each other. It was as if they had started home and just hadn't made it very far. Sir Lionel's sedan chair was under a tree. One of the runners was asleep in it. Ned wondered where the rest of the Society members were.

As if in answer, he heard a hacking sound, then the loud noise of a piss that seemed to go on forever. Finally, when he was done, Sweeney came stumbling from around the side of the house, buttoning his breeches.

This was not how the gentlemen of the Logical Men's Society were to comport themselves; another crime he laid at the duke's door.

Sweeney squinted toward them. "Thurlowe? You are here? Who do you have with you?" He scratched his privates and Mrs. Estep ducked her head as if to hide a laugh or her embarrassment. He didn't blame her either way.

"I'm here to see His Grace."

"Oh," Sweeney said, the amount he'd had to drink slowing his words. "He's—" Sweeney looked around as if he'd been in charge of the duke and had misplaced him. He looked up to Ned, confusion on his face. "He's here. I don't know where."

"Stay on the horse," Ned said to Mrs. Estep, and he hopped down.

"Wait, this is a big horse," she said. "You can't leave me here on top of him."

"You will be fine. He's a lamb. Aren't you, Hippocrates?" The response was a heavy sigh and cocked leg as Hippocrates demonstrated he understood he was to stand and take care of Mrs. Estep. That being settled, Ned walked up to the door, stepping over the two men in front of it, and rapped smartly.

A wigged servant in Winderton colors answered. "Yes, sir?"

"I'm here to see His Grace. Send him out."

His eyebrows lifted all the way to his wig. "I beg your pardon, sir?"

"Send out the duke. Oh, never mind." Ned backed off the step, avoiding the two men and stood where he could see the upper-floor windows. He called in his loudest voice, "*Winderton,* come out here."

"Sir, you can't do that," the servant said.

"I am doing that," Ned answered, opening his arms to show he had no tricks before raising his voice. "*Winderton.*"

The servant shut the door.

The racket caused the men on the step to rouse themselves. Sweeney stood to the side, gaping like an idiot. Ned picked up a stone and threw it at one of the windows. "*Come out, Winderton.* Come out here, you *coward.*"

In truth, it would have been impossible for Ned to make the duke do his bidding. Except the word *coward* awakened the others to the duke's defense.

"His Grace is not a coward," Dawson mumbled.

"Then have him come out here."

To Ned's surprise, Dawson scrambled to his feet and went inside the house.

Mrs. Estep spoke, her voice almost urgent. "Mr. Thurlowe, have you gone mad?"

"No more mad than a woman who stands in the road tossing eggs at me."

She made an impatient sound. "You've proven your point. Let us leave."

"No, I haven't proven my point yet."

"Except I believe you."

"I'm not here because of you," he answered. And that was true. This was a reckoning. If Winderton was allowed to continue with his nonsense, Mrs. Estep would bear the brunt of most of it. And that made him unreasonably angry. Nor was he doing this just to bring the duke in line. He wanted them *all* to be brought to heel. "*Winderton.*"

The door opened.

The Duke of Winderton came out. He was in

shirtsleeves, breeches, and boots. His hair went every which way as if he'd just been awakened. He hadn't been shaved and his eyes were bloodshot. Dawson fell out behind him.

"Thurlowe, what are you doing here at this hour?"

"Challenging you."

"What?" Now the duke was waking up. "You are being a fool, Thurlowe." He turned to reenter the house.

"No, I'm stopping a fool. What happened last night to Mrs. Estep was not right."

The duke paused. "Last night—? Ah, yes. Last night. Did *Gemma* enjoy our surprise?"

Dawson and Sweeney smirked.

"Come here and ask her," Ned challenged.

The duke looked up sharply, finally noticing Mrs. Estep on Hippocrates. "Sorry, I don't need to." The duke would have closed his door, but Ned blocked his movement by slamming his hand on the wood.

"You are a coward, Your Grace, and a fool. It is a terrible combination. You can't do whatever you want around here. Maidenshop is not London and you are not that entitled. Bad behavior has consequences. There was a time when I respected you. But you are changing, growing more selfish. I'm here to knock some sense into you."

"You would *knock* me, Doctor? I doubt if you could."

"Let us see."

"Mr. Thurlowe, please," Mrs. Estep said. "He admitted they put the chickens in my place. I believe you now."

Except this wasn't about her.

Ned had paid a terrible disservice to the Logical Men's Society when, in his eagerness to see his lectures a success, he had recruited these men. They had turned the high standards of the Society into rubbish. No one respected the group anymore, including Ned.

Well, he was going to correct his mistake and the only way to do it was to show Dawson and the others that he was stronger than Winderton in every way.

"Go home, Doctor," the duke said. All benevolence had left his expression.

"Not until I accomplish what I came to do."

"Pistols at dawn?" There was a sneer in the duke's voice—although Ned doubted he'd ever dueled. At least the old Winderton, the one before he'd gone off to London who had been somewhat naïve and very earnest, would not have.

Ned named his terms. "No, bare fists. Right here. Right now."

The others' eyes widened. This was language they understood. Behind the duke, in the doorway, Ned noticed movement. The servants were listening.

Winderton frowned. His lips started to curve as if he was going to say no, until he seemed to realize what was at stake.

"Well?" Ned prodded.

"We shall." Winderton acted surprised he was saying it. "Right here, right now. Are there rules?"

"Do we need them?"

"I suppose not."

"Very well." Ned walked back to his horse.

"Mr. Thurlowe," Mrs. Estep pleaded, but he wasn't interested in what she had to say. He removed his jacket and laid it on the saddle behind her.

He turned around—and that is when he realized that Winderton had followed him. The duke hit him hard right in the mouth. He fell back against Hippocrates, who was not happy.

"Right here, right now, eh?" the duke taunted.

Thankfully, the horse hadn't budged far. He looked at Ned as if to say, *Go on with it.*

And so he did. The duke's punch had caused him to bite his tongue. He could taste blood. He'd tasted it before. Ned had learned his fighting skills fending off bullies who would corner him in school. Boys knew no other way to sort out their differences, and he should have anticipated the duke's attack because there had been no rules then, either.

However, the others, even Dawson, shouted their disapproval. They had some decency in them when they had to think for themselves.

Ned came back, ducking his head and barreling into Winderton, who was about his size. They were evenly matched. It also became apparent that Winderton had had his share of schoolroom brawls. Ned got in two good facers before the duke walloped him against the side of the head.

For what seemed like ages, they battled. Ned felt himself tire and yet the stakes were too high— especially for Mrs. Estep—to let Winderton win. The lads would make her life miserable.

And perhaps that is what gave him the advantage. Winderton was younger and actually stronger. However, Ned had purpose. He was also more cunning. He used his understanding of the human body to ensure his every blow was a powerful one.

Furthermore, he hadn't been drinking all night, and eventually, that was what won him the day. But not before he took a beating.

Both of them were sweating heavily. Ned's arms felt as if they weighed two stone. His knuckles hurt and he wasn't certain he could go on until Winderton dropped to one knee.

"Enough," he said.

Ned had never heard a better word spoken. He didn't let down his guard. "And?" he prodded.

"No more chickens."

"Or any other nonsense."

Reluctantly, the duke nodded. "We were in our cups."

Ned wasn't going to give him a sobriety lecture. His mother could do that. He dropped his guard and offered the duke a hand up. "That was a good match, Your Grace."

Winderton's head shot up as if to see if Ned was mocking him. He wasn't.

"I didn't expect a doctor to fight so hard."

"I may have had more practice. You live in a boys' school where everyone knows your mother is a whore, you learn quick."

Winderton gave a begrudging smile and then frowned with a sniff. "What is that yellow stain on your shirt?"

Ned looked down. "Egg. Mrs. Estep has a temper. You owe her an apology, Your Grace. You all do," he added, raising his voice.

The duke looked to Mrs. Estep sitting on the horse. He sighed and walked over to her. Her expression grew apprehensive until he stopped. "I beg your pardon, Mrs. Estep, for my boorish behavior." He looked to the others. "Come here. You need to show some manners."

With that the other three made their apologies to Mrs. Estep. She sat as if in shock at the turn of events, her brows buckling in concern.

"Will you break your fast with us, Thurlowe?" the duke asked when he'd seen the last of his minions apologize.

Lingering any longer was the last thing Ned wanted to do. The weight of the duke's blows were starting to make themselves known on his body. He kept his voice steady and cordial as he commented, "I wish I could, Your Grace. However, I am late for patients."

"Ah, well, perhaps tomorrow."

"Possibly. Thank you for asking." On those words, Ned managed to mount Hippocrates. It took effort and he prided himself on looking reasonably good doing it.

"Thank you, gentlemen. Your Grace." He gave a short bow and, lifting the reins, put them on their way. He didn't ride far. Every step Hippocrates took was a jolt.

"What was that about?" Mrs. Estep demanded.

"Chickens," he murmured.

"No, there was something else taking place. Why do men pound each other with their fists, and then shake hands as if nothing happened?"

"I fear you wouldn't understand."

"You are probably quite right. If someone hit me, I would be angry for ages—Wait, where are we going?"

Ned had set Hippocrates on the path to his favorite destination—a spring-fed pond a quarter of a mile off the road. Few beyond the locals knew of it because it was on Winderton's land and because of the shelter of trees around it.

Reaching his destination, he brought Hippocrates to a halt, and then practically fell to the ground. He caught himself by grabbing the saddle. Every muscle hurt and all he could think about was relief.

Ned pulled off a boot, then another.

"What are you doing?" Mrs. Estep asked.

He didn't answer. He didn't have the energy.

When he'd finished the fight, he'd not bothered to put his coat or hat back on. Now he practically clawed at his neck cloth as he walked toward the pond. He tossed it on the ground. Then he pulled loose the hem of his shirt and lifted it over his head.

"Mr. Thurlowe? *What are you doing?*"

His answer was to walk straight into the icy-fresh water of the pond.

Chapter Fourteen

Gemma watched Mr. Thurlowe march straight into the pond, uncertain if she trusted what her eyes were witnessing. She slid off the back of the horse, keeping the reins in her hand. Mr. Thurlowe disappeared completely under the water. It was as if the pond swallowed him whole.

She looked at the horse. The horse looked at her. "Does he do this often?"

Was it her imagination that the horse nodded? Then, he yanked on the reins, pulling his head down, letting her know he wished to graze. She held on, not knowing what to do.

After several minutes there was a disturbance in the water. Mr. Thurlowe's head popped up. He pushed his wet hair out of his eyes. "Drop the reins. He won't step on them."

As if seconding the order, the horse gave a snort and another annoyed pull of his head. Gemma dropped the reins . . . but not because of a conscious effort.

No, she dropped them because Mr. Thurlowe had started walking out of the pond. Water sluiced down over his naked torso in rivulets that followed his muscles. Every stitch he still wore molded almost obscenely to his body, and yet, she was not offended.

She'd been married. Many of her patients were men. She was accustomed to the male anatomy. It was no secret that Ned Thurlowe was an excellent specimen of masculine beauty in its prime.

But no man, not even her husband, had made her jaw drop in lascivious admiration as if she had the manners of a sailor. She couldn't stop herself.

Or control the sharp yearning that radiated from the pit of her stomach to the essence of her being. Even her breasts tightened, and it took all her strength to bite back the half whimper before it escaped her lips, and fortunately the only one who heard was the horse, who cocked an ear and then snorted his opinion.

Paul Estep's looks had turned heads, even hers. She had been flattered that, out of all the lasses in Manchester, he'd singled out her.

But never, not once, had he inspired in her this almost overwhelming reaction to his body. She wanted to step forward into Mr. Thurlowe's arms, to see if he was as strong and safe as she remembered.

He, on the other hand, acted completely oblivious to her. He raked his hair back from his face as he made his way to the bank. Reaching the grassy area, he threw himself upon the ground. He rolled to his back, closed his eyes, and groaned.

The sound of pain broke through her ogling.

She reached for his jacket she'd draped over the saddle. She walked over to the prone body. "Mr. Thurlowe?"

He didn't move. His eyes were closed.

Had he lost consciousness? Was there something wrong with him internally? She'd been appalled at the beatings the doctor and the duke had given each other.

She dropped to her knees beside him and tucked the jacket around his chest. His skin was cold to the touch. She cupped his face in her hands. "Mr. Thurlowe? *Mr. Thurlowe?*"

He shook his head as if she had startled him from sleep. "What?" He squinted up at her.

Gemma sat back, a touch chastened that she'd laid her hands on him. "I was checking if you were all right."

Wincing as he propped himself up by his elbows, he declared, "I'm not. There isn't a muscle in my body that doesn't ache like a bloody—" He stopped eyeing her as if her presence was an annoyance and finished tamely, "With pain. I ache with pain."

"You didn't need to correct yourself. I am not critical of strong language. Sometimes it has its place. My father was quite fond of it."

He looked at her as if she spoke gibberish and lay back down.

Gemma sat in silence. Not asking questions

went against everything her gran had taught her.
Her purpose was to heal.

She leaned over him. "I have a salve—"

Without opening his eyes, he shushed her.

"I could run back to the vill—"

He snapped his fingers. "No."

She had to try again. "It will help you feel
better."

"What would help me feel better is—" He
paused as if for dramatic effect.

"Yes?" she prodded.

"If I would stop fighting with men younger
than I am."

Gemma sat back, confused. "You make a habit
of fighting?" That was contradictory to her image
of him.

His eyes opened with a frown. Golden eyes.
Annoyed eyes. "No, I don't make a habit of it.
However, today was not wise."

"Why did you do it?" He pinned her with a look
that said she should know why . . . that, possibly,
he was defending her, a thought so disconcerting
she heard herself begin to rattle on. "You know
he could have called you out. Then you would be
honor-bound to fight a duel and kill someone. Or
be killed. That doesn't make sense, does it? When
I reflect upon the matter, what happened was
actually much better . . . *if* you are going to go
around doing something like this."

His gaze changed from annoyance to pity.

She frowned back at him. "So if you knew it
was a foolish thing to do, why did you do it?"

"Because I wanted them to stop harassing you."

He *had* been defending her.

She'd suspected it. She wanted to be furious. She was making her own way, and yet, something shifted inside her, just as it had the other night when he'd carried her through The Garland. It was hard always being alone. Hard not trusting, even after the harsh lessons she had learned. She knew she should be wiser about men . . . especially this one who seemed to do the right thing.

Ah, yes, but how many times had her trust been betrayed before?

Gemma hardened her jaw, trying to drum up anger. "I can defend myself."

He appeared as if he could see right through her, to what she wasn't saying—and perhaps even why she said it. He closed his eyes. "You could." There was a beat before he tacked on, "Except you were outnumbered. Besides, I am responsible for that lot."

"Couldn't you have just told them to stop?"

"I tried that more than once. The time came to take action." He sat up, wincing as his rib cage moved. He reached for the shirt he had carelessly tossed aside. He pulled it over his head and she felt a twinge of regret. "Of course, today I discovered six years is a considerable age difference. I'm always one to learn a good lesson when it presents itself." He bent at the waist, stretching his back forward.

"How are your ribs? Is anything broken?"

"Thankfully, no. He did give me a good bruising."

"He did. I can wrap your ribs for you."

"Not necessary." And then he groaned.

"I'll be the judge of that, if you will let me help."

"Mrs. Estep, I'm—"

"A doctor. A *trained* doctor. I know. You are a pest about it."

"I'm a what?"

Now she had his full attention. And she was not going to repeat herself. Instead, she reached out to press her fingers on the pulse at his neck. He tried to duck her and she lightly tapped him. "Don't be silly." He gave her another frown, except this time he let her feel his pulse. "Strong and steady," she observed. "I was concerned."

"I told you I was fine. Just bruises. In fact, now after it is over, I have to admit it has been a long time since I've ever felt more alive." He said this last almost to himself.

"And you beat him."

His head lifted. The corners of his mouth rose in a cocksure grin. "I did, didn't I?"

"So why did you walk into the pond?" she pressed.

He fell back onto the ground. "You are relentless," he said bluntly.

True. "Why did you walk into the pond?"

"Because the spring water is cold. Not only did it feel good after that fight, I also hope it will stave off some of the bruising. And, because I smelled like egg."

Eggs she'd thrown.

Was he angry with her?

He gave her a side glance. "Don't look that way."

"What way?"

"Like you are about to be flogged. I was jesting. Well, not about smelling like eggs, but that I hold a grudge."

"About any of it? Including losing The Garland?" She had to ask . . . because it would be nice to have a true truce between them.

He seemed to weigh his answer, his sharp gaze considering her, and then he said, "Mrs. Crisp had piles and instead of telling me, she told you."

"Oh, yes. Is she better?" The change of topic confused her.

"How would I know? Most of the women in this parish aren't talking to me anymore. And I don't understand it. I'm a good physician."

"One of the best I've met," she admitted.

"And yet Mrs. Crisp would rather suffer than speak to me? And why does cream relieve piles? Where did you find that notion?"

Gemma shrugged. "From my gran, who had it from her gran. Someone learned cream helps and so we share it. I have no idea why it works."

His brows came together as he digested this. He grunted a response before saying, "And my other question? The one you don't want to answer."

How did he know?

"*Well?*" he demanded. "I've come to expect honesty from you, Gemma. Do they tell you they don't want to speak to me?"

"No," she said, startled by the thought.

"Would *you* not talk to me about your health?"

"I would heal myself," Gemma answered.

"If you *weren't* a healer," he clarified with some exasperation. "Would you be shy?"

"There are men who are shy," she said in her defense. "They don't like to talk to women about private parts of their body."

"Health comes before modesty."

Gemma gave an exasperated sigh. "Not if there is a choice. And," she said, pausing thoughtfully, "is this why you are so angry with me? Because I told Mrs. Crisp to use cream?"

"I've been very clear why I'm angry—"

"You are jealous."

The words just came out of her. There was no conscious thought and yet, there it was, the truth. The damning, disappointing truth.

He looked as if she'd slapped him. Of course, he scowled.

"Yes, go ahead, frown at me," she said. "That is all you do, as if that is some sort of explanation for your bad moods. And you know what?" she continued, rising to her feet. "I have no idea what your true question is. Seriously, I don't. So I can't give an answer. Are you angry that I gave someone advice that worked or that I sold someone foot soaks? Or are you angry that I am encroaching on your sacred territory? Oh, dear, that's a disaster," she said with a mock shudder. "Or that some women are very modest and feel uncomfortable talking about private matters? I have no control over what anyone thinks. I imagine it is different for every patient. *Male* and female. But I believe you know that. And if you don't, then I question your powers of observation. However, what I am not here for is your grumpiness. No matter what I do, you find fault." She shook out her skirts and started for the horse. "I'm going to ride back. *You* can take another dive in the pond—"

Suddenly, his hand grabbed her arm and whipped her around. He was on his feet. He'd moved with astonishing speed. Before she realized what was happening, his lips came down upon hers.

His lips.

On *hers.*

Gemma was so shocked, she let out a gasp . . . that evolved into a sigh.

Heedless of his damp body, she leaned into him. His arms came around her, gathering her close. Their lips fit perfectly. Her hips met his. Her breasts pressed against his chest. And she found herself greedily wanting more, yearning to be close to him.

This was how she'd imagined a kiss should be. Her husband's kisses had been slobbery and port soaked, and a test of her endurance.

Mr. Thurlowe's kiss set her heart pounding madly. He tasted sweeter than honey. She wanted to bury her fingers in his hair—and a memory came back to her.

Years ago she'd asked her gran why, if she missed her daughter so much, she had let her go away with a man to Manchester. And her gran had said, "I had to let her go. When she kissed him, she told me she saw stars."

Gemma had forgotten the story, and yet here it was—she *was seeing stars*. Bright, beautiful, exploding ones. She could kiss Ned Thurlowe all day, all night, all—

Abruptly, he broke the kiss. He stepped back. Gemma wasn't ready to let go. She started to follow. He held her at arm's length.

Cold air brought her to her senses. They had been kissing out in the open. If anyone had seen them, if the matrons caught wind of this, or worse, Miss Taylor . . .

The expression in his eyes appeared just as confused as she felt. He spoke first. "I shouldn't have done that."

She didn't trust herself to speak.

Then he added, "I have no regrets."

Neither did she. Stars. She'd seen stars—

She found her voice. "We can't do that again."

"It wouldn't be wise."

"No."

He dropped his arms and looked to the pond, turning from her. "Take Hippocrates. I'll help you up. He knows the way to the village. When you reach The Garland, throw the reins over his head. He'll go home on his own."

"What are you going to do?"

"I need to stay here a bit."

Gemma didn't move, her hands at her sides, her palms against her skirts. "I think perhaps we should talk—"

"I think we shouldn't," he answered, cutting her off. He turned completely from her now. "There is nothing to say. I should not have done that. I was out of bounds. This is not like me."

It was not like her, either . . . and yet, Gemma knew she'd not forget that kiss. Ever.

She drew a steadying breath, released it. "You have nothing to worry about from me. Clarissa is a friend. I would never betray that friendship."

"I know. The fault is mine alone."

That was not true and they both knew it.

He broke the silence between them. "Let me help you mount." He didn't meet her eye as he passed her. Almost woodenly, she fell into step behind him.

He picked her up and put her in the saddle, his touch gentle—protecting her. Caring for her.

"There is something I don't understand," she said, picking up the reins.

He was adjusting the stirrup. He looked up at her.

"You don't truly have any feelings for Clarissa, do you?"

He stiffened. Didn't answer. Instead, he walked around the horse to lift the other stirrup so it wouldn't bump the horse as she rode sidesaddle. Finally, "I admire her."

She had no doubt that was true. Everyone in the village admired Clarissa. "Why did you offer for her?"

The corners of his mouth tightened.

"I understand," she said. "We *should* keep a distance from each other."

He nodded in agreement, his expression pensive.

"I don't want this, either," she told him. "It was not my intent."

"Understood."

Except she *did* want him.

He stepped back. At last he looked at her. "I've never kissed her." He made the statement as if it explained everything, and then added, "She is a good person."

"And the matrons want her to stay in the village."

His golden eyes darkened with concern. "I've always been an outsider until I came to Maidenshop. You know Miss Taylor's story?"

"That she was found as a babe on the parsonage doorstep in a basket."

He nodded. "Of course you have heard it. Everyone knows it. All her life she has been *that one*. I understand what she is up against because I was *that one*." Then he said quietly, "I had no right to touch you."

"Yes," she agreed, a heavy sadness coming down upon her. "It was the moment," she suggested. "Just a passing moment."

A *very good* moment.

"Gemma—"

She held up a hand to cut him off. "Let's not make it seem more than it is." Her words seemed heavy in the world around them.

His expression falling into lines of gentlemanly politeness. "Of course."

There. They were done.

She lifted the reins but then had one more thought. "You may hold your lecture at The Garland."

His expression changed to gratitude. "Thank you, Gemma. Thank you."

"There is one condition."

He tensed, wary. "Yes?"

"You must invite the women. Men aren't the only ones interested in the goings-on of the world or the cosmos. Besides, I'd pit my intelligence against one of the Dawson lads any day."

That made him laugh.

And in that moment, when he was pleased, when he was trusting her . . . she realized she could fall in love with him.

The idea rose unbidden in her mind. *She* could fall *in love* with *him*.

But she mustn't. She couldn't.

If anyone learned that they'd kissed, that *she'd liked* that kiss, well, the matrons would protect Clarissa—whom Gemma considered a friend.

"I need to go back," she said. Her voice sounded strained, a combination of both being around him and realizing she could never have him.

"Yes." He didn't sound happy himself. "This is it, right?"

She didn't pretend to misunderstand him. "If we care for Clarissa."

He nodded, then stepped back. "Go, Hippocrates. Take her home."

The horse gave himself a shake as if he'd been sleeping. He chewed the bit a second and then took a step toward the road, when the doctor suddenly put up a hand and stopped him.

Ned looked up at Gemma.

"Yes?" she prodded, not wanting to leave him. Not yet.

"I was wrong when I said fighting Winderton had made me feel more alive than I had for a long time. It was nothing compared to kissing you."

On those words, he said, "On with you now. Home, Hippocrates." The horse began moving.

Gemma turned in the saddle, watching Ned until the shelter trees hid him from her view, wishing she had his words written on paper, even though she knew she'd never forget them.

As she let Hippocrates take her toward Maidenshop, Gemma lifted a hand to her lips, tracing the line of her lower lip with her finger. They'd been changed. They seemed softer now . . . and not because of the kiss, but because he'd let her know she mattered to him.

And he could never be hers.

Clarissa would have Ned.

Meanwhile, Gemma would have The Garland, her herbs, her vision of a shop, and a tea garden. She would have her dreams. She prayed it was enough.

Hippocrates picked up his pace at the outskirts of the village. However, when she pulled on the reins in front of The Garland, he was obedient enough. After she slid off, he trotted smartly on his way.

It was almost noon. The streets were busier

than they had been earlier when she'd thrown the eggs. In her yard she saw a cluster of three hens scratching at the dirt she and Fitz had over-turned for planting. They were probably looking for worms.

Then she thought of the mess waiting for her inside. Gemma sighed and opened the door to be greeted by the sight of Mrs. Warbler, Mrs. Burnham, Mrs. Summerall, and the dowager. They sat at the only clean table in the room, their faces pinched with distaste.

"Hello, Mrs. Estep," Mrs. Warbler said in the coldest tone. "We have been waiting for you."

"Yes," the dowager echoed. "We wish to talk to you about Mr. Thurlowe."

Chapter Fifteen

Gemma closed the door, uncertain. She faced them. "What of Mr. Thurlowe?"

They couldn't know that she'd been with him. The pond had been well sheltered. No one had happened by. Not that she'd noticed. Then again, her mind had been focused on him.

Or was there evidence of his kiss upon her face? A mark? A different look about her? *That*, she could believe.

"You created quite a scene this morning," Mrs. Burnham said.

"I did and for that I apologize. I was upset."

"Why were you carrying on that way?" Mrs. Summerall asked. "I hear your actions were most unseemly."

"I woke to find The Garland filled with chickens. It was a prank on the behalf of the Logical Men's Society. Logical *Child's* Society is more like it." Gemma's temper flared again. "You can see the damage that has been done. I will spend the rest of the day scrubbing."

"Oh, dear," the dowager said. "We wondered when we came in here why you had allowed chickens inside."

"I didn't allow it. I'm also tired of them thinking they can walk onto my property whenever they feel like it."

"You should lock the door," Mrs. Warbler replied.

"Do you lock your door?"

Her neighbor blinked at her. Of course not. No one locked their doors in Maidenshop. Gemma continued, "I was gathering the eggs when I saw Mr. Thurlowe and I regret to say I took out my temper on him, because he was not responsible. In fact, he went to battle for me."

A look was exchanged among the ladies. "He did?" Mrs. Warbler said, her tone carefully noncommittal.

"Yes, that is why he let me ride his horse home." Gemma was feeling her way here. She suddenly understood how it must have looked for Mr. Thurlowe to just lift her up onto the saddle in front of him. She'd literally been riding in his lap. "He took me to confront the duke and—" She paused, realizing what she'd said in front of the dowager but gamely went on, "The other culprits." She wasn't going to tell them that the duke and Mr. Thurlowe had exchanged physical blows. Who knew how that information would be received? "They had stern words," she finished.

Silence met her story.

The duke's mother broke it. "Stern words?"

"Very stern," Gemma said, nodding.

"My *son*, the seventh Duke of Winderton, was involved in filling The Garland with chickens?"

Gemma's hands suddenly felt sweaty. She pressed them to her skirts. "I don't know how involved," she lied, and had to add, "However, the place reeks of them."

"Mr. Thurlowe was *not* involved?" The dowager behaved as if she needed clarification.

"I should not have thrown the eggs at him," Gemma confessed.

The dowager looked to Mrs. Warbler. "I wonder why, Elizabeth, we heard that my son and the doctor were exchanging blows over the matter?"

They had known all along. Hadn't Gemma been warned? Nothing escaped the matrons.

And then the dowager with fire in her eyes swung her attention to Gemma. "Do you lie to me? I will not tolerate it."

"I'm sorry, Your Grace." It was all Gemma could say.

The dowager came to her feet. "I will send servants to help with the *scrubbing*. Accept my apologies. If my son instigated this, it was without my knowledge."

Aware of her own culpability, Gemma mumbled out, "I understand that, Your Grace. I would never believe you were involved."

But the dowager's attention had already shifted

to her friends. "You may all take care of the rest," she said. "I have a *personal* matter to attend. I know you, my dear friends, will understand." With that she left, ignoring the faltering curtsey Gemma offered.

After the door had closed, Gemma looked to the others. "What is *the rest*?"

"Mr. Thurlowe," Mrs. Summerall said, not unkindly.

"What of him? I know I shouldn't have made a scene."

Mrs. Warbler took charge. "Gemma, you went with Mr. Thurlowe to confront the duke. We know they came to blows. The whole parish probably does by this time."

Little more than an hour could have passed. "How did you find out so soon?"

"Gossip like that?" Mrs. Burnham said. "It travels on the wind."

"We didn't know exactly what had happened here," Mrs. Warbler said. "Or why you were throwing eggs or for what reason Mr. Thurlowe went riding off with you. However, once we heard about the fight, we realized that there was more to your angry egg throwing."

Relief flooded Gemma. They just wanted answers. That was why they had been so stern with her when she'd first walked in. "I'm sorry for the scene—" Gemma apologized again only to be cut off.

"What we want to know is where were you and

Mr. Thurlowe for the time between the fight and when you arrived back here? Riding his horse, no less."

Now Gemma understood why people were cautious around the matrons. It dawned on her that just as they had given their blessing to her tea garden, they could withdraw it. Would her dream survive?

Gemma proceeded warily. "Mr. Thurlowe and I discussed his lecture. I've agreed to let him have it here."

Three stony faces stared at her.

She had the urge to elaborate. She fought it.

It was hard.

But they already seemed to sense what she wasn't saying.

Mrs. Warbler looked at the other two. "I shall manage from here."

"Yes," Mrs. Summerall agreed. "You know what must be said."

The other two ladies left. "Sit down, Gemma," Mrs. Warbler ordered, nodding at the chair across the table from her.

Gemma did as she was told. "I've done nothing wrong."

"We know you haven't, dear. Of course, from the first, you and Mr. Thurlowe have been at cross purposes."

"He wanted to take The Garland from me."

"Yes, he did . . . except there was also some-thing else we sensed."

"And what was that?"

"An attraction."

Gemma made a sound that was a cross between a laugh of denial and a choke. She started to get up. "I don't know what you are talking about—"

Mrs. Warbler's hand came down on the one Gemma used to push herself up from the table, holding her in place. "You do know."

Gemma retook her seat. "You are questioning my word? Should I be offended?"

"You may be offended but hear me well. Clarissa Taylor has few options for her life. She has no one except us. We are her family and we've treated her well. We've seen that she was educated, that she is clothed, that she has a roof over her head. From the moment she was discovered on the church step, *we* have taken care of her. She will make an excellent doctor's wife. And she looks forward to it. You don't want to rob her of her future, do you?"

At that moment, almost as if she'd been summoned, there was a light knock on the door a second before it opened and Clarissa came in. Her cheeks were flushed as if she had been in a great hurry. Her gaze looked around the room and then went straight to Gemma.

"I heard what happened. I couldn't believe that someone would be so monstrously mean-spirited as to try and undo your hard work. Who did this?" She looked young, fresh, defenseless. Gemma knew how hard Clarissa's life would be if she didn't marry. She knew too well because those had been her father's fears for her.

Mrs. Warbler gave Gemma's hand a squeeze that was both a warning and an order. She looked to Clarissa. "This is a mess, but have you heard what Gemma did?"

"They say you pelted Mr. Thurlowe with eggs, and well you should. I'm shocked that he would be a party to this—"

Gemma cut her off. "He wasn't. It was the idea of others." Gemma now knew better than to accuse the duke.

"I'm so sorry. I came to help clean." Clarissa looked around the room again, shaking her head. "Have you started? Should I fetch water? And to think today I was going to help you hang the shelves Mr. Haskins built for you."

She was all that was kind. Mr. Thurlowe would be an excellent husband. He'd not leave her without money or an understanding of his whereabouts and his actions. And although he and Clarissa would not be a love match, Ned would honor his vows. He would always provide for his wife, even upon his death. They might even, in time, learn to love each other. Perhaps Clarissa already had strong feelings for him. The conflict Gemma had sensed in her friend might have been her own imaginings—because the matrons were right. There had been an attraction from the beginning.

But none of the turmoil inside Gemma betrayed itself in her voice as she said, "Mrs. Warbler and I were discussing the best way to proceed. Yes, please fill the bucket with water."

Gemma rose to her feet. To her surprise, the earth was solid beneath her, and yet, she felt as if she was falling through a hole and there was nothing to grab ahold of to help her. "You will find it in the kitchen, which is an even worse mess. I don't know where Athena has gone off to. She may be a good mouser but the chickens gave her a terrible fright."

Thankfully, Mrs. Warbler jumped right in. "*I* have a bucket," Mrs. Warbler announced. "And soap. Jane and I will help. Once again, we will have this place shining."

"Thank you," Gemma said, the words hollow inside her.

Mrs. Warbler didn't seem to notice. Neither did Clarissa.

And Gemma knew better than to pine. After all, she and Ned had never had a chance. She didn't even have a right to consider it.

Still, as she and Clarissa began gathering cleaning supplies, Gemma had to say, "You are fortunate that you are marrying Mr. Thurlowe."

Clarissa set water in the iron pot over the fire to heat before carelessly answering, "I am. He's a good man."

She smiled at Gemma, her expression without guile. It also didn't quite meet her eyes—and God help her, Gemma had to press the issue. In all the time that she'd known Clarissa, her friend had rarely talked about her intended, except in approving platitudes. "He's handsome, too."

"Yes, he is." Clarissa straightened, gave a little

shrug of her shoulders, and with one of her sunny smiles that could say everything and say nothing, said, "He'll do."

Yes, he would.

LUCY, THE Dowager Duchess of Winderton, didn't knock on the door of the Dower House where her son had been staying for the past several weeks. He may own the house, but she was still the authority at Smythson.

A footman crossing the front sitting room stopped midstride at the sight of her in the hall. His shirt was untucked, his wig askew, and he was in the process of buttoning his breeches. If she hadn't had those clues, Lucy would have still known what he was up to by the guilt on his face.

The man turned abruptly as if to walk away and pretend he didn't see her.

That was not about to happen.

The time had come to end this nonsense.

"Don't you dare move," she said in her most imperial voice. "Hodgeson, isn't it?"

At that moment a giggling maid came around the corner, the man's neck cloth in her hand. "You forgot this, lovey—" she started and then closed her mouth and shut up at the sight of her mistress.

Lucy eyed the girl. Her uniform was ill fitting, which didn't make sense. All of the Smythson uniforms were tailored to the wearer. "I know all the servants in my employ. I do not know you.

What is your name, girl?" She used her tone that could chill water.

The maid had the good sense to curtsey. It was awkward and poorly done, but she did it. Hodgeson stood frozen as if he feared for his immortal soul.

"Cora Belks, Your Grace." Another inept curtsey. Really. Her most trusted servant, Randall, who had been the Smythson butler from before she'd first arrived as a bride, had recently retired out of service. Lucy had not been terribly satisfied with his replacement, Andrews. The man had come highly recommended except Lucy had noticed he was lazy. Did he believe that just because she was widowed and her son too young for common sense that she would turn a blind eye to foolishness on her staff?

She looked to Hodgeson. "Where is Mr. Andrews?"

"He is at the main house, Your Grace."

"Fetch him."

"Yes, Your Grace."

"And where is my son?" she asked before the footman could make his bowing escape.

"His Grace is in his chambers, Your Grace."

She noticed Cora trying to stealthily back out of the room. "Stop right there, missy. And stay there until *I* return." The girl dutifully froze.

Lucy started up the stairs. She spied another servant lingering in the back of the hall. Word was spreading that she was in the house. Good.

She didn't bother to knock on her son's door. Lucy wanted the element of surprise. She received it. The heavy drapes were all pulled shut. However, in the shadowy darkness of the bedroom she couldn't mistake his naked buttocks as he was spread out on the bed with an equally nude young woman under his arm. A host of empty bottles surrounded the bed.

For a long moment, punctuated only by her son's light snores, Lucy glared at the scene. She expected the couple to come awake from her presence alone, and then realized her son was too far gone.

Fighting . . . carousing . . . whoring? When had he come to this? Christopher had always been sensible.

And spoiled.

Her brother Brandon had warned her. Growing up, if Christopher didn't have his way, there were often tantrums and later just pouting. But he was one and twenty. The time had come for him to be a man, and not one with loose morals.

"Christopher."

He didn't budge.

"*Christopher.*"

The girl came awake and gave a squeal of surprise. Lucy expected her to jump up and run from the room. Instead, the bold puss frowned. "Who are you to bother us?"

Was she truly that stupid?

"Who are you?" Lucy asked succinctly in a tone only a duchess could use.

Now the girl looked nervous. She glanced at the still-sleeping duke. "I work here."

"Not anymore," Lucy replied.

"The duke hired my sister and me."

"Cora?"

A line of concern appeared between the girl's brows. "Yes."

"She doesn't work here any longer, either. Now go. Put on your clothes. Run away."

"The duke won't like that. He expects me here. Wants me in his bed whenever he needs me." She made it sound as if she was being a good soldier.

In answer, Lucy walked over to the bed, kicking the bottles aside as she made her way. She grabbed her son's head by the hair and lifted it up. His breath was foul as he began coughing and coming to his senses. Bruises marred his handsome features. A squinting eye appeared blackened.

And then Christopher realized he was looking at the face of his mother.

His reaction was everything she could have wished. He scooted to the other side of the bed, pushing his companion to the floor. She landed with a thud while he grabbed the sheet and wrapped it around his privates.

"*Mother?* What are you doing here?"

"Delivering an ultimatum."

"A what?" He frowned and scratched his whiskered jaw as if his mind was still sleep fogged.

"I hope that Mr. Thurlowe looks worse than you do."

"He doesn't."

"Ah, so you can admit that."

The girl stood up. She'd found a shift on the floor to cover herself and pulled it over her head. Placing her hands on her hips as if she was a princess of the realm, she frowned at Christopher as if he should be defending her. The unlucky chit was about to learn a harsh lesson.

Lucy focused on her son. "Dismiss the girl. She is no longer welcome on this property."

"Mother—"

"Dismiss her."

He frowned. He didn't like being backed into a corner . . . still, a part of him was her beloved son. "Sarah, be on your way. My mother and I need to talk."

"She said I don't have a position here. Cora, either."

"We will talk later, Sarah."

The cheeky lass looked from the duke to the duchess and then tramped out.

After the door slammed behind her, Winderton said, "You have no right to walk in here like this, Mother. I am the duke."

"And I'm your mother. That gives me higher rights than you will ever have. You are done here, Christopher. You need to return to London or wherever you wish to go."

"I wish to be in Maidenshop."

"That is not possible. You will not stay here and shame this family with your behavior."

"I've done nothing shameful—"

Lucy's hold on her temper snapped. *"You certainly haven't done anything ducal.* I know that much of the resistance Gemma Estep has received over The Garland is of *your* making. Whose idea was it to fill her establishment with chickens? *Who* among that sorry band of followers you have been cultivating has the resources to secure that many chickens? It must have taken you days."

"I thought it would be a lark."

"A schoolboy lark, yes. Unfortunately, that is not what we expect from a duke."

"The fellows thought it was fun."

"I don't. And obviously, neither did Mr. Thurlowe."

"He made his point."

"Now I'm going to make mine. I accept that you thought yourself in love with my brother's wife. She never encouraged you, Christopher. You were the only one who believed she had. I had hoped your going away to London would give you some Town bronze and help focus you on your duties and responsibilities. Instead, you learned how to whore, to use your position for hedonistic reasons."

"A man is a man."

That statement infuriated her. *"No,* a man is someone who stands for something. Your father was a statesman. Not a drunkard. Not a prankster. Not a *sore loser.* Kate chose someone else. Instead of proving her right for not choosing you, why don't you behave in a way to make her question her decision?"

"She is obviously happy with my uncle." Oh, he spoke so stiffly, so full of misplaced pride.

"Yes, because he truly loves her. He cares about her and doesn't give two snaps for what other people think about their love. That is the sort of man a woman wants."

"I could have been that man."

"If she had returned your feelings. She didn't. And now, here you are busy pleasing Sarah Belks, who is on her way to catching the pox if she hasn't caught it already." Lucy came around to the end of the bed. "You chose to return to Maidenshop. And for what? Christopher, your future does not lie here. Go on, out into the world. Become the man that I know you are."

"I don't wish to leave. I like Maidenshop."

Lucy sighed, confronted with her own culpability. Her poor son. In her grief over her husband's death, she had kept Christopher too close. "We will always be here. This is your family seat, your home. And I am not ordering you to leave because I don't respect you. I love you more than my own soul. However, this"—her hand came out to encompass the room, the bottles, the soiled sheets—"isn't who you are. You are Winderton . . . and that must stand for something."

Then the thought struck her—what if it was too late? Had she spoiled him to the point that he might never become what she and her dear husband had envisioned? Had she ruined him?

She blinked back her tears. Now was not the time for him to see her falter. Not if he was to succeed. "You must go."

Lucy left the room.

NED KNEW it was a risk to see Gemma.

Still, he could not stay away.

He waited until most people were gathered around their dinner table. This was the loneliest hour of the day for him.

Except now there was a deeper twist to what he was feeling.

He followed the bank of the Three Thieves until he reached the back of The Garland. One thing the Logical Men's Society understood was how to avoid detection by the matrons. Coming up onto the lawn, he had to admire what Gemma had accomplished. She was well on her way to having her bowling green back here. He was also impressed with the size and the arrangement of herb and flower beds. Some things were already planted; such was the blessing of English weather.

And then he stopped, his gaze on the closed back door. He had to see her, but now, what should he say? Well, other than he wanted to kiss her again. He *needed* to kiss her. To hold her, to be close to her . . .

There was light in the kitchen, a sign she was home. All he had to do was knock on the door and yet, his feet didn't move—

The door opened. Gemma came out the back carrying a heavy bucket.

Without hesitation, Ned moved to her. She started as if she didn't expect anyone to be out there in the night. Of course, after the experiences she'd had, no wonder she was nervous.

She recognized him and went very still. He wrapped a hand around the bucket handle, taking it from her. She watched, her expression wary in the kitchen light.

"I had to see you." No flowery phrases. No excuses. Just truth. "Perhaps I can come in—?"

"No." She took a step back.

He sensed something was wrong. "We need to talk."

"And say what?"

"That is the part I've been trying to reason out. So many words flood my mind—"

"Then don't say anything," she answered woodenly and would have turned away—

"*Gemma*, I—well, today, we kissed. And I thought I would be able to put it out of my mind, save I can't."

"You must." Her breathing was shallow and tight. This was not what he wanted.

He set the bucket down. Came forward. "It is not that easy. I thought I could let matters lie, and yet, all I can think about is you—"

She held up a hand, stopping him. "The kiss meant nothing. We discussed it. It's behind us."

Her denial brought a flash of anger, until he realized she didn't meet his eye. "You're lying."

She stiffened, before whispering, "I'm lying." Expressive eyes met his. "I'm so lying. But there can't be a *we*. No *us*. You are promised to someone else."

"Yes, I've been thinking about that. It is a difficulty—"

"A difficulty? You gave your word to one of the kindest, most defenseless of women in not just the village but the world. Mr. Thurlowe—"

"Ned."

"What?"

"My name is *Ned*. I want to hear you use my given name as you say what I believe you are about to say."

"We can't do this . . . Ned."

He turned. Stared into the darkness before picking up the bucket and tossing the contents across the lawn. He faced her. "We can."

"We mustn't. And we don't even know what *this* is. I barely know you. I *annoy* you. We are *enemies*."

"I love you." The words flowed out of him.

For a second he didn't know who was more startled—her or himself. However, once spoken, once released to the night air, the power of that simple statement reverberated around them.

She closed her eyes. "No, Ned, don't. You can't."

"But I already do, Gemma. I love you. I also know you have feelings for me. It was there in your kiss."

Her eyes opened, her gaze clear, troubled, honest. "Feelings that should never be acted upon."

"And yet, we did. Now they are here, and how can we deny them?" She started to shake her head, to offer more resistance. He wouldn't let her. "We don't have to live here." He'd never imagined he would say such a thing. Maidenshop was the only true home he'd ever known. The only place where he'd felt welcomed.

Except, he sensed he could be happy wherever he was, if he was with Gemma. "We can find a place that is ours alone."

"Ned, life doesn't work that way. You know that. And we are two people with big dreams. We'd come to hate each other if we did this the wrong way."

She was right.

"And it is more than our running away," she continued. "My husband betrayed me with many women. He didn't honor his vows. I *hated* the way he made me feel. I can't do that to Clarissa. She doesn't deserve it."

"Let Mars marry her," he said. He spoke desperately. He knew that would never happen.

"And yet, you are the one who asked her. Could you truly renege on your promise, Ned? Without you, she has no future—except being a governess or a companion . . . and you and I know how cruel the world can be for anyone without family."

He did know. Too well.

Ned didn't want to let go of these fledgling feelings he had for Gemma. He didn't completely understand what was happening. He'd never experienced wanting to open his life to another, or to even trust a woman. To have her by his side. What swirled inside him was, yes, desire and lust and need, but also a yearning to be the man he'd spent the afternoon imagining he could be with Gemma in his life. He could see it clearly now. She, alone, held the key.

There was no other for him.

"Gemma," he said, her name a plea, and a blessing. "I don't trust very many people, and none who are female, and yet, I'm placing my heart before you. I can't imagine my life with any other." He leaned toward her—she stopped him with a shake of her head.

"No, Ned. *No.*" Before he realized it, she stepped back and shut the door.

He stood there both stunned and angry. He wanted to break things. He wanted to rip down the door. He wanted to leap into the past and call back his promise to Clarissa because he'd been a fool to not imagine that Gemma would come into his life.

Instead, he leaned his palms against the door. He could sense her there. Waiting.

He whispered, "Gemma, I am not a man who pays attention to feelings. They make you vulnerable and then people can hurt and even destroy you . . . except I don't feel that way about you. Please, help me. Since the moment we laid eyes on each other that first morning, you have rarely been far from my thoughts. It defies logic. I don't understand what is happening or why, except I've never needed anyone in my life. I've refused to need them . . . until you. You challenge me, you argue with me, you infuriate me, and I love you. We can't leave it here."

Her answer was silence.

Damnable silence. And then, slowly, he accepted that she was right.

The realization made him push back from the door.

Maybe tomorrow she'd come to him—and then he would have to be the one strong enough for the both of them to say no.

That didn't make this moment any easier.

He lightly rested his palm against the weathered wood of the door. She was still there. He believed he could feel her heartbeat in the air between them.

He loved . . . and that alone for a boy who had grown up abandoned was a miracle.

Ned left. He didn't bother following the water. Instead, he walked for the road. As he reached it, he glanced over at Mrs. Warbler's house. There was no light in the window, or lurking figure. That didn't mean she wasn't watching. She was known to be a clever spy.

However, at this point, he didn't care. He made his way home.

Chapter Sixteen

$\mathcal{L}$ife had a way of continuing whether a person wanted it to or not. Ned had learned this lesson through many disappointments . . . but none had left him as unsure about himself as parting with Gemma.

And, yes, he understood he barely knew her. Yet, from the beginning he'd been drawn to her. He'd blamed it on the vibrant color of her hair, the determined set of her chin, her claim to being a healer. Now he understood that what had truly caught his attention was her fearlessness. She hadn't hesitated in challenging him—something Clarissa Taylor could never do, and not through any fault of her own. He was her only chance to cling to the only life she'd known. She lacked Gemma's boldness.

Now, instead of riding by The Garland, as had been his custom, he made a point of taking a different route the next morning and every day after. He didn't want to see Gemma. He knew when their paths did cross, they would be cordial and undeniably distant. He wasn't eager for *that* moment to come.

A few days after the kiss he ran into Agnes Woodman driving her dog cart down the road.

Mrs. Woodman suffered headaches and complained about them constantly. Ned had advised that quiet and sitting in a dark room with a warm compress against her brow would give her some relief. She'd informed him briskly that when a woman had nine children, sitting was not an option. He could not argue.

Actually, what he suspected was that she used her "headaches" to keep her husband away from her, especially at night. Daniel Woodman had bent Ned's ear more than once complaining about how her headaches stopped him from enjoying his marital sport. "She used to be as ready as I was," he'd complained. "Now she goes to bed early and refuses to even look at me."

The truth was, little could be done for headaches. Many people had them; often those people were women. It was an unsatisfactory answer to both husband and wife. Ned had given her powders. She swore none of them worked.

However, today Mrs. Woodman greeted him gaily. "Good morning to you, Mr. Thurlowe."

He tipped his hat. "Good morning to you. I see you are looking well."

She pulled over. "Aye, that I am." She adjusted her shawl around her shoulders. "I have not had a headache in over a week."

"Excellent. You are taking my advice?"

"No, I went to see Gemma," the woman proudly informed him. "She gave me a powder she concocted and I haven't had an incident since. And I'll tell you, my husband is happy with the change."

He tamped down the sting to his professional pride. Kate's reminder went through his mind that sometimes women would not confide intimate details to a male, even a professional like himself. Had he missed something? A clue that could have unlocked the secret to her pain? One that Gemma, being female, had understood?

"What was in the powder?" he asked.

"I don't know but it works like a miracle far better than the ones you gave me. In fact, if it keeps working, there will be a tenth baby in the Woodman household." She laughed as she bragged. He'd never seen her so carefree.

"That is good news." And then he had to ask, "How does the powder present itself? What does it taste like?" What did Gemma know that he didn't?

Mrs. Woodman made a face. "It's a foul taste. The powder is dusty black and finely ground. I only use a pinch in some mayweed tea. She gives me that, as well. Then I'm to follow up the tea with a half a glass of rum. I'm to take the cure several times a day as I need. And there you have it. No headache."

Clever, clever Gemma. He was certain the powder was charcoal and had little effect on headaches. He knew nothing of mayweed tea but presumed it was fine. However, he suspected the rum was adding to Mrs. Woodman's new attitude about life.

And Gemma claimed she didn't use spirits.

Actually, he should have thought of this solution himself. Daniel Woodman was not an easy man on his best days and nine children, with the oldest being fifteen, would certainly be enough to make Ned need to drink.

"I'm happy it is working for you," he said.

She nodded, almost giddily, and took off down the road.

An hour later Ned was sharing this story with Balfour and Kate.

"It's genius, actually," he admitted. "All this time I was taking Mrs. Woodman's complaints as a medical issue when actually, she was just overwhelmed."

"Well, a tenth child won't help," Balfour observed.

"I can't even imagine living through a pregnancy ten times," Kate murmured. She appeared tired today. She stretched as if her back ached.

Ned wondered if she had been eating properly. He had given her the lecture, that she had to force herself toward nourishment, whether she had an appetite or not. "You don't have much longer. It will soon be over," he assured her.

Her response had been a weak smile.

Looking at her now, he sensed something bothered her. He could only hope she went into labor soon. Once this was behind her and she held her baby in her arms, she would recover whatever strength she lost.

At that moment they were interrupted by the arrival of none other than the Earl of Marsden.

Mars charged into the room, a force of nature. His eyes were clear, his skin healthy, his energy intact. The opium was once again behind him.

His gaze went straight to Ned. "I knew you'd be here." Without waiting for an invitation and with the familiarity of longtime friendship, he threw himself into a chair close to Ned and leaned forward. "What is this I hear about you giving Winderton a drubbing?"

"What?" Balfour sat up. Even Kate grew alive.

"You haven't heard?" Mars said to them. "I feared I was the last one. Why is it, Thurlowe, that your closest friends do not know you used fisticuffs on our young duke?" His eyes danced with anticipation of the story.

"I don't know why you haven't heard. Everyone else in the parish seemed to know minutes after it happened."

"Did you give him a blow in the middle of his arrogant face?" Balfour asked. "Please say you did."

"Brandon," Kate said in surprise and then started laughing, a sound neither Ned nor her husband had heard for some time.

Balfour's eyes met Ned's. He was pleased. As if he wanted to encourage the topic if it made her happy, Balfour declared, "I've wanted to land a facer on him many times when I served as his guardian. And when he had his eye on you." He sat on the chair next to the upholstered one where Kate was. "Let me say that when he showed up in the area recently, he was smart to not come calling on us."

"No, apparently, he was busy making Thurlowe's life difficult," Mars chimed in. "So what is the story, Doctor? And did it really involve chickens?"

"Chickens?" Kate repeated, and Ned had to oblige with a telling. He started with the attempt to steal Gemma's papers. He didn't tell about her being attacked. Fitz had become one of Gemma's most ardent admirers, and Ned didn't see a purpose to bringing up the matter other than to mention that, "Winderton had instigated some other nasty pranks to pester Gemma. The locals would do whatever he suggested."

"Which must please him," Balfour murmured.

"Pleased, in the past tense," Mars said. "Winderton has left the area."

"Where did he go?" Ned asked. "And why did we not know this?"

Balfour answered, "Because we don't have time for gossip."

That was true. Especially since Ned had been keeping to himself.

"Where did he go?" Mars shrugged. "Wherever dukes who need to grow up go. Probably London."

"Poor Mrs. Estep," Kate observed.

"To be honest, and I mean this as no criticism of you, Kate, but since you broke his young, unruly heart, Winderton has been at loose ends," Mars said. "He was cutting quite a path in London when he was there . . . for a time. The rumor was he was not making the right friends. Or honoring his obligations." He referred to gambling debts.

Kate frowned and Balfour took her hand. "This has nothing to do with you, my dear. I've lectured Winderton on the dangers of flying too high and keeping bad company. He was warned. Now it is up to him to heed those warnings."

"Perhaps he should stay away from London," she said.

Mars shrugged. "He is a grown man. I had to learn to navigate the waters at a young age and so should he."

She nodded somberly then looked to Ned, the sparkle returning to her eye. "Tell us about the fight."

How could he refuse? Of course, he embellished it. They all studied his face and could see no marking. Mars announced that he'd heard Winderton had appeared completely battered.

It was a good afternoon. One of shared friendship. Kate sent word to the cook to prepare a light supper and the Three Bucks enjoyed being together again.

Kate didn't stay long with them. She had barely touched her food when she stood, bringing them to their feet, and announced, "I believe I need to rest." She placed her hand on the small of her back. "I hear that most women when their time is near feel a surge of energy. Tonight will not be the night. Enjoy your evening, gentlemen."

Balfour started to escort her out of the room. She waved him back. "I can go up the stairs alone. Stay and talk to your friends." She kissed his cheek and left.

Still, her husband trailed behind her to the staircase before returning.

The three friends gathered at the table. Mars launched into telling a story of one of his adventures in Parliament. He was not the most earnest member of the Lords and he appreciated the gossip more than the legislation. He was also an excellent mimic so his stories were engaging. He was interrupted by a maid in the doorway, her eyes wide with fear.

"Sir, Mrs. Balfour, she is on the steps. She has been there. She can't get up—"

The men jumped to their feet and raced each other to the front stairs. Kate sat on a step two-thirds of the way up. She looked down at them, her face pale. "I think the baby is coming."

The hem of her gown was wet. Her water had broken, or, at least, Ned hoped it was water. Her skirts were a dark blue so it was hard to tell.

Mars discreetly stayed at the foot of the stairs as Ned and Balfour went up to her. She held her arms out to her husband. "I don't feel anything. I think she wants to be born, but I don't have any pain the way they said I should. What does this mean?"

The water breaking without contractions was not a good sign, but Ned didn't want to say anything until he knew more. He forced a smile. "It means we should see you to your bed right now." He looked to the maid standing at the top of the stairs. "Is her bed ready?" He had already spoken to Kate and her housekeeper about what would be needed when the time came—blankets to protect the mattress, soft rags, and pitchers of warm water.

His question sparked the girl to action. She went running down the hall.

"Can you stand, Kate?" Ned asked.

She was very pale. "I don't know."

She'd barely finished the words before Balfour lifted his wife into his arms and carried her to their bedroom. The maid who had notified them followed in his wake and ran ahead when they reached the top of the stairs to open the bedroom door.

Ned followed them. In the bedroom, the maids hurriedly made preparations. A heavy blanket was thrown over the bed. It was soft wool. Balfour sat his wife upon it. Kate started to lie back and then stopped when she saw the expression on her husband's face. Balfour had noticed the swipe of blood on her white stockings. She had not yet. She now looked down.

Ned stepped forward and pulled a blanket

folded on the end of the bed up over her legs.
"Kate, all will be well." Or he hoped it would be.
The few human births he'd participated in had
started with contractions. This was different. He
sensed it in his bones.

He was not going to say that to Kate or Balfour.
He looked to the servants. "Please make your
lady as comfortable as possible." He grabbed Balfour's arm at the elbow and directed him out of
the room.

Of course, his friend resisted. "I don't want to
leave her."

"You must. I need to examine your wife, and
she will not want you here."

"Then I'll be right outside the door," Balfour
declared, speaking to his beloved wife as if to offer reassurance, except Ned heard an undernote.
If anything happened, he would be held responsible.

Once he had Balfour outside, Ned went to
work. To his relief, there were contractions. They
were just very mild and still a good fifteen minutes apart. An examination showed her body was
preparing for birth. The only difficulty was she
seemed to be carrying the baby too high and that
bothered him. What was holding the baby back
from the birth canal? And why was there a small
amount of blood in her water? He didn't know.

The hours passed. The contractions eventually
started coming closer. Now Kate felt them. She
was a strong woman and she bore them in good

grace. Ned reminded himself that some births took time. And, yet, he couldn't shake the sense that something was wrong.

The maids were a godsend. They put compresses on Kate's brow, they cooed encouraging words, they massaged her shoulders. Her husband and Mars paced outside.

But as the long hours of the night gave way to morning, then afternoon, Ned could see in the women's eyes that they were growing worried. One had a child. She understood what was happening. Kate was now in the active throes of labor. Her cries understandably upset her husband, who kept knocking on the door. Ned knew Balfour hated being unable to do anything for his wife. Ned felt powerless as well.

Kate's body seemed ready for birth, except the child had not dropped. Ned knew Kate could labor like this for days, and it would cost her life and her baby's—unless something was done. And having too-tired maids for help was not going to be enough. They had stopped their encouragement. They knew what was happening. Fear had silenced them.

Fear. And he was supposed to be the strong one.

Ned knew he had to do something. "I'm going to step out a moment," he said. Battered by contractions, Kate gave him a weak smile and he took that as assent.

Balfour was waiting right by the door. He was unshaven, and worry gave his face a mask-like countenance. He practically jumped on Ned. "What is going on? Does it usually take this long? It's been almost seventeen hours."

Mars had been stretched out in a hallway chair, attempting to sleep. He came to his feet.

"Sometimes it does take this long," Ned answered. "Or longer."

"How can she continue in pain?" Balfour asked. "Can't you make her comfortable?"

"Balfour, this is childbirth."

"I don't know if I can stand it much longer." He ran a hand over his face. "I don't even know if I believe you if you say it is normal."

Ned studied his friend for a moment. He hadn't made that claim. Balfour had assumed and he deserved some honesty. "It will grow worse."

His friend practically pounced on him. "Nothing is going to happen to her, is it?"

"I'm doing my best to see her through."

"And you will?"

God, there it was again. That demand for a promise. "Kate is strong. She's *strong*," he repeated as if words could make it true. "I'm also going to need help."

Balfour appeared almost pathetic in his desire to be of service to his wife. "Of course. Anything."

"You need to be here," Ned told him. "However, Mars?"

The earl stepped forward, almost as eager for action as Balfour.

"Fetch Gemma Estep."

Chapter Seventeen

*N*ed was never far from Gemma's thoughts in spite of her doing everything she could to keep busy.

She told herself she had regrets about turning him away. She was also grateful that he had come to her . . . that her feelings, especially the depth of them, were not one-sided. *He loved her.*

And she believed him. After so many betrayals, she hadn't lost her ability to trust. Who knew that would be such a gift?

She also loved him enough to let him go. To do what was best for both of them.

Even if she and Ned defied convention, if they eloped or ran away, the giving up of dreams that had meant so much to them would hang over their heads.

No, the only option was to do what was honorable. Or so she kept telling herself.

Her only antidote was work. She and Fitz had hung shelves and then she'd finished creating smelling salts with the awakening scent of peppermint. Her soaps were almost ready to be wrapped in paper and string, and she'd put her ointment for joint pain in small tins that Mr. Pointer, the tinker, had found for her.

That man was a godsend. She'd given Mr. Pointer a list of things she wanted and when he had them, he paid a call. Other items had to be ordered in the post, which took forever and was usually more costly.

She'd focused on what she could have, not what she couldn't. Just as she must with Ned Thurlowe.

Except . . . he had told her he loved her. Loved *her*.

And she held those words very close in her heart.

They were well into the afternoon when she heard a pounding on the kitchen door. She opened it cautiously. Lord Marsden was outside.

"Good afternoon, my lord."

"Gemma, I don't have time for manners. I require your assistance immediately. Mrs. Balfour is in labor and Thurlowe requested your help."

"My help? I'm not a midwife."

"I only do what I am told. Please come."

"Let me gather my herb bag."

"As long as you do it immediately."

Within minutes she was sitting behind Lord Marsden on the biggest horse she'd ever seen. She'd thrown on a cape but she'd been in too much of a hurry to fool with a bonnet.

"Hold on," he warned, and it was a good thing Gemma listened. Otherwise, she would have rolled off the back of the horse when the animal leaped into motion and hit the ground at a gallop. They raced through the village and would probably have run over anyone silly enough to step in their path.

Cradling her bag of herbs, teas, and salves between herself and Lord Marsden's body, Gemma prayed she would survive this trip. The horse continued to pick up speed as if he was some ethereal creature.

Gemma had never been to the Balfour home, although she'd heard much about it. Mr. Woodman was one of the carpenters and his wife, Agnes, always had tidbits of gossip lavishly shared amongst the matrons.

Now, charging up the drive, she could see Mr. Balfour pacing in front of the house, waiting for them. The beast came to an abrupt halt. Mr. Balfour had hurried forward and offered a steadying hand, which Gemma appreciated because she was ready to fall off the horse. Without a word to Lord Marsden, Mr. Balfour directed her up the stairs and through the front door.

"I am Brandon Balfour. Thank you for coming, Mrs. Estep," he said as they walked. He hustled her up the stairs.

"Gemma," she said, correcting him. "Please call me Gemma, and I am *not* a midwife."

"She's adamant that we know that," Lord Marsden said, following up the stairs behind them. He'd handed his horse off to a stable lad and hadn't bothered to remove his gloves or hat.

"Thurlowe sent for you and that is all that matters," Mr. Balfour said as a way of explanation. Like his friends, he was a broad-shouldered, handsome man. "Please, this way." He escorted her down a carpeted hall. The walls showed signs of where repairs were being done. "Pardon us," he murmured. "We are making changes to the house."

Gemma had heard of the renovations the Balfours had undertaken. She was curious. After all, she was making her own changes to The Garland. However, now was not the time to exchange thoughts on their projects.

From a door at the end of the hall came the sound of a woman's sharp cry of pain. A cry Gemma remembered too clearly coming from her own lips.

She tried to slow her step. "I'm not a midwife," she repeated almost breathlessly, when in truth, what she didn't want was to relive those moments of her own daughter being born. The daughter who she'd longed for and who had not lived.

Except, Mr. Balfour kept pushing her forward. He wasn't about to let her resist. They reached the door. Mr. Balfour knocked.

It opened. Ned was there. He appeared tired, exhausted . . . and she sensed something else. He was afraid.

In that moment, her reservations about helping with this birth vanished. Instead of herself, she thought of a patient in need, and the man she loved—and she did love him—asking for her help. When he looked at her with an expression that conveyed his need for her presence, all resistance ceased to matter.

He pulled her in. He shut the door, and she felt as if she'd entered a different world.

The drapes were pulled against the afternoon sun. The golden lamplight cast globes of light on the huge four-poster bed with its white sheets. There was a surreal calm inside the bedroom punctuated by the sound of a woman's breathing as she prepared for her next contraction.

Kate Balfour lay in the middle of the bed. She was pale. Too pale. She almost blended with the sheets. A maid held her hand while another sat in a chair, her head down as if defeated.

"How long has she been like this?" Gemma murmured.

"Labor started yesterday evening." Ned drew her to a far corner of the bedroom. He whispered, "I believe the cord is entangled."

An entangled cord? Anytime she'd heard of an entangled cord, it had meant death. The cord prevented the baby from leaving the womb. Gemma knew that much. The cord could suffocate the child, who would then need to be removed from the mother, an always dangerous and tragic task. Or, if the labor continued on without respite, both baby and mother would eventually die.

"Dear Lord." She looked up at Ned, wanting to help him and knowing she couldn't. "I'm not a midwife."

"I know. I didn't ask you here for that purpose."

"Then what can I do? I'm willing to help. I will do anything."

He smiled. "I knew you would. What I need is for you to work your Gemma magic."

"What?"

"Your Gemma magic," he repeated calmly, even as Mrs. Balfour gasped in pain.

Gemma's immediate response was to go to her. Ned turned her to face him. "I could lose her. I could lose the baby. I don't know how I can face Balfour if that happens."

Her heart broke for him. "This isn't in your hands, Ned."

"Right now it is. I must do something that may be unorthodox."

"Have you done it before?"

"On ewes."

Gemma blinked, uncertain she heard him correctly. "I don't know if this is the same thing."

"I'm hoping it is. Birth is birth and I learned what I'm about to do from an old shepherd. It worked."

It had to work. Gemma knew he had no choice—except, deep emotions threatened to take over. Life was so fragile.

He noticed. "Are you all right?"

"I'm not as strong as you believe I am." She couldn't speak above a whisper. "I lost a baby."

"Gemma, I'm sorry. I didn't know." His arms came around her and she leaned into him. Almost two years ago she'd been so alone . . . and she'd longed for this empathy. "I shouldn't have asked you here."

There was another contraction. Another gasping groan. Oh, yes, Gemma knew what Kate Balfour was going through. Gemma could almost feel the way pain racked through her body.

"Was your baby stillborn?" he asked gently.

"No, she was born. She was perfect. She died a few days after. I put her in the crib and when I checked on her not even an hour later, she was gone." She couldn't take her eyes off Kate Balfour. She might not have the opportunity to hold her baby. "What do you want me to do?"

He let out his breath as if in relief. "Be there for her. She is the one who told me women tell each other what they won't say to men. I want you to talk to her. Guide her."

How could she refuse him? "Has there been movement?"

"A little."

"Then we'd best start."

His arms tightened momentarily around her. "Right." He spoke to the maids. "Ladies, I need to ask you to leave."

The maid beside Mrs. Balfour shook her head. "We need to be here for the mistress. We must."

"And you have been excellent," Ned assured them. "The time has come for Gemma to spell you."

The maids exchanged looks.

Then Mrs. Balfour helped. "Go on." Her voice was faint.

The maids bowed and left.

After the door closed behind them, Mrs. Balfour said, "So you are Gemma."

Gemma crossed to the side of the bed. "I am." The woman didn't have much energy left.

"I've heard . . . much about you—" A contraction robbed her of words. Gemma took her hand. She dared to sit on the bed so that she was closer to the patient.

Gemma said, "When I went through this, I was told to breathe deep." Mrs. Balfour squeezed her hand, a sign of the pain she was in. "And to be brave," Gemma offered.

A tear escaped Mrs. Balfour's eye. "I'm not very brave right now. I want this over. I want this over."

Any lingering reservations Gemma had evaporated. Kate was a woman in need. Gemma untied the strings of her cape, letting it slip off her shoulders. "It will be over soon."

"I don't think it will end," was the tortured response.

"It will," Gemma assured her. "And I'm going to tell you a secret that helped me when I gave birth—you don't go through childbirth often in life. At least, that is true of most of us. Yes, it is painful but the reward is worth it, especially if you embrace this process. Don't fight it."

"Something is wrong, isn't it? There is something wrong. I was afraid this would happen."

"Shush now. You must help your baby. You need to relax if it is possible."

"Relax?" Mrs. Balfour sounded as if she would have boxed Gemma's ears for the suggestion. Except she was too weak.

Soothing her voice, Gemma said, "Work with us."

Mrs. Balfour stared at the ceiling. "Dear God." Whether she was entreating the Almighty, or begging Gemma to be quiet, she did not say.

Ned now came to the bed. He had greased his hands.

At that moment Mrs. Balfour cried out, this one stronger than any before. It was practically a shriek.

The door flew open. Her husband came charging in. He stopped, stood as if uncertain, and then shut the door. "I *won't* leave. I don't know what is happening, but I'm not leaving Kate."

His wife started to speak but was robbed of words by another contraction. They were coming hard now.

Gemma said close to her ear, "Breathe deep. We are all here."

Kate looked at her as if she wished they were all someplace else.

Gemma took that as a good sign.

Mr. Balfour pleaded his case to Ned. "I'm not leaving. I lived in India. Things are not as distant there as they are here. I've seen childbirth."

"Could I make you leave?"

"No."

"Then stay," Ned answered. "But do not interfere. Do you understand? You will *not* interfere."

"I won't interfere." He came around the other side of his wife's bed.

"What is happening?" Mrs. Balfour asked. She sounded almost desperate.

"Mr. Thurlowe is going to help your baby be born," Gemma responded carefully. He was already folding up the sheet covering Kate's legs.

Mrs. Balfour was no fool. Her brows came together. "Is something wrong? Something is wrong, isn't it?" Gemma didn't know if she should answer. Mrs. Balfour grabbed her husband's hand. She used it as leverage to try to rise.

"Kate, relax." Ned spoke with authority.

His patient stopped struggling.

"Your baby wants to come out and he can't. I believe the cord is wrapped around him and I'm going to reach in and see if I can feel exactly where the problem is. If I can, I hope to free him from the cord."

"You can do that?" she asked.

"Of course," Ned answered as if she'd asked him to walk across the room.

Gemma leaned close to Kate. "Look at me," she ordered.

Kate obeyed.

"It will all be fine. It will."

Kate nodded mutely, and then flinched as Ned checked on the baby. He spoke as he did so. "I can feel him. He is a good size. Feeling for the cord now." Tense moments passed—

Abruptly, Ned jumped up on the bed, boots and all. "Back off, both of you."

To Mr. Balfour's credit, he did as ordered, in fact, quicker than Gemma, who was confused. To her shock, Ned picked up Kate's heels and lifted them. "Balfour, help me."

"Help you what?"

"We are going to shake her upside down."

"What?"

But Ned was not in an explaining mood. He'd already had Kate up in the air. While Mr. Balfour stared dumbstruck, Gemma rose on the mattress to help. She had no idea what Ned was doing, but she trusted him.

Yes, trust. She believed in him as she had no other. She helped him give Kate several hard shakes. Kate was like a rag, doing whatever they wished.

"Let her down," Ned said, and then he reached in. "Yes. That is what it took."

"What?" Mr. Balfour asked again.

"The movement loosened the cord." Ned freed his hand. "I managed to lift it off."

"Lift it off his neck?" Mr. Balfour repeated.

"Kate, *push*," was Ned's answer.

Gemma scrambled across the bed to position herself behind Kate so that her back was against her chest. "Yes, Kate, push. *Come, push.*"

The woman was beyond exhausted and yet she found that extra bit of energy.

"He's coming," Ned said. "*Push*, Kate."

Mr. Balfour stood by the side of the bed, his face an expression of fear, then shock, and then wonder as with deep shuddering breaths of ex-

ertion his wife brought his daughter into the
world.

And when the first cries were heard, he fell to
his knees.

Ned held the baby up as if she was a trophy.
"Congratulations, Mr. and Mrs. Balfour."

Kate began laughing and crying. Her husband
climbed onto the mattress to rain kisses all over
her face.

Gemma extricated herself from the celebra-
tion, rising from the bed. Ned handed the baby
to her and she carefully carried the wee one to
a basin to clean while he took care of the after-
birth. The child was perfectly formed. Ten toes,
ten fingers, two eyes, and a mouth that let the
world know that her coming into the world had
not been easy.

The baby settled after Gemma had cleaned her
and wrapped her in a cloth. For a second, she held
the child before taking her over to her mother.
"She's beautiful," Gemma murmured in wonder.
"She's just beautiful."

Mrs. Balfour found the strength to take her
daughter in her arms. Tears welled in Gemma's
eyes as she remembered holding her child the
first time. Her baby had been perfect, too. And
such a gift, even for the short span of her life—

Her memories were interrupted by a knock on
the door. Lord Marsden called, "I'm out here. All
of you are in there. Is everything fine?"

He sounded so comical that they all laughed.

Mr. Balfour kissed his wife one more time before he walked to the door and opened it. He proudly announced to his friend and the servants, "I have a daughter. A *daughter.*"

There was a smattering of clapping. Lord Marsden called out, "Congratulations, Kate. Well done. And do we have a name for the newest Balfour?"

Looking down at her child, she smiled as she said, "Anne. For Bran's mother." Her husband leaned over and kissed the top of his child's head as if giving a blessing.

Then he did something that truly moved Gemma. He kissed his wife's cheek. A simple, heartfelt kiss. And was it her imagination? Was there a tear of gratitude in his eye?

How different this was from when Gemma herself had given birth. She'd been alone with no one but the midwife to attend her. She hadn't even been in the house of her birth, having been evicted by the man who had won it at the gaming tables from Paul only a few months before.

But that was the past.

And right now, in the present, she had witnessed a miracle.

No midwife would have had the knowledge or the daring to save this baby. Any other doctor of her acquaintance would have backed off. Certainly, they wouldn't have been as involved in seeing the birth through. Ned had been bold. He'd saved that baby. Without him, the scene in front of her would have been a far different one.

Maids entered the bedroom and began cleaning up. They fluffed pillows so the new mother could relax.

Almost as if from a distance, Gemma heard Ned suggest, "Shall we go?"

He was speaking to her. He'd scrubbed himself clean and had donned his jacket. He held her embroidered bag with his medical case. He looked the same—and entirely different. The air around him seemed to move, to single him out. He was like no other—

"Gemma?" He smiled, offered his hand. "We should leave," he prodded in a soft voice.

She nodded mutely and was actually surprised that her legs could move. That no time seemed to have elapsed, and yet, everything had changed. *Everything*. She took her cape from the maid who held it.

Just as they reached the bedroom door, Kate said, "Gemma, thank you for coming. You helped."

"She did, didn't she?" Ned said proudly. "I'll be by to check on you tomorrow."

"Enjoy your baby," Gemma said. She wanted to add that they were lucky to have their wee Anne. That if it hadn't been for Ned . . . Well, perhaps they understood that already. He touched her arm at the elbow and left the room.

Down in the front hall, Lord Marsden was preparing to take his departure. A stableman had brought up his big, bold horse. He set his hat on his head at a rakish angle and admitted, "I don't know how you did that, Thurlowe. Things weren't as easy as we hoped, were they?"

"A touch more difficult than I had anticipated."

And Gemma had to jump in. "That is an understatement, sir. That child is *alive* because of you."

His golden eyes met hers. Did he realize how deeply she admired him? Their gazes held—and in that second, she knew he understood everything she wanted to say . . .

Lord Marsden cleared his throat in the sudden silence. "Well." He glanced from Gemma to Ned and frowned with interest. Could he feel the attraction between them?

Did she care?

"You succeeded and that is all that matters," the earl finished as if they had been having a conversation. And then he followed it with, "I think I need to find something to drink. And my bed. I feel as if I am the one who's given birth."

Gemma gave his comment a wan smile, but truth be told, she could not pull her gaze from Ned's.

"Good day to you, Gemma. Thurlowe."

Ned glanced at his friend as if surprised to see him still standing there. He pulled his attention from Gemma. "Good day to you, my lord."

They watched him leave with his loose-limbed stride. He climbed on his beast of a horse and Gemma leaned close to Ned to say, "I knew you were a good doctor, but this was different. You have a rare gift."

He laughed as if her praise embarrassed him, as if to disavow her words—and that, too, made her love him. Oh, yes, Ned could be stubborn and resistant to anything he couldn't control, but he was also kind and fair-minded and humble. His strengths, his faults . . . made him practically perfect.

The butler interrupted them. "Excuse me, sir, Mrs. Estep. The master ordered a coach to bring you home. It is outside now." And so it was. Gemma hadn't even noticed the hansom team and vehicle that had apparently arrived after Lord Marsden had left.

"I have my horse," Ned said.

"A lad is already riding your horse to your home and will see him put up. Mr. Balfour's orders."

"Thank him for us, please," Ned said.

Us. They were an *us.*

He looked to Gemma. "Are you ready, then?"

"Yes." She knew she sounded distracted, and yet, she sensed he understood.

The sun was setting as Gemma and Ned climbed into the coach. She was surprised that the day had grown so advanced. She'd lost all sense of time in the birthing room.

Everyone in Maidenshop knew this coach was new and Mr. Balfour's pride and joy. Plush velvet covered the vehicle's seats and walls. The quarters were also tight. There was no way for her leg not to brush against his, especially once the coach started moving . . . not that she was interested in pulling away. She looked down at their ungloved hands that were inches from each other.

He leaned back and closed his eyes. He had to be spent. Gemma understood the herculean effort he had made for his friends. It was a challenge to stay alert and aware by a bedside for hours on end. The labor had been difficult but also boring for those in attendance. Then there was always a moment of reckoning—one wrong move and they'd be mourning instead of rejoicing.

Except *he'd* guided them through. *He* had saved the baby and the mother.

And suddenly, all the common-sense objections to why she should keep her distance vanished.

Life was fragile. Fleeting.

Before she could process her actions, before she could tell herself to stop, Gemma leaned over and kissed him fully on the lips with all the passion in her being.

Chapter Eighteen

Gemma was kissing him.

Or was he dreaming?

Ned was exhausted. The nervous energy that had driven him for the past days had left him weary. At the same time, he was very aware of Gemma's scent of lavender and spice. Or that his hand was close enough to hers that if he just moved his fingers he could touch her.

She'd come to him today. He'd needed her support. He'd trusted she wouldn't panic, that she would help Kate through this and he'd not been disappointed.

Now, Gemma, who days before had rejected his love, was kissing him. A burst of energy sang through him.

He pulled her up into his lap, the better to be close to her. Her hands cupped his whiskered face. Their tongues met. The kiss deepened.

God, he could feel the heat of her. *She* wanted him. He could have shouted his joy to the heavens, but he didn't want this kiss to ever end. He wrapped his arms around her. She moved to straddle him.

Was he dreaming . . . ?

His hand began searching for the hem of her skirts, pulling the material up her leg until he could feel the flesh of her thigh. She twisted the button of his breeches.

If this was a dream, it was a *very* good one.

There was no pause in her unbuttoning. There was nothing coy about her—and that was one of the things he realized he adored about her. She was direct, bold, and as hungry for him as he was for her. He cupped her bottom, feeling himself free of his breeches and strong and proud. It pushed between them. They were quiet, aware of the coachman.

Gemma shifted and then sank down on him.

Just like that. No preamble, no flowery phrases— she was perfect in every way.

The kiss broke.

She gave a shuddering sigh that he caught in his mouth, letting it echo through him. She was hot, tight. He kissed her gently, then deeper, then deeper. Slowly, matching the sway of the coach, he lifted his hips and moved in her.

The world centered on their joining. Ned kissed her lips, her chin, her throat. Gemma met him for every thrust—this was so bloody good. So satisfying in a way he'd never experienced before. She felt right.

He felt right being here with her.

Her muscles tightened. She held him. *"Ned."*

That one word. His name. He loved hearing it on her lips. She pressed herself against him. He could feel the wave rolling through her, and he rode it with her. And then he thrust once, twice, and found his own blessed release.

Her body collapsed into his arms. Her breath was hot against his neck. He held her as both their hearts slowly returned to normal. He stretched out her arm, entwining his fingers with hers.

And all was perfect in the world.

GEMMA DIDN'T believe she could ever move again, and she had no wish to. She wanted to stay right here, connected with him, until the end of her days.

So, *this* was what the world acclaimed. The *pinnacle of desire* praised by poets in flowery language.

They had not lied.

Once she'd started kissing Ned, she'd not been able to keep her hands off him. It was as if touching him bewitched her.

She had not been fond of the act during her marriage. It had seemed vulgar, senseless, and messy. Paul had always enjoyed himself and she'd done it because she'd wished to be a good wife. She'd never once thought about desire.

She'd never once initiated their coupling.

What she'd just done to Ned had been out of character. Except, his touch, his response to her kiss, had opened something inside her. She had not been able to stop herself from jumping in his lap. She believed she'd acted wanton—but he did not seem to mind.

In fact, with Ned, she was always herself. She never repressed her thoughts on any subject. She spoke her mind, and he spoke his.

In that moment, the intensity of what had just happened between them upended her doubts about men and women. Something shimmering and bright hovered in the air between them. It beckoned her to trust, to let herself believe again—

The coach started to slow. They had reached Maidenshop.

She slid off his lap and pulled her skirts down. Ned didn't move. Instead, he turned his head toward her. His lips curved into a satisfied smile. Dear Lord, he was so handsome, but not because of the arrangement of his eyes and his nose. No, what made him handsome in her sight were his values, his willingness to give his all, his intelligence, and even his stubbornness.

"Do you think we can ask him to drive up and down this road a few times more?"

His question startled a laugh out of her. "What a good idea." Her body still hummed. She felt full, content . . . and eager for more. Unfortunately, one of them had to have their wits about them. "Although, we'd best put ourselves together before the coachman catches us."

With a regretful sigh, he began rebuttoning his breeches.

She glanced outside. The sun was almost down on a mild early evening. Mr. Burnham was out in his front garden talking to his brother, the blacksmith, as if they had finished up late and were parting company. The lights were on in Mrs. Warbler's house.

She prayed the woman didn't see her arrive in the coach and notice her companion. There would be more lectures and who knows what recriminations—

No. Gemma would not entertain any regrets. Not one. She would never apologize for what had just happened between herself and Ned.

The coach rolled to a stop in front of The Garland.

Ned jumped out and offered Gemma his hand. As he helped her down, she gave his hand a squeeze. He lifted it to his lips. "We're not done here—" he promised.

She prayed he wasn't, and yet common sense was returning. Her strongest desire was ready to throw herself at him again. She was saved from doing so by Mrs. Warbler calling to the coachman. She was on the other side of the coach and had not yet seen them.

"Here now. Are you from the Balfour estate?"

Ned's mouth flattened in annoyance. "She knows this is Balfour's coach. She is the one who shared the news when he purchased it."

And then Mrs. Warbler was coming around the coach. "Oh, Gemma, there you . . . are." The woman's steps slowed as she took in Mr. Thurlowe's presence . . . and that he still held Gemma's hand. "Oh." The word sounded faint, dismayed. It was followed by a stronger *"Oh"* as her neighbor formed her conclusions.

He released her hand.

"Mr. Thurlowe," Mrs. Warbler said, acknowledging his presence. His name was a statement in and of itself. She seemed to force the next words out. "Do we have good news about the Balfours?"

"We do. Mr. and Mrs. Balfour are the proud parents of a baby girl. I believe they are naming her Anne," he said as if tossing the woman a bone of gossip.

"Ah, isn't that lovely?" Her words would have been more sincere if the clock wheels of her mind weren't turning frantically. "Gemma, do you feel quite the thing?"

That was an odd question. "Yes, I do."

"Your lips are very chapped. They are red and a bit swollen. Your skin on your cheeks seems a bit chapped, as well."

From *his* whiskered jaw.

And her lips were still remarkably sensitive.

Gemma laid her hand against her face. "I feel a bit hot. There must be something in the air. If you will excuse me?"

She would have made her escape, except Mrs. Warbler wasn't done with her. "Were you with Mr. Thurlowe this afternoon?"

Such an innocent question. Such a silly one.

He answered, "She was. I requested her help. Sometimes a woman will share with another woman what she is too shy to say to her doctor. As a healer, I thought Gemma would be great help, and she was."

"Was she?" Mrs. Warbler echoed. "I mean, I didn't know that you knew about childbirth, Gemma."

"You doubt me, Mrs. Warbler?" Gemma asked.

"Oh, no. I am one of your greatest supporters. And we do need a midwife. We can't rely on Mary."

"Actually," Gemma said, "Mr. Thurlowe was a most excellent male midwife."

"Although I am not going to do it as a regular calling," Ned was quick to add.

Mrs. Warbler studied them both for a moment, her suspicions obvious.

Gemma remained stoic, meeting her eye, refusing to feel guilty, and also knowing she should. What they'd done had been wrong, so very wrong . . .

The coachman interrupted the tension of the moment. "Are you ready to be driven to your house, Mr. Thurlowe?"

"Actually, I will walk from here," Ned said.

"I'm obliged to drive you, sir," the coachman answered. "The master was quite clear."

"It's a nice evening. The air will feel good," Ned said. "You have done your duty."

"Very well, sir." The coach pulled away to the

crossroad and made a huge circle before he drove past them on his way home. The three of them stood, watching. Gemma knew Mrs. Warbler's mind was a hive of questions—questions that were not going to be answered.

Questions she needed time to consider.

She pretended to yawn, the action allowing her to withdraw her hand from his. "It's been an eventful day." That was an understatement. "If you will excuse me?" Before she left, she turned to Ned. "Thank you. You are a remarkable doctor." *And so much more.*

Their eyes met. His were laughing. Did he not know the anger Mrs. Warbler could bring down upon them?

Gemma didn't want to have regrets over what had happened in the coach. But now, back to her everyday life, she needed to sort things out.

Ned took her hint. "Good night, Gemma, Mrs. Warbler." On those words, with a tip of his hat, he went walking down the road.

"He is feeling very good about himself," Mrs. Warbler observed.

"As he should. He saved that baby."

"Ah, the baby. What are the details about the baby?"

"Her name is Anne. It was a long labor."

"Did she have hair?"

"Mrs. Warbler, I must say good night." Gemma moved toward the door. "Please excuse me."

"I'm disappointed you don't have more information."

"Perhaps on the morrow, Mrs. Warbler." Gemma opened the door. She gave a little wave so as not to offend and then slipped inside.

The moment she closed the door, she fell back upon it. All was silent . . . and she felt very alone. Her body still reverberated with the passion of what she'd just done in the coach. She never wanted to let this feeling go, because it could not happen again. Her conscience and reality had returned.

Nothing could come of a liaison between her and Ned. "Clarissa Taylor." She whispered the name. She had to remember Clarissa's claim on him . . . and yet, she would not trade one second of having him inside her. Of being that close to him. Of knowing the taste of his skin or how well their bodies melded together.

"Do not feel guilty," she warned herself. She pushed away from the door and walked across the darkening rooms to the kitchen, her footsteps echoing hollow.

Who knew if she could ever allow another man to touch her?

Carefully, she stoked the fire and added more wood. The flames sent a golden glow around the room. Tea would be nice. Would be settling—and that is when she finally let it hit her, how alone she was.

And yet, this aloneness was different than what she'd experienced with a husband who had ignored her. Or having to build a life for herself. This came from a sense of loss.

She was being silly. "You can't love him." *Oh, but she could. She did.*

"He's not yours." *No, he wasn't.* Which made having him in her arms more poignant.

"I'm going to go mad," she assured herself. *You already are—madly in love with a man you admire.*

"And can never have," she reminded herself, her jaw beginning to ache from fighting back tears she had no right to shed. Instead, she reached for the kettle and saw that she needed more water.

Of course.

She picked up the pail to go fetch it but as she opened the door, a figure stepped into view. There he was, filling the doorway as if her arguments had conjured him.

She dropped the bucket. "Ned."

His answer was to swoop her up in his arms. He walked her back into the kitchen, kicking the door shut. Their lips locked, his fingers already unlacing her dress.

Gemma didn't question. She acted. She tugged on his shirt and pushed his jacket down his arms. He loosened her dress. It fell to the floor between them. Her breasts were already firm and hard and his breeches were full. She started to unbutton them. She'd have him right here, on the brick floor if necessary—and then that voice inside her said, *No.*

"We can't do this." She sounded crazed. She *was* crazed.

His hands started to come down on her shoulders. "Gemma—"

She caught his wrists, not trusting what would happen if she let him touch her further. "We can't, Ned."

Once she'd tried to deny Paul and he had been furious. She looked up into Ned's eyes, begging him to understand. "We mustn't. It will just be harder. And then what will happen the next time we are tempted?"

His jaw tightened. She braced herself, and then his weight shifted. He leaned back, away from her. She let him go. "Did the matrons corner you again?" He didn't sound angry. Although it was hard to read what he was thinking.

"No, this is me. Ned, I'm sorry. I shouldn't have in the coach—"

"*We* shouldn't have," he corrected. "God help me, Gemma, do not apologize. I was as much a participant as you were."

"It was wrong—"

"*I love you.* It can't be wrong to want you in my arms, in my bed?"

"And I love you, too. I so love you."

In the stillness of the kitchen, her words seemed to wrap around them. *They loved . . . and they shouldn't.*

Her chest felt tight. She held herself very steady. She broke the silence. "When I first arrived in Maidenshop, I believed that love was some child's tale told to women to make them line up and obey. I was tired and I was angry. I felt betrayed. I also didn't like you very much."

"We were at odds." A slight smile softened his features. He stood with his hands at his sides. The light from the candle and the fire played across the handsome features of his face, his shoulders. "But you are not the only one who resisted, Gemma. Not the only one who was angry. I didn't believe women were to be trusted. You've proved me wrong. Slipped past my guard. I've come to know you as one of the most generous, intelligent of souls. More important, I trust you. You were the only one I knew I could turn to with Kate and her baby. I believed you would come, and you did."

"I also attacked you in the coach."

Her words hung in the air a moment before he tilted his head and laughed.

She was entranced. She'd never heard Ned laugh. The sound of it was better than music . . . until he sobered.

"We are standing almost naked in your kitchen. There is a bed in the other room."

She placed her hand against his hard jaw. "Are you willing to jilt Clarissa Taylor?"

His manner changed. He tensed. "I love you."

"Will you jilt Clarissa?" Gemma repeated.

A bleakness came to his eye. "It would ruin her."

"I know."

"She doesn't love me. She barely knows me and that is more my fault than hers."

Gemma nodded, her throat tightening. He was right because once Clarissa knew the full measure of this man, she couldn't help but love him as much as Gemma did. And that hurt.

He looked away and released his breath slowly. "We can't do this, can we?" He indicated the clothes on the floor at their feet, the room, their love.

"I can't hurt her that way. Neither can you." And then, to her horror, the dam broke inside her. A sob escaped and she would have collapsed save for his arms coming around her.

He carried her to a chair at the table and sat. He held her in his lap as if she was precious to him. She placed her head in the crook of his neck and let the tears come until she was spent.

For a long time they were quiet. She never wanted to forget the scent of him or the feel of his arms around her.

Or the way he looked so earnest when he said he loved her.

A rooster crowed in the distance, too early for it to be dawn. Athena appeared from where she hid and observed them solemnly before padding off into the darkness of the taproom and beyond.

"You must go," she whispered. She traced the profile of his face with one finger. He caught her finger with his lips and then pressed his face into her palm.

"Gemma," he said, her name a benediction— and then she rose to stand aside.

He came to his feet, as well.

A last kiss was tempting . . . They both turned away. He picked up his jacket from the floor, buttoned what she had undone, and left.

Gemma watched him go, and then realized she'd been wrong—her tears had not been spent. She collapsed to the floor and let them come.

NED BEGAN to feel as if he was living two lives.

One was as that of the doctor promised to a lovely, congenial woman whom he had no desire to kiss.

The other was as a man who had lost his best friend, his chance for happiness, and often, his equilibrium. What sort of world brought Gemma into his life when he could not have her?

His wedding day was fast approaching. He still called on Clarissa for fifteen minutes every Friday for the short time they had left. He sat with her and her guardians during Sunday services. He struggled to keep his gaze from drifting to wherever Gemma was sitting, especially when the banns were announced.

Any planning for the Frost lecture he turned over to Royce . . . because it would be too difficult for Ned to share this project closest to his heart with the woman who owned The Garland and not make a fool of himself. He gave instructions and his faithful man carried them out, offering Ned a report almost every evening. Ned discovered his dream had lost its luster.

However, to his surprise, many of the village women were interested in the topic of the heavens and the stars and were excited to attend. Because their wives were interested, more married men were committed to attend than last year. And that was without the lure of all the ale they could drink and rook pie.

Gemma had also opened her tea garden. From all accounts the gardens themselves were a mere shadow to what they would become by summer. People didn't mind. The Garland presented itself as a cozy hub for the community, especially once the tinker found the duckpins Gemma wanted. Immediately, the Logical Men's Society returned to the tavern.

Oh, Ned didn't go at all and neither did Mars very often. However, as the spring days grew longer, the lads, the same ones who had plotted an attack on Gemma and filled her rooms with chickens, became her strongest supporters. They now spent hours in the evenings bowling. Ned even heard they were good-natured when Gemma informed them that they'd had a wee too much to drink and needed to go home.

Their mothers were very happy.

Occasionally, Ned would come face-to-face with Gemma where he had to speak to her. He'd turn a corner in the village and she would be there—so many chance meetings. And while each and every time he wanted to gather her into his arms, they acted cordial, distantly polite . . . and no one, Clarissa or the matrons, seemed the wiser to his true emotions swirling beneath the veneer. One thing Ned had learned in his growing up was how to pretend all was fine.

Of course, in truth, most in the village were

more interested in the plans for the upcoming Cotillion, the annual dance that was the social event of Maidenshop. The matrons organized it and they were a flurry of activity with plans and meetings.

No one gave a care about star-crossed lovers.

Or that Ned's newly discovered heart was broken, and might never be repaired.

Chapter Nineteen

$\mathcal{I}$t was late afternoon, the day of the Cotillion Dance.

The whole village was wrapped in excitement for the event and while there had been bustling earlier in the day, the street had become deserted as women and men took to their homes to prepare for the evening.

Gemma was not going. She couldn't. It was hard enough seeing Ned when it came to patients or passing him on the street. She didn't know if her fragile heart could weather watching him at an event where he would be expected to dance with his intended or where she'd hear congratulations and all the good wishes a couple received up until the wedding.

Her decision was not a popular one. She'd lost count of the number of times she'd been stopped on the street and asked if she was going. One of the Dawson lads—she *still* couldn't tell them apart—had been hinting broadly he hoped to see her at the dance. That he wouldn't mind "escorting her out onto the floor." He said this as if he was bestowing a great favor.

Jonathon Fitzsimmons had also shyly said that he looked forward to seeing her at the dance. She knew he was sweet on her, something his mother wanted to encourage.

The one who was the most persistent was Mrs. Warbler. "You are an attractive woman. You should remarry," had become her persistent refrain. "There will be men from far and wide at the Cotillion. You won't believe what an important event it is."

"I'm certain I won't," Gemma always murmured and tried to change the subject; no small task with her neighbor.

It had taken a good amount of time and all Gemma's effort to tamp down her disappointment at losing Ned. Work was a salve. She threw herself into her tasks because they helped keep thoughts of Ned at bay.

The worst moments were when she'd wake in the middle of the night, discontent, lost, adrift. That was when she'd truly lose herself in self-pity. Her gran had warned her that she had a dramatic mind. Gemma now understood what she meant. In those wee hours of the night, she'd start imagining scenarios of a long, empty life saved only by Ned's arrival when she was on her deathbed.

And it was all so silly.

And, yet, it hurt so bad that sometimes her soul couldn't breathe.

Nor did it help that Clarissa was such a lovely person.

At the same time she was also more than a bit naïve, more than a bit sheltered, more than a bit unaware of what marriage entailed. It seemed to Gemma that her friend looked at marriage as just a step in life. It was what women did. Off she goes!

And Gemma knew because that was the way she'd once been.

So she'd made it clear to one and all who asked that she didn't enjoy dances. She said she was too busy preparing for the lecture. She had responsibilities, a business, a life that had no room for frivolity.

Eventually, Mrs. Warbler and the others became too involved in their own plans to worry much about her, which is how Gemma told herself she wanted it.

The Cotillion morning had been very busy, although no one complained of headaches and pains and illness—not when there was a big dance to attend.

No, what had kept her blessedly busy was the number of visitors from the area who had come for the dance. Many mentioned they planned on attending the next day's lecture. They called on The Garland because they'd heard about her soaps and creams, her salves and teas. They complimented her on the changes to the building and the grounds.

However, by afternoon, trade had slowed to

a stop. Gemma was certain everyone had gone home to press their finery, style their hair, and pinch their cheeks to add color. She used to spend hours readying herself for dances in Manchester.

Now she had hours to not think about what was happening down the road in the old barn owned by St. Martyr's where the dance was held. She set to work wrapping more soaps for sale and dividing the salts into packets. It was messy but a welcome task because it kept her mind busy. She didn't worry about tomorrow's lecture because all was ready. She'd even plotted how she would avoid spending more time than necessary around Ned.

Oh, no, she did not need to see him this evening, although she was very aware that evening had fallen—

The bell tinkled in the main room. Who would be calling at this time? She thought everyone knew she was closed. She started to rise and then heard Clarissa's voice. "Gemma?"

"I'm in the kitchen."

What was this about?

Clarissa burst into the room looking more lovely than ever. Her honey-colored hair was piled on her head and her dress was a green so pale it could almost be white. She wore a locket around her neck and long gloves that had been a gift from the matrons.

"Clarissa," Gemma said in wonder. "You could pass for a lady of the first water."

Her friend laughed, pleased by the compliment. "Do you think Mr. Thurlowe will like me?"

There it was.

Gemma took a deep breath and spoke the truth. "He will believe you are the most beautiful woman there."

Clarissa's eyes sparkled. "I hope so." She took a step closer to Gemma. "I'm going to see if he'll kiss me tonight."

This was not a conversation Gemma wanted. "Clarissa—"

"He's kissed me," the woman charged on, speaking over Gemma's protest. "But I had to practically beg for it. Tonight, I want a real kiss."

"And what is a real kiss?" Gemma was thankful she was sitting.

"One he wants to give me. One from his heart."

"Ah." The word seemed to hang in the air and then, realizing more should be said, Gemma managed a weak, "I'm certain you will be successful—"

Clarissa cut her off with a gloved hand on her shoulder. "But I'm not here about my plans. Gemma, you must come to the dance."

Gemma picked up the tray of salt packets and rose from the chair, wanting to put distance between herself and Clarissa's idea. "I don't enjoy dances."

"I can't believe that is true," was the bold reply. "When I first met you, we talked about the dances you attended. You said you loved to dance."

"I've changed."

"Why?"

Gemma frowned, put out. "Where is this coming from? Who are you to tell me what I like and don't like?"

"Exactly." Clarissa straightened. "Now you are the person I know. I have no idea why you are hiding away, but please don't. This is going to be great fun and, to be honest, I need you there."

"Because?"

"Because I feel alone much of the time. And I wish I were like you. I wish I were brave enough to go out into the world as you have. You never appear to worry about what other people think."

Genuinely touched, Gemma said, "Clarissa, you are well loved in this village."

"Unfortunately, not always included. The Nelson girls have already let me know that I am not to dance with any of the young men they have an eye on, which is half the parish. People will congratulate me on my upcoming marriage and then whisper once I've passed that I'm an orphan, that I don't belong. It would be nice to have someone there I trust."

Someone she trusted. Gemma could relate to those words.

"Besides," Clarissa said, "you are a part of this community. You *need* to be there. This evening is about celebrating all of us."

The front doorbell tinkled again. A woman's voice called, "Clarissa, *come*. You only said you would be a minute."

Clarissa looked to Gemma and made a face. "That is Jane." Jane was one of Squire Nelson's daughters.

"The Nelsons are waiting for you?"

"Yes, out front. I begged them to let me talk to you."

"Clarissa, you must go," Gemma answered.

The girl placed a hand on Gemma's arm. "Please come. Please don't stay away. You are one of us. And I need you."

"I will think on it."

"Thank you." The words were heartfelt and then in a swirl of muslin as light as air, Clarissa left the room. A second later the door tinkled as it was closed.

And Gemma was alone. Hiding.

It wasn't very brave of her.

Her mood began to shift. Two months ago she'd come to Maidenshop with a determination she, herself, at Clarissa's age didn't know she had possessed. Today she was a member of this strong little community. Sooner or later she had to face Ned with Clarissa. She had to stop pretending to hide. Why, she'd see him tomorrow and probably her friend, as well.

Gemma walked to her bedroom. On a wall peg hung the dresses from her former life. Three dresses from when she'd been a rich man's daughter.

The time had come to shed her black, to stop moping about what could not be changed. She needed to be strong for herself.

Gemma reached for a dress of the deepest blue in a figured silk. It had been her father's favorite. He'd claimed it had been well worth the cost and she hadn't worn it since his death. She also hadn't been able to part with it.

If she was going to live in Maidenshop, Gemma knew she had to make her peace with Ned's marriage to Clarissa.

That meant finding the courage to go to the dance.

THE OLD barn where the Cotillion was held had apparently been a donation to the church a century or so ago from one of Mars's ancestors. Mars claimed it had to be a penance offering for some past lord's black soul. Whatever the reason, the village had held all important celebrations here ever since.

Last year's dance had dissolved into a brawl that would never be forgotten. The men had thought it good sport and the matrons were determined such a disaster would never happen again.

Therefore, they had stationed members of their group around the room, the doyennes of proper conduct in the village—and Ned, dutifully standing beside Clarissa, didn't know if he was sorry they were there. Or annoyed.

He resented the matrons, even though it had been his own damn empathy that prompted him to step up and offer for Clarissa. On one hand he could see reason, on the other, he felt trapped.

For her part, Clarissa appeared lovely. She was in a dress that brought out the green in her eyes. Many had looked at her covetously, and yet, she seemed oblivious, even toward him. She stood smiling and poised and he didn't have one idea of what was going through her head. Or a care to find out.

The Balfours had chosen not to attend. Baby Anne was doing well and they acted content with their simple life. Who knew when anyone in the village would see them again?

Meanwhile, everyone else was either on the dance floor, stomping to their heart's content while musicians churned out one lively tune after another, or standing in clusters grousing about the lack of a significantly strong punch this year. Apparently, last year's punch was blamed for the fight that broke out. It was no secret the lads had laced last year's punch with strong spirits, and now the matrons were guarding the bowl as if it were one of the crown jewels.

Mars came up beside him. The tall earl always cut a fine figure in his black evening dress. Most of the men were dressed more like Ned—they wore their best but they were country men, meaning polished boots and a clean jacket were fine.

"This place is as deadly boring as Almack's." Mars referred to the famed club in London known for its insipid punch and rigid rules.

"I wouldn't know. The hostesses of Almack's wouldn't let me past the door," Ned answered.

"You aren't missing anything. And I don't think I am missing anything here."

Clarissa pinned him with a look that would make a governess proud. "Instead of complaining, why don't you ask someone to dance, my lord?"

"I've already let Miss Nelson trample on my feet. And the Moncrieff chit has been stalking me as if I was a deer she'd set her sights on."

"She wouldn't if she knew you better," Clarissa answered.

The ghost of a smile crossed Mars's lips. "Perhaps you will enlighten her."

Clarissa grimly smiled her response.

Mars wiped that smile from her face by drawling, "Your training as a matron is advancing splendidly."

"What does that mean?"

"That I feel I'm caught between two children," Ned answered. Then realizing how petulant he sounded, he suggested instead, "Let us dance."

She nodded and offered her hand. As he led her toward where couples were taking their places for the next set, she said, "We usually don't have the opportunity to dance. Last year patients needed you and you had to leave early. The same thing happened the year before. Or were you even able to attend?"

"You know it is my calling, Clarissa."

"I do. I do. I'm just surprised, that's all." Her smile was tight. She had suggested several times they take a walk outside for the air. Ned had put her off. He wasn't in the mood to be alone with her tonight. He had the lecture on his mind . . . and that, too soon, they would be alone forever—

A movement by the door caught his attention. There was a flash of blue, of sun-gold red hair. A murmur of greeting went up, and then the crowd parted, and there was Gemma.

She was spectacular.

Her hair was piled high on her head with the regal manner of any London lady. Her dress was the deep cerulean of a summer sky. It set off the creamy perfection of her skin—

His feet tripped over themselves. He almost knocked Clarissa over, saving his dignity at the last moment.

And he didn't care. Gemma could have been wearing a sack and he would still have thought her the loveliest woman in the room.

Many greeted Gemma warmly and called to her to join their company.

Immediately, several men lined up to ask her to dance. Gemma was quickly claimed by a prosperous gentleman farmer from Newmarket.

Ned knew all of this because he was watching every movement around Gemma. Fortunately, the farmer didn't lead Gemma to the floor close to Clarissa and Ned so he was forced to give his intended his attention. That didn't make it any easier for him.

This was what his life was going to be like, he realized. He'd spend his days living for a glimpse of Gemma and then be eaten alive with jealousy as other men paid attention to her until, what? The *end* of their days?

Or she married? That realization was the specter of a fresh hell. How was he to keep his sanity?

As the evening progressed, Clarissa tried several times to practically pull him to Gemma. She succeeded just as Gemma had finished dancing with a very attentive Mars.

Ned wanted to grab his friend by his elegant jacket and dunk his head in the watered-down punch. Instead, he had no choice but to smile and pretend all was fine. He hated every second of this farce, especially the small talk.

Then, suddenly, for whatever reason, he and Gemma were alone.

Mars was dragged away by Mrs. Summerall, who claimed he owed her blushing niece from Haversford a dance. Miss Nelson begged Clarissa to retire to the lady's necessary room with her. Apparently, from the whispers Ned overheard, something had gone wrong with Miss Nelson's dress.

And he and Gemma were alone . . . in a room full of people milling about, laughing, enjoying themselves.

A million words were in Ned's mind, and not one could he speak aloud. Not here. So he stood, mute, aware that she wouldn't look at him. He wanted to tell her he understood. This was not easy.

It was *never* going to be easy.

Then abruptly, she turned and left, not just him but the dance.

He watched her go out the front door. He glanced around. Had anyone noticed?

Apparently not. The dancing went on. Sweeney was complaining about the punch. Fitz was trying to work up his nerve to ask Miss Lindlow to dance. Mrs. Warbler was eyeing a couple who were standing *too* close to one another.

No one seemed to have noticed.

Nor was anyone paying attention to him.

In that moment he had a vision of him and Gemma escaping from not just this gathering but also from the world . . . so he followed. He went out the door, making his way past those gathered outside. He looked down the road toward The Garland. He didn't see a figure in blue.

He walked around to the side of the building where it was quiet and dark. She was there. He sensed her presence before she stepped out of the shadows. "I couldn't stay there. It was suffocating."

He understood.

"You are beautiful," he said. He could see her blush in the darkness, and then she turned and began walking toward the back of the building. He followed, his step coming into line with hers.

Their hands met. Their fingers clasped. And that was all it took. He gave her a small tug and she whirled around and into his arms. She buried her head in his shoulder. "I can't do this."

"I know." He tightened his hold. "I will talk to Clarissa. She needs to know."

"And will we be able to live with ourselves when she is the topic of every gossip?"

"We will be talked about, as well," he reminded her.

"Except, we will have each other. And we won't be able to stay here, Ned. If you think you were branded for having a courtesan for a mother, wait until you feel the burden of having destroyed someone as innocent as Clarissa. Especially in a place like Maidenshop."

She was right. He dropped his arms and stepped back. "What do we do now?"

Gemma gave him a sad smile. "We don't meet like this again."

"No."

"And no kisses. Because seeing you alone like this, I feel as if my heart is being broken all over again. Ned, we must stay apart."

"That won't be easy."

"It is what you owe your wife . . . and your children when you have them."

He thought of the baby she'd lost, of her alone.

"Gemma, I love you."

"And I love you with a passion so fierce it frightens me—but we can't." And then, as if to belie her words, she kissed him. One last kiss.

This was madness, a glorious one.

He loved this woman. She was a piece of him that had been missing. However, she was right. He owed Clarissa his loyalty. Honor demanded it.

Ned just wanted to hold Gemma a heartbeat longer—

A soft gasp was all the warning needed.

Gemma heard it, as well. The kiss broke, they turned, and found themselves looking at Clarissa.

Chapter Twenty

$\mathcal{T}$ime stopped. Gemma couldn't breathe, couldn't think. Now she understood why women swooned. Anything to escape this terrible moment, and yet, she was made of better stuff than that.

For her part, Clarissa stood poised as if caught in midstep. Her eyes were wide and round, as if she couldn't understand what she was seeing, until she did. Her brows came together. The confusion left her expression and just as suddenly as she had arrived, she turned and sprinted off.

Gemma pushed against Ned. *"Clarissa."*

He held her firm. "I'll talk to her."

She frowned. "She'll never forgive me."

"You did nothing wrong. *I* followed you out here."

"When you speak to her, what will you tell her, Ned? How can we explain? I don't want to hurt her."

"No, that isn't who we are, is it? We live for

others. Come, let me be certain she isn't inside denouncing us."

"If she is?"

"Then we brazen it out. If she isn't, it means she wants the marriage."

"Ned—"

"Gemma, no more. Either way, each of us is in our own little hell, caught up with honor, expectations, and the choices we've made."

"If she isn't inside?"

He suddenly looked very tired. "Then I find her, apologize abjectly, and let her decide what she wants."

"I'm sorry, Ned. I should have stayed home."

"No, this had to happen. We'll just see our way through."

He took her arm by the elbow and guided her toward the front of the building. He went in first and then returned to the doorway and gave a small, discreet sign to Gemma that it was safe for her to go inside. He himself took off into the night in search of his intended.

CLARISSA DIDN'T know where she was heading. She just knew she had to put as much distance between what she'd seen and herself as possible.

She didn't bother going back into the dance. She didn't even think about it. She was too stunned by the sight of two people she trusted kissing each other.

He'd been kissing Gemma.

Clarissa had begged him for a kiss. She'd swallowed her pride and asked for *any* show of emotion from him that could waylay her fears about the marriage. What she'd received was little more than a brotherly peck on the cheek.

And she knew what was going to happen next. They would search her out and then make excuses, the sort of excuses that always made it sound like it was Clarissa's fault and not their bad behavior. Hadn't that been the pattern of her life? She was always blamed, no matter what she did. She was also always expected to be well behaved and accommodate others because she was the orphan . . . the burden . . . the village project.

However, her future was at stake now. She was not ready for confessions or questions. She also feared that when that moment came, she might completely break down. Ned was her only chance for freedom. Why else had she patiently tolerated his reluctance to marry her?

She needed time to think. She also couldn't walk all the way back to Squire Nelson's house. First, she wasn't about to return to the hall to let her hosts know she was leaving. She didn't wish to make an announcement. She also couldn't just disappear. The worst would be if, when the dance was over, they started looking for her and discovered her gone. She didn't want to hear the lectures that would come out of that. She'd be chastised for being irresponsible, and she didn't believe she could stomach *that* accusation, not tonight.

What she needed was a place where Ned and

Gemma couldn't find her. She didn't want them to tell her that what she saw hadn't been the truth. Living with different families over the years, she'd heard that more than once. *Don't believe what your eyes see, Clarissa. Or your ears hear. Only believe what we tell you.*

Therefore, the best place to go, the only place, was over by the horses. The coaches, carriages, and even pony carts were lined up in the shelter of some trees. There had to be at least fifty of them, and the sounds of the animals would provide cover if she gave in to a good cry. The area was dark and appeared safe. The local lads hired to watch that all was safe had gathered as far away from the front door of the barn as they could. They were busy telling stories and wouldn't notice her as she picked her way through the vehicles, searching for a place to hide.

Her intention was to wait here until the dance was over. She knew the Nelsons were so preoccupied with watching their daughters, they would not even notice Clarissa wasn't in the room until she joined them as they left. And they were not going to leave until it was over, not if the Nelson sisters had their way.

She spied a covered barouche located in the deepest night shade. It would be a perfect spot to wait. Quietly, so as not to alarm the horses, she moved to the door, opened it, and bit back a shriek of surprise when she saw the shadows move and a grumbly voice said, "What are you doing here?"

Clarissa frowned at Lord Marsden, who had

spread his long body across the interior of the vehicle. "You gave me a fright. What are *you* doing here?"

"Drinking."

Her eyes adjusted to the shadowy darkness. She could see the glint off the flask as he held it up.

"You should be inside dancing," she said, rather sanctimoniously.

"Thank you for ordering me about, Miss Strait-laced," he countered.

He'd called her that before. She was not in the mood to ignore it tonight. "I don't see that having morals is a bad thing."

"Of course you wouldn't."

Clarissa made a face. She was in no mood for his whims. She'd find shelter elsewhere. She started to shut the door. He stopped her by pushing one booted foot against it. "What are you doing skulking around out here?"

"I don't believe that is your business." She tried to shut the door again. He kept his boot in place.

"Oh, come, I told you what I was doing."

"It isn't a mystery," she replied, nodding to his flask. And then, because she was in a foul mood, she had to ask, "Do you tire of behaving like a ploughman?"

He appeared to consider her question, and then, taking a good draw on the flask, answered, "If a ploughman does whatever he likes, I believe I'm fine with it."

Of course. What was it Mrs. Taylor had always said? One can't talk sense with a simpleton.

Or, apparently, an earl.

Clarissa decided to leave the door open. She didn't have time for this. She made a fast turn and would have headed off to search for a place with more privacy, except he sat up then and hung out the door.

"Oh, come back. Don't be a ninny."

Those words stopped her. Slowly, she faced him. "What did you call me?"

He grinned. There was the devil in that expression. "You heard me."

How dismissive. How rude. How *everything everyone* expected her to swallow.

Clarissa rounded on him. "I am well aware that for some reason I annoy you, but I have no idea why. Fortunately, I do not concern myself with your affairs. You mean *nothing* to me." She emphasized her words by snapping her fingers, except her snap wasn't very good, not in gloves. It ended up being more of an angry gesture and less cavalier than she would have liked.

He frowned and stretched his back. "Oh, please, Miss Taylor. No dramatics. However shall I stand it?" he finished with mock horror.

"I'm not being dramatic."

"I'm *not* being *dramatic*," he mimicked, and Clarissa felt like a pot ready to boil.

She never let herself be angry. Anger was the first step to sin. That is what the Reverend Taylor had always said. And although she didn't know her feelings about sin, she knew those she depended upon wouldn't be pleased with her if she spoke her mind or had a bout of frustration.

So she didn't know the depths of her temper. She'd never allowed herself to experience it, until this moment.

Clarissa grabbed hold of the door with both hands and shoved it with such force, the earl fell back, holding his flask high so that he didn't spill a drop.

"You, you, *you*, YOU." She didn't know why she was repeating the word except it felt good to give voice to her feelings. "I am *tired* of your attitude, my lord. Of you acting as if you know what *I* think or of judging me and always finding me coming up short. You are a small-minded man."

"Ouch, that hurts," he responded and then laughed.

"*What is the matter with you?* My life is falling apart. Everyone I thought I could trust is either gone or they have—" She paused, needing a word strong enough, and found it. "*Betrayed* me." Oh, yes, that was a good word. "Of course, I don't know what you would understand about the matter. You are *his lordship*. You live in your big house. You have generations of *family* behind you and never have to worry about being thrown into the streets if you don't act pretty or if you say the wrong word and the family's daughters complain. No one criticizes you or gives you the silent treatment. Oh, *I hate* the silent treatment.

"And the worst," she continued, "is that I have

so wanted to escape *that* house. And now *I can't.*
I won't ever be able to leave. And I have to tell
them and they will be furious. They want me
gone. There will be a big meeting and everyone
will talk about me. *Poor Clarissa, what are we going
to do with her? She has no one. She has nowhere to go.*
And I'm trapped. I will live my life *trapped.* Don't
you see how terrible it all is?"

To his credit, Lord Marsden, who appeared
stunned by her verbal assault, had the good sense
to merely nod.

"And I have to *live* with this," Clarissa said. "I
trusted he was going to come through for me.
Instead, I see him choosing another. He *chose* another."

Lord Marsden found his voice. "Who did?"

With all the disdain she could muster, Clarissa
said, "You *men* are so *blind*."

"Perhaps, but will you give me a hint?"

She ignored his request. Instead, she admitted, "I really didn't care for him that much." She
talked more to herself than his lordship. Saying
those words aloud was like uncorking a bottle.
"He was kind. He was *being* kind. However, I am
tired of *kind*. I did trust him. I believed he was
true to his word. I wouldn't have waited otherwise, and now I don't know what to do. If I don't
marry him, what will become of me?"

"Ah, *that* is who you are talking about. What
will become of you if you *do* marry him?"

Lord Marsden's question caught her off guard.

"The answer is obvious. I'm safe."

"And if you don't?"

Her imagination took over. Everyone had given her dire predictions of the fate of women alone. "I will have to take a position being some old lady's companion. Or I could fall into bad hands—"

"Bad hands?"

"Yes, I could be carried away by brigands."

He leaned to hang out the window, his elbows on the door. "Being carried off sounds far more entertaining than marriage."

"Are you mad? It sounds scary."

"Well, life is scary."

She frowned at him. "Only because you don't have any challenges."

"I have challenges."

"Oh, yes? Such as?"

"There are so many expectations on my shoulders it is as if I am weighed down by blocks from ancient pyramids—"

"Blocks from pyramids? What are you talking about?"

"The big stone blocks that they used to make the pyramids." He acted as if she should understand. "I feel as if I'm weighed down by one of them, much like Sisyphus, who had to roll that stone up a steep hill for eternity, except his is round and mine is rectangular."

Clarissa frowned, and then she said carefully, "You are foxed."

He held up the flask. "Here was your first clue. I do carry it off well, don't I?"

"Not if I can notice."

"I miss Old Andy."

His change of topic caught her. "We all do. He was a kind man."

Lord Marsden hummed his thoughts and then said, "He always gave good advice. Occasionally, he'd take me to task. He was the only one who would. See," he said, wagging a finger at her, "that is what you are missing. Someone who can help you sort out what is bedeviling you. Of course, I have a sense of what you might need."

"You do? You know nothing of me."

"I have some clever powers of deduction." She snorted her derision. He ignored her. "I am certain this all involves Thurlowe, who is one of my closest friends. He is also deadly dull. I admit it. I would say it to his face. In fact, I believe I have a time or two. All he thinks about is science, and studies and lectures and studies. And *purpose*. This is a big theme of his—"

"And Gemma." The words were out before she realized it. She was shocked at herself and clapped a hand over her mouth. She knew how to be discreet. That was not it.

Lord Marsden appeared to sober. "So that is the lay of the land. I can see it. No wonder he gave me a look that could fry bacon after I danced with her. He thought he was being discreet. He wasn't. And it makes sense. They both probably entertain each other talking about rashes and poxes."

"No, that isn't how they entertain each other."

He gave a sharp bark of laughter. "Why, Miss Taylor, there is some humor in you."

"I see nothing humorous about the situation. He was *promised* to me. I waited for him to come up to scratch for two years. *Two years* of his *weekly* calls where he'd *bore* me because he never said *anything.*"

"I told you he could be dull," Lord Marsden said with a shrug.

She waved him off, too lost in her catalog of complaints to care. "In truth, he was just *there*. A placeholder in my life. One of many, it turns out."

That was the gist of it.

He'd wasted her time, and she was a woman. The matrons warned her time was limited for a woman.

"Then you will have to do something else," the earl said reasonably, and Clarissa thought she would scream. She turned on her heel and went marching off. The dance was better than arguing with Lord Marsden.

She forgot her intent to hide, to escape to someplace to think. Consequently, she almost ran into Ned.

He caught her by the arms before she barreled over him. "Thank heavens I found you."

She yanked away from him and he let her go. "I am not interested in anything you have to say to me."

"I understand, and you have every reason to be upset—"

"Why, Ned, *why*? *Why her and not me?*"

Regret crossed his handsome features, and something else akin to wonder before he said, "I fell in love with her."

"Love?" She took a step away, wishing she hadn't heard him say those words, wishing she hadn't seen him kissing Gemma. Wishing, wishing, wishing . . .

And hadn't her wishes always led to disillusionment? Nothing was ever as it seemed.

She faced him with what she hoped was some maturity. "What do we do now?"

The moonlight caught on a muscle working in his jaw. His expression was so bleak, he could have been carved from stone, and then he said, "We marry."

She wasn't certain she heard him correctly. "You are serious?"

"Clarissa, I gave my word."

Relief flooded through her. She wasn't going to be humiliated. He was going to honor his promise. She'd be free from having to live under others' roofs or to be alone. "Thank you, Ned. Thank you very much. I will be the best wife. I promise. I will do anything you wish."

There was a heavy beat of silence, and then he said, "I know." He shifted his weight, turning from her. He drew a deep breath and released it and then said, without true energy or desire, "Shall we go inside?" He offered his arm.

This wasn't the way she wanted it. In a world of her making, he'd kiss her and tell her *she* was the one he loved.

But then, no one had ever loved her. She was the burden.

She took his arm. "Yes, let's." Hers was a false

cheerfulness, and a signal of determination to be true to her word—she would be a good wife. She'd not offer complaint, she'd do as he suggested, and she'd keep her own emotions and feelings carefully in line with his. After all, she knew how to walk a very narrow line.

And out of the corner of her eye, she caught movement.

Another glance told her that Lord Marsden had come out of the barouche. He'd probably heard everything—and had an opinion, one designed to make her feel guilty. Well, she wouldn't. He was not her judge. He knew nothing of her life, of how hard it was to manage the world when one had nothing.

Besides, she really, really, really did *not* like the Earl of Marsden.

She just wished his words didn't haunt her, especially as she returned to the dance and pretended everything was all right.

Chapter Twenty-One

Gemma had left the dance by the time Ned returned with Clarissa on his arm. It disturbed him that he couldn't ask anyone where she'd gone. He had no right to worry whether she'd made it home safe—if home had been her destination.

No, he had to stand beside Clarissa and behave as if all was right in his world, even as he felt himself crumbling apart inside.

Eventually, the evening came to an end. Ned escorted Clarissa out to Squire Nelson's vehicle and dutifully waved as they drove off.

Mars sidled up to him. It was obvious his friend was in his cups. "I didn't see you most of the evening," Ned said.

"I've been to one Cotillion too many," was the response, and then the earl added, "Run away, Thurlowe. Don't marry her."

Ned didn't like hearing his deepest desire put into words. "You have been against the marriage from the beginning. You know one of us has to do it."

"No, I don't know that. Nor do I jump because the matrons issue a command."

"I'm not marrying her for that reason."

"No, you are doing it because good Doctor Ned Thurlowe takes care of everyone. Someday you need to start caring for yourself." On that he walked over to his horse and mounted, leaving Ned alone.

Most of the attendees were gone. Even the musicians and the matrons had packed up.

And Ned dared to walk by The Garland. All was quiet . . . and life moved on.

The next day, after a sleepless night where Ned had reviewed in his mind the confrontation with Clarissa, he was heavy-eyed and not particularly anticipating the Frost lecture, something he'd believed would be the highlight of his year.

What he wanted was to see Gemma.

He arrived at the back door, hoping to catch her alone in the kitchen before everything started. He didn't know what he was doing. He just needed to lay eyes on her.

She was in the kitchen but unfortunately not alone. Mark Dawson and Fitz were there helping her. Or rather, they were there in her way.

But there could be no doubt in anyone's mind they were wooing her, each in his own clumsy way.

"Hello, Doctor," Fitz said. He was in shirtsleeves.

"Since the day promises rain, we've moved everything to the main room."

"Ah, well, that is good." Ned's gaze met Gemma's.

She'd pinned her hair at the nape of her neck instead of wearing her braid. Once again, she'd left her black. Her dress was green with sprigs of violets printed on it. He thought she looked beautiful—even though she refused to meet his eye and used Fitz and Dawson as buffers. He couldn't blame her.

Other members of the Logical Men's Society and Royce arrived to help prepare seating for the lecture. Sir Lionel and Fullerton did not come. Since the activities of the Society had stopped revolving around drink, they had been notably absent. Ned hadn't even seen Sir Lionel at the Cotillion, either. However, he hadn't been so lost in himself not to notice Fullerton escorting Mrs. Warbler through a set or two of the more sedate dances.

Around noon the villagers started gathering for the lecture. There were more women than Ned had anticipated and, to his alarm, some children. Their mothers went to great pains to assure Ned the children would stay outside.

"Even in the rain?"

"Children don't melt," one mother promised him. He prayed that was true.

Gemma busied herself serving sherry, ale, and thick sandwiches that Ned had paid the Widow

Smethers to make. The bread was fresh and the meat the finest the village could offer.

Because so many from the surrounding areas traveled to take part in the Cotillion, there were a number of new faces for the lecture. This was how Ned had designed his venture. His purpose was to introduce scientific ideas to the largest number of people possible. To open minds. A noble purpose, and right now he wasn't certain if anything mattered.

Mars arrived with Balfour, and it was good to have his two best friends present. When Squire Nelson cornered Balfour to talk about a drainage issue he was having, Mars leaned over to Ned. "Has a night's sleep brought you to your senses? Are you still determined to marry her?"

"Stop it."

The earl shrugged. "Well, then, go greet your betrothed." He nodded to Clarissa, who had arrived with Mrs. Warbler.

At the same moment Clarissa looked across the main taproom to Ned. Her face was pale, as if she hadn't slept well, either. Their gazes met and then *she* looked away, her expression cold.

God help him. He was badgered from every side.

"Run," Mars whispered again and went off to pay his respects to the dowager, who had surprised Ned with her appearance. He wouldn't have imagined her interested in astronomy. Or were some women here just to be present?

Gemma came up to Ned. "I believe your lecturer is at the door." These were the first words she'd said to him since he'd arrived.

And there was so much he wanted to say to her—except, standing in the middle of all of Maidenshop crowded into the tight space around them was not the time.

So he went over to greet his guest. Thaddeus Frost, an officious man with graying hair, thin legs, and a protruding belly. Frost's clothes appeared as if they had been stored in a hamper and just been removed.

Ned held out his hand. He knew Frost would be happy with the size of the gathering. There were twice as many people as Ned had promised. "Sir, it is my pleasure. I'm Mr. Ned Thurlowe. I invited you."

Frost ignored his hand. His priggish eyes narrowed behind his wired spectacles. He surveyed the gathering with distaste. "What is this?"

"This is the crowd gathered to hear your lecture. Impressive, no?"

"No."

"No?"

"Are you deaf?"

Ned was taken aback. "I hear quite well. However, I may not have understood you. I have the impression you are offended. Is something the matter?"

"Something the matter? I came here to speak to scholars."

Ned nodded with understanding. "Trust me, there are some keen minds in the room. Of course, many are laymen with a casual interest in the topic you will present." That was just remotely true. "It is my fervent hope that your ideas will be so engaging, you will spur many of us to want to know more."

"I don't *engage* people." Frost moved to the side of the door. "I pontificate."

Conscious that this conversation was starting to draw attention, Ned kept his manner pleasant. "Ah, well, we are ready for pontification. In fact, it is almost on the hour. May I summon a refreshment for you? We have a podium set up for you over here." Last year Woodman had built one for Ned and he was quite proud of it.

"Are you deliberately mistaking my meaning?" the academic demanded, his voice rising. Others in the crowd became quiet. "I can't speak to these people."

"Why not?"

Frost looked around the room, unperturbed that his people had quieted. He returned his gaze to Ned and said, "There are *women* here."

"Yes, there are."

"I was told that I was speaking to the Logical Men's Society."

"And our guests." Ned knew very well exactly what he'd written in the invitation.

"But some are *women*." Frost spoke as if that should explain everything.

"Yes, some. Some are not."

"Women will never grasp the concepts of my ideas."

A year ago, even a few months ago, Ned would have agreed. He'd never attended a lecture that included women. He'd never intended for *his* lecture series to have females in the audience.

That was before Gemma.

Gemma, whose bright mind captivated him. Gemma, who insisted he discuss matters with her as an equal. Gemma, who understood types of healing far better than he.

Ned looked into his guest's nearsighted eyes and realized that before Gemma, he'd been in danger of being like Frost. The man's narrow-mindedness curdled his stomach.

Ned spoke. "Knowledge, especially pertaining to natural philosophy, should be of interest for everyone. We all live in this world and I believe it is important to understand it. The people here, including the females, have gathered to honor you by listening to your theories, sir, something you are not allowed to share in London. The women gathered here have sharp intellects and a curiosity that rivals their male counterparts. I will not have you insult them. Now, are you ready to speak? It is growing past the hour."

By now, everyone was paying attention. The room was very quiet as if all waited for the lecturer's response, and it was one few would forget.

Frost's face grew an alarming shade of purple. "I do not share my ideas with women. I see no reason to waste the words. Good day, Doctor." On that announcement, Frost marched right out the door.

Ned had a good mind to grab him by the collar and drag him back into The Garland so he could throw him out. He'd paid the bastard ten pounds to make the trip and speak.

And for what? So that he could walk into the village and insult people who mattered to Ned? Who were part of his life?

The sound of clapping pulled him out of his haze of anger.

Ned looked around. Men and women were applauding him. The sound grew as they came to their feet.

"Well done, sir," Royce called.

"Excellent," the dowager said.

"That was better than any lecture," Mars announced, a sentiment that was seconded all the way around.

However, the opinion that mattered to Ned was Gemma's. He searched the room for her and found her standing next to Mrs. Warbler *and Clarissa*. Gemma was clapping as hard as anyone. He wanted to tell her that he'd found the wherewithal to refuse Frost's demands from her.

She'd changed him. He was not the man she'd first met.

Gemma spoke up, telling people they would still enjoy themselves. "There is plenty of food."

The Dawson brothers announced they would take on all comers bowling, at least until it started to rain, and the matrons quickly gathered to gossip. Ned marveled at how his friends and neighbors all made the most of what, to him, had been at first a disastrous situation.

Instead, he realized he was surrounded by good company.

That is when Clarissa chose to speak.

No one heard her at first. Ned saw her lips moving; he didn't know why—and then she stood on one of the chairs. *"Please,"* she shouted. "I have something to say."

Because she was standing over them, people grew quiet and looked up at her with curiosity.

Clarissa appeared nervous. Ned's first thought was fear that she was about to publicly denounce him and Gemma. He wished he was standing beside his beloved. Their gazes met across the room. She appeared concerned and yet resigned. He understood. He nodded. Whatever came, they would meet it head-on.

"I have something to say," Clarissa repeated.

"Then say it," William Dawson said. "We want a game in before it rains." He was shushed by his betters.

"This won't take long," Clarissa answered him. She looked around the room. Her eyes settled on Squire Nelson and his wife. "I'll say I'm sorry before I start. I know my news may not be received well."

"Clarissa—" Ned started. She was confirming his fears.

She ignored him, announcing in ringing tones, "I call off my betrothal to Mr. Thurlowe."

That stopped him. It stopped everyone. The whole room seemed to freeze, even the Dawson brothers.

Seeing that she had, at last, commanded everyone's attention, Clarissa said to Ned, "Sir, you paid me a great honor. However, I find I must release you from your promise. I do not wish to marry you." With that, she stepped down from the chair and walked through the stunned crowd and out the door.

Ned was the first to recover. He went after her.

Clarissa stood not far from the front door beneath the shade of a sheltering tree. As he approached, she said, "Did I catch you by surprise?"

"You caught us all by surprise." He didn't know what he expected but it was not seeing her stand so calmly and self-possessed.

"Yes, myself, too." She waited until he reached her before explaining, "I wasn't going to do that. You have made me very angry, Ned. And you've hurt me."

"You have the right to those feelings. I am completely at fault."

"I've had many thoughts since last night. Some far from charitable. My plan was to make you honor your promise. I'm scared, Ned. I don't know what will become of me now."

"First, you will have Gemma and me. We will help you in any way possible."

"Thank you," she said, the words barely spoken. She looked down. "My hands are shaking."

"No one in there could tell."

She nodded and then crossed her arms as if she was cold.

He had to ask. "What changed your mind? Why did you release me?"

"You told your lecturer that women have fine minds. You didn't think that way before. There were times I sensed you didn't really like women."

"I wasn't close to any."

"You were close to me."

What could he say? He'd never given her the opportunity to be anything to him other than an obligation. "I'm sorry."

She nodded before admitting, "I am, too. I actually thought you were quite admirable when you told him what you thought." Her shoulders straightened. "Very well. I'm going back in there. I needed a moment for the initial shock to wear off. This won't be easy. I know the Nelsons are rather anxious to unburden themselves of me—"

"Clarissa," he started, but she shook her head as if not wanting his sympathy.

"I'll talk to the dowager and Mrs. Warbler and . . . we'll see. There will be a place for me somewhere. I'll find my way."

"Let me come with you to explain—"

"*No.*" She studied him a moment and then said, "I must do this myself, Ned. I'm tired of leaning on others to guide me. The time has come for me to make my own decisions and stand by them."

"I will always be here for you, Clarissa."

She gave him a sad smile. "This isn't your fault,

Ned. Don't blame yourself. You see, I've come to realize I want to marry someone who truly wishes to kiss me. I'm done settling for anything less." On those words, she walked back to The Garland.

And that is when he noticed Gemma. She'd come around the back of the building and had been watching them. She approached. "What happened? How is she?"

"She knows I love you. I told her last night. She knows I can't live without you. She's also decided that she deserves something more than what I offer. She's right."

"Still, I worry."

"And how does that help her? She has her own life to live and I pray she finds a love as strong as the one I feel for you." On those words he bent down on one knee. "She freed me, Gemma, so that I can offer my heart, my name, all of me, to you. Please, say you will be my wife. I can't imagine my life without you."

"Ned—"

"I know. I understand. We are caretakers. We worry about others. It is our lot in life . . . but now, this is about our happiness. Clarissa has given us a gift, Gemma. Please, say you will have me."

Her answer was to throw herself into his arms, and he was never going to let her go.

So IT was that Gemma and Ned stood before the Reverend Summerall as soon as the banns were announced. He couldn't wait to make Gemma his wife.

And they were not alone when they celebrated. The matrons understood they couldn't stand in the way of love.

The wedding breakfast was held at The Garland and it rivaled any that had ever come before it. No one was left out. Marsden and the Balfours, including baby Anne, were there. The matrons ruled a corner of the room, and Clarissa, who had agreed to take a position as a lady's companion in London, sat among them. She would be leaving the next day so the party was also a farewell to her.

"I'm nervous," Clarissa had confided once she'd accepted the position. "They tell me Mrs. Emsdale is of a cranky nature. However, the pay is very good and she can't be worse than Jane Nelson when she can't have her way."

"Even if it doesn't work out, we'll be here for you," Gemma had promised.

"And we'll keep an ear cocked for a position closer to home," Ned had added.

"I appreciate that. I've not known anyplace else other than Maidenshop."

"Then it will be an adventure," Gemma had said.

Clarissa had smiled bravely at that and then murmured, "At least it will free me of that obnoxious Lord Marsden. If the man accuses me of becoming a matron one more time, I shall not be responsible for my actions."

Ned had said, "That should keep Mars on his best behavior," and the three of them had laughed because they knew the earl feared no one in Maidenshop.

Of course, the members of the Logical Men's Society were at the breakfast. They celebrated harder than most, and their good wishes seemed to be heartfelt.

However, the truth was, Ned was happily no longer a member of the Logical Men's Society, something he had never imagined conceivable. He'd once believed they were his only family. Now, with Gemma, he had a world of new possibilities.

He also discovered that the word *wife* was one of the sweetest in the English language.

And as he gathered her up in his arms after, finally enjoying her in a proper bed, he watched her sleep, marveling that *love*—a word he had considered a myth—had changed his life completely.

Never again would he be alone . . . not with Gemma by his side.

Author's Note

Dear Readers,

I'm writing this during a good portÑn of the pandemic. It was easy for me to get lost in the research. We humans w²l believe, or *want* to believe, anything if it promises a cure. History does repeat itself, especially when it involves human nature.

Fortunately, there were talented healers like Gemma who kept track of successful recipes, handed down one generation to the other— especially when it came to women's health, which is a relatively new specialty. There were also enlightened doctors like Ned who had suspicions about the spread of disease, without understanding the true cause. Germs would not be discovered for several decades. God bless the fastidious who washed their hands. Humanity might not have survived otherwise.

In truth, all medicine is trial and error, observation and intuition. Keep in mind, so many of the medical tools we take for granted, such as the stethoscope, weren't available to Ned. It wasn't invented until 1816, a year after our story takes place.

Well, enough of this—yes, there is another book coming. Clarissa is in the hands of Mrs. Emsdale. Will it be an adventure or a nightmare? And someplace in the world is the hapless Duke of Winderton. Hopefully, he is growing up a bit.

And let us not forget Mars, who may be in need of a recovery meeting or a sharp whack against the side of his head. We'll see.

I hope you enjoyed Gemma and Ned's story. I value your support and pray you all stay happy and healthy until we get together again.

All my best,

Cathy Maxwell
Buda, TX
July 31, 2020

Keep reading for a sneak peek at

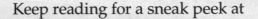

His Lessons on Love

By Cathy Maxwell
Coming January 2022

Chapter One

"Women do have their place in society ... although I'm not quite certain where."

–Book of Mars

The moment Mars had charged into Mrs. Warbler's house and handed his infant daughter off to Miss Taylor, he wanted to collapse with relief.

Dora was safe. She was here with *women. They* would know what to do. For the first time since this baby had been dumped on him by an angry mistress, he could breathe.

Of course, he would rather Miss Taylor not be here. He didn't have the patience, especially right now, for her self-righteous huffing and puffing. Oh, she was easy on the eyes with her golden hair and well-endowed figure. Possibly one of the loveliest women in several parishes around— but then she would open her mouth and a more rigid, narrow-minded soul Mars had yet to meet.

Wasn't she supposed to be off being a companion to some old, rich hen in London? Isn't that what he'd heard?

Well, apparently she had returned and was sipping tea at Mrs. Warbler's table along with Reverend Summerall's wife. Damn his luck.

Miss Taylor held Dora up. The two of them seemed to have a good look at each other, and then the corners of the baby's mouth turned down. Mars had already learned this was a precursor to a soul-rattling cry. He braced himself by reaching for the only bottle on a table covered with teacups. He had missed his strong tea and port this morning and he dearly needed it. "Please tell me this is port?"

"Sherry," Mrs. Warbler answered.

"Her nappy is soaking," Miss Taylor declared as if this was news to Mars.

"Yes," he agreed. "It is." He'd felt that soaked nappy against his chest all the way to Maidenshop. She'd been so wet, it had gone through the thin blanket he'd wrapped her in. "She needs a dry one."

"And with all due respect, my lord," Mrs. Warbler said, "is this a social call?" He understood her suspicion. There wasn't a soul in the village who didn't know that he avoided the Matrons of Maidenshop. They were barely on cordial terms and yet here he was.

"Do you have a *dry* nappy?" Miss Taylor demanded as if he would deliberately withhold a nappy from her.

"Sherry will have to do," he muttered to himself just as Dora broke down into tears—again. He turned to the maid. "I need a cup of *very* strong tea."

The maid glanced at Mrs. Warbler who, thankfully, nodded her assent. Mars didn't know what he would have done if his request had been denied. Probably tipped the bottle right in front of them, and that would have outraged their feminine sensibilities.

Then he remembered he owed answers. To Mrs. Warbler, he said, "This isn't a social call but a desperate plea for help." To Miss Taylor, "No, I do not have a dry nappy. Or even another wet one."

She shot him a look that said clearly, *What is wrong with you?* followed by a glance in the direction of the other women as if to say, *Isn't he a disappointment?*

He was.

Mars didn't know about nappies. Or what to feed babies. Although, to find the answers, he'd braved putting himself into the center of the coven known at the Matrons of Maidenshop. That must count for something. It also made his daughter's crying easier to take now that he wasn't the sole one in control. He hated feeling inept.

"Did you even bring a sucking bottle?" Miss Taylor wondered.

"A sucking bottle?" he repeated blankly. "*Yes,* that is what she needs. She's hungry. But what to feed her?"

"Where is her mother?" Mrs. Summerall asked.

"Gone." He wasn't going to tell them that Jane had foisted the baby on him before she went off to accept another man's protection. Or even make the excuse that he was a responsible lover who always took precautions with his partners, because quite obviously, he had not been completely successful.

No, he'd keep all of that to himself because poor Dora didn't need any more counts against her than being abandoned. He'd seen what Miss Taylor had endured over the years. *His* daughter would be treated better.

Miss Taylor shifted the baby into her arms with a practiced ease and did something he would never have thought of doing—she crooked her finger and offered the baby a knuckle. Dora latched on to it as if desperate. "She is starving. When did she last eat?"

If he didn't have nappies or a sucking bottle, Mars didn't understand why Miss Taylor thought he'd have a clue about Dora's eating schedule. Before he could frame an answer, the maid returned to the room holding a cup and sauce and a pot of tea. He could have cried at the sight. She sat the dishes on the table in front of him and poured the steaming brew into cup. He uncorked the sherry and topped the cup off. "Bless you," he whispered to the maid and the world. "Bless you, bless you."

"Well, I'm so pleased that we have met *your* needs, my lord," Miss Taylor said.

"You don't sound pleased." He took a swallow

of tea. The sherry wasn't half bad and his body wanted to groan with the pleasure of it. "And I wish I could answer your questions, except I don't know the answers. Dora has been in my care for all of—what? An hour? Maybe a bit more?"

There was a beat of silence, and then Miss Taylor said, "*Who* in their right mind gave *you* a baby?"

He had asked himself that question several times on the ride from Belvoir to Maidenshop with a sobbing child tucked against his chest. It was just not one he wanted to hear from *her*. Still, he did have an answer.

"God," he said with great finality. "God gave me a baby." He drained the cup of tea, not even minding if it burned his mouth a bit.

"She's *yours*?" Mrs. Warbler asked. "With the dark hair?"

"She is. Do you think I would be doing all of this if she wasn't?" He answered Mrs. Warbler, but he spoke directly to Miss Taylor, daring her to make a sharp comment . . . except, for the first time in their acquaintance, she appeared speechless.

NEW YORK TIMES BESTSELLING AUTHOR

Cathy Maxwell

The Brides of Wishmore

The Bride Says No

978-0-06-221925-1

Blake Stephens is the bastard son of a duke, arrogant, handsome, and one of the most sought-after bachelors in London. He is promised to one woman, but discovers his soul is stirred by . . . the chit's sister! And now he must make a choice: marry for honor . . . or marry for love?

The Bride Says Maybe

978-0-06-221927-5

Pretty, petted, Lady Tara Davidson planned to marry for love, but her profligate father has promised her hand to Breccan Campbell, laird of the valley's most despised clan. Breccan loves nothing more than a challenge, and he's vowed to thoroughly seduce Tara—and make her his in more than name alone.

The Groom Says Yes

978-0-06-221929-9

Cormac Enright, Earl of Ballin, is determined to find the man whose testimony sentenced him to a hangman's noose. Protecting Mac is Sabrina Davidson, the man's daughter, the most entrancing, frustrating woman Mac has ever met. And it doesn't help that he's already tasted her beguiling kisses.

CM5 1215